"I've got to calm down!"

But Melodye couldn't keep her eyes or her mind off Jim Ryan, the detective assigned to investigate her husband's murder. To make matters worse, she'd sat closer to him than she'd intended. She imagined she could feel the side of her thigh tingle as it brushed against his. She fantasized that they were the only two people in the room. But they weren't the only two people in the room. And in fact, Jim was in the middle of interrogating a suspect.

This is a serious affair. A man has been murdered, Melodye thought. Her husband and the father of her twins had been murdered, and all she could think about was how hot the detective working on how his case was?

"Cool off, girl," Melodye said to herself. She willed her brain to fixate on something besides the handsome detective sitting at her side. But no matter how hard she tried, her glance kept sliding to Jim. And every time it did, she felt a funny little thrumming in the pit of her stomach....

Books by Francine Craft

Kimani Romance

If Love Is Good to Me
Never Without You…Again
Designed for Passion

Kimani Arabesque

Still in Love
Wedding Bells
"Love's Masquerade"
Star Crossed
Betrayed by Love
Forever Love
Love in Bloom
"Love's Masquerade"
What Matters Most
Haunted Heart
Born to Love You
Give Love
"Kisses and Mistletoe"
The Best of Everything
Wild Heart
Dreams of Ecstasy
Passion's Fool

FRANCINE CRAFT

is the pen name of a Washington, D.C.-based writer who has enjoyed writing for many years. A native Mississippian, she has been a research assistant for a large psychological organization, an elementary school teacher, a business school instructor and a federal government legal secretary. Francine's hobbies include reading, photography and songwriting. She deeply cherishes time spent with her good friends.

Designed for PASSION

Francine Craft

KIMANI PRESS™

ISBN-13: 978-0-373-86057-9
ISBN-10:   0-373-86057-9

DESIGNED FOR PASSION

Copyright © 2008 by Francine Craft

All rights reserved. The reproduction, transmission or utilization
of this work in whole or in part in any form by any electronic, mechanical
or other means, now known or hereafter invented, including xerography,
photocopying and recording, or in any information storage or retrieval
system, is forbidden without written permission. For permission please
contact Kimani Press, Editorial Office, 233 Broadway, New York, NY
10279 U.S.A.

This is a work of fiction. Names, characters, places and incidents are
either the product of the author's imagination or are used fictitiously,
and any resemblance to actual persons, living or dead, business establishments,
events or locales is entirely coincidental.

® and TM are trademarks. Trademarks indicated with ® are registered in
the United States Patent and Trademark Office, the Canadian Trade Marks
Office and/or other countries.

www.kimanipress.com

Printed in U.S.A.

Dear Reader,

Few prejudices are meaner than the ones toward the plus-size woman. Many plus-size women are beautiful and Melodye Carter is one of these. However, long savaged by her model-thin mother and sister, she grew up with poor self-esteem.

Melodye thought she had escaped the prison of rejection when she married, but her marriage was not a happy one. Her husband didn't want children, and when she had her twins, he turned nasty. By the time he was killed, their marriage was in tatters.

Then Melodye is enlisted to help Detective Jim Ryan, a man she knew in high school, find her husband's murderer. As they work together, Melodye and Jim discover they have something in common. Both are bitterly hurt and want nothing to do with love, but neither can resist the powerful attraction that develops between them.

I certainly hope you'll write and tell me what you did and didn't like about Melodye and Jim's story. I love hearing from you and will always answer.

All blessings,

Francine

www.francinecraft.com

hol718@aol.com

Dedication

To Mavis Allen, one of the savviest editors in the industry, who graciously shares her extensive knowledge with writers.

To Tracye White, a chocolate diva who is beyond her years, beautiful and who is a true Christian and a good friend.

Acknowledgment

Always give thanks to God for His endless blessings and guidance. I thank Charlie Kanno for his unfailing patience and superb work.

Chapter 1

It was the last Sunday in May and Melodye Carter frowned as she answered her door. She was rushing to leave for her boutique and design studio for the plus-size woman, and she wanted no distractions. The twins were with their godmother for the day, so Melodye could bring sketches back home to work on.

Looking out of the peephole, her heart nearly leaped into her throat as she saw the tall, familiar figure. She opened the door to Detective Jim Ryman, one of Crystal Lake, Virginia's police department's finest. "Oh, Jim, come in."

The man grinned, stepped inside and hesitated. He wanted to hug her, but something held him back. He hadn't seen her since he'd investigated her husband's death in a robbery over two years ago.

"I haven't seen you in far too long. You're looking fabulous."

His eyes roved her face and voluptuous body. She'd gotten even more beautiful than he remembered. Her straight, off-black hair was worn in a shoulder-length flip with bangs made to order for her oval face. Yeah, he remembered the thickly fringed, long black lashes. He smiled a little as he looked into her dark eyes.

He apologized for stopping in on a Sunday. She said it was okay. He knew then why he hadn't hugged her. She was fine wine and she went to his head. And he didn't like it one bit. He wasn't looking to be romantically drawn to a woman anytime soon…and maybe never again.

His face grew somber then. "What I'm here to see you about is going to hurt you and I'm sorry." He gave her a minute to prepare herself. "I've been assigned to your late husband's cold case and I've collected enough evidence to tell me Rafael's death was a premeditated murder. It wasn't just your ordinary business robbery."

"Oh, my God," she breathed as dizziness set in, and he reached out to steady her. Electricity flashed between them, startling both. He drew a deep breath and guided her to the sofa where they sat down. She was trembling and it wasn't from what he'd just told her.

"I'm going to need your help, Melodye. I've been able to pinpoint who I think is behind this, but it's liable to be the devil to prove. We think there's at least a small mob tie-in."

She looked at him steadily as a finger of dread traced along her spine. "Am *I* in danger then?"

He looked at her keenly, shaking his head. "I don't think so, but there'll be protection for you just in case. We're moving fast on this one so far, and the guy knows he's in our crosshairs."

"Do I know him?"

"Turk Hylton, Rafael's partner."

Her heart lurched and she felt cold. Turk had come on to her the whole time she and Rafael had been married. After her husband's death, he had gotten bolder until she'd turned him away.

"I see," she said, "I'll give you every bit of help I can."

Jim drew a quick breath. He saw he was making her nervous, but he couldn't stop feasting his eyes until they landed on her moist and full, luscious lips. Without wanting to, he imagined sucking the bottom lip, his eyes nearly closed with desire. He was fighting it all the way. Since Elyssa's death, he hadn't been with another woman.

"How're your twins? Mom still talks about them and their terrible two's," he said.

Melodye smiled with her head slightly thrown back in that way he remembered from their high school days. His mind flooded with memories of the days when they'd been friendly, although they'd moved in different crowds. She had been shy and one year behind him. She hadn't dated, but boys had admired her full figure extravagantly. He used to wonder if she was shy because they came on to her so hard or if they came onto her because she was so shy.

She was busy with her own memories of high school. "They're fine, with plenty of the two's left over. Their godmother has them for the day. Hey, I'm delighted to see you. Your mom told me you were coming back and I thought I'd run into you before now."

"Yeah," was all he said.

How calm she sounded, Melodye thought, as if he'd come by with good news instead of this shocker. And as if he were just any man and not a six-foot-two hunk. He had always carried an edge of danger that thrilled her.

It was warm for May. He was dressed in a long-sleeved white tee that failed to hide his rippling pecs, biceps and abs and stonewashed jeans. She stifled a groan at what his body did to her. His voice was still slightly husky, as if he were recovering from a cold. The coal-black hair, straightgrained and rough, the stormy hazel eyes and the thick black silk brows made her stomach ache a little with wanting to run her fingers over his long, angular face.

The trouble was, after Rafael, she felt she never wanted another man to hurt her the way he had. It was okay, she told herself. She could handle her feelings for Jim. It was simply physical hunger and the desire to be wanted, the way Rafael wanted her in the first years of their marriage.

"Have you had coffee?" she asked.

"Just one cup, and that only starts me for the day."

"Have another. I made fresh coffee from beans I ground myself."

Again she thought how calm she sounded, as if a thousand butterflies weren't fluttering in her stomach. He was giving her a chance to digest his news and she wasn't sure how she felt about it. She wasn't surprised. Her late husband had long had dangerous friends and lived a dangerous life.

Jim was the detective assigned to Rafael's robbery. It was his first case after moving back from New York. Jim himself had been shot in a street robbery not too long before Rafael's death. Both cases had gone cold. She tensed. She didn't want to think about Rafael. He had hurt her enough.

They took their coffee and raspberry Danishes to the breakfast nook, which was flooded with sunlight. In the morning light she was beautiful, he thought. He smiled inside, remembering that he sometimes brought her home in his souped-up hotrod.

But her mother had put a stop to even that. Melodye had looked sad when she told him. Jim raced cars and was the community heller who had more than his share of girlfriends. Everybody wondered how his mother, that sweet Miss Belle, and his strict father, Paul, could raise such a son.

"Hey, you're lost," Melodye gently prodded him. "What're you thinking?"

Jim laughed then, his head thrown back. She drew a sharp breath as she watched his wide, wickedly sensual mouth. Heat ran rampant throughout her body.

"You don't want t'know." His eyes were half closed. He'd been thinking about the steady, raunchy pipe dreams he'd had of Melodye in their youth. She was stacked, even then. Voluptuous with her womanly hips and large, perky breasts. From the top of her head to her beautiful feet she was fine, he reflected, and she hadn't changed.

He grew somber then. "You're still beautiful," he told her, feeling his crotch begin to swell and tingle. The heller he had been as a boy had turned into a man who brooded and kept his own counsel. People considered him aloof, but he was talking to her, paying her compliments. Something about her still seemed to need reassurance and he was more than happy to provide it.

She shook her head. "You always said that, and I never was. I was always too big, too awkward. I'm out of fashion and you've never realized that. Out of fashion. Out of season."

He smiled, his eyes on her. "But you're coming back into fashion. The rail-thin woman is going out of style."

As he looked at her, Jim felt his loins tighten. This wasn't going to do. These weren't just friendly feelings, but he had sworn off anything like desire and passion since Elyssa and his unborn son died. He had lived a bleak life since then. It was getting better, but there was no room anymore for love and romance. *Plough on,* he told himself. *You didn't come here to ogle her.* Still, he found himself saying it because she looked wistful and a little lost, the way she'd looked long ago.

"You never knew you were beautiful," he told her. "I used to want to drill it into your head that you were. Those few times I ran into you and we talked. I know Papa France and your grandmother told you, but you always chose to believe your mother and your sister. You're Cinderella, babe, and I thought by now you'd know it."

She shrugged. "I'm just another overweight sister who doesn't look too bad."

His leg brushed hers, and she thrilled, fever running throughout her body, then fought it.

"Sorry," he said.

"Don't be. He didn't have to know that every nerve in her body was thrumming with excitement. What in hell was wrong with her? If she could handle his raging teenage hormones, she surely could handle her feelings now.

For a moment, Jim held his breath. She was feeling something for him; he was sure of it, but he didn't intend to lead her on. "We need to talk about Rafael's death again. What happened after I left?"

She breathed shallowly, remembering that time. "Not much, but one thing, Turk Hylton asked me if I'd found a large sum of money he said Rafael left for him. I searched and found nothing. I told him, but I don't think he believed me. I've never been able to bring myself to go through Rafael's study…."

She hated talking about Rafael, remembering only the shattered dreams and what he'd put her through.

He cleared his throat. "You miss Rafael, I know, and I can't tell you how sorry I am. The worst part of being a detective is breaking news of a murder to the spouses and families."

She longed to tell him then that Rafael had long destroyed her love for him by the time he died. At first, he had been everything she'd dreamed of in a husband. Well, maybe not everything. From the beginning, he'd been hard to get along with. He had wanted her to have an abortion when she found out she was pregnant with twins. He'd railed that he didn't want children. He'd never told her that when he was courting her.

She'd been adamant. No abortion. He'd sulked and stayed away later. After the twins were born, he'd criticized her for not being good company. "Hell, they're your whole life. Where do I fit in?" He'd been drunk half the time and spent more and more time at *Steeped In Joy*, the nightclub he owned with Turk Hylton. She'd suspected he cheated and she'd thought about hiring a private investigator, but by then, it hadn't mattered. He also gambled heavily, something else she hadn't known before they were married.

"I don't miss him," she said flatly, and he looked at her, startled at the vehemence in her voice.

His head went to one side, keenly interested, empathetic. "Want to talk about it?"

She thought a moment before scalding tears stung her eyes. "Later," she said, "and thank you."

What had hurt so much was the brutal way Rafael had criticized her person. She had gained little weight with her pregnancy, but he said she had and that he didn't like it. The final straw had been when he compared her unfavorably to Lucia, her thin, fashion-model sister, saying, "You two sure aren't cut from the same cloth. Take a page from her book. I'm putting you on a diet."

She hunched her shoulders, still too vividly aware of him. She wasn't looking for a man, not even Jim. "Do you still miss Elyssa?"

He thought a moment and found he couldn't talk about it. It still hurt too much, even after almost three years. He shook his head. "As you said, later. Mom told you I moved back."

"Oh, yes, she told me even when you were planning to. She needs someone since her heart attack. She misses your father."

He wanted to talk about his pain and how much it had hurt that he wasn't going to get to be a father. Suddenly his attention was caught by a large framed photo on the table beside them. "The twins," he said, and picked it up. God, they were beautiful, each with an arm wrapped around Melodye's neck. He could only croak out, "Very nice," and it was like saying a brilliant sun was nice. Not nearly good enough.

"They're a handful," she said, laughing. "They're often sick and I wonder about it."

"I understand children are. Fevers, that sort of thing."

She pressed her legs back against the chair so his leg wouldn't brush hers again, and bit her lip.

Jim looked thoughtful. "We know Rafael was a heavy gambler, but not a very good one. You would know he went everywhere from Vegas to Monaco…Atlantic City."

"Yes." That was one of the things they had quarreled about.

"I think he was a hit. We've questioned Turk Hylton. His kind would hire it done, of course. I think Rafael double crossed him. Turk's got mob ties…."

She shuddered. "I think he's a dangerous man."

"He knows how to play it safe. I don't think he'll bother you."

She crossed her arms over her breasts, and he noted the protective gesture. "Like I said, I haven't gone over Rafael's things because I haven't wanted to face what he left behind, but you'll need me to, won't you?"

"Yeah. I'd appreciate it if you did."

She felt cold then. "I don't like danger, Jim. If I'd known there was any chance that Rafael even knew a mobster, or that he gambled heavily, I wouldn't have married him. By the time I found out, it was too late."

His heart went out to her. He wanted to talk about old times, but now wasn't the right moment. They had to talk about Rafael's murder. He drew a deep breath, asked her what she remembered about the night Rafael died. She told him everything, thinking back to the shock and of that night. Rafael had been a night owl, especially with owning and running a nightclub. He had been killed at 3:00 a.m. His wallet had been missing, but not his expensive diamond ring and watch. He was known to carry large sums of money and it seemed a simple open-and-shut robbery case.

Jim listened intently. Finally he asked, "Men living the life he lived have enemies. Do you personally know of any?"

She shook her head. "He kept his business to himself. He wasn't fond of Turk, although they'd once been best friends. He often talked of buying him out, but Turk wasn't selling. One thing he did tell me when we were close…"

She was silent and he gently prodded. "One thing…"

She drew a deep breath. "He said he was loosely connected to the New York mob, that he couldn't get where he wanted to go without them. He was worried that they demanded more and more and he thought Turk was really in bed with them. The police never said anything about that and I didn't tell them. I was just too much in shock."

Jim nodded. "That's understandable."

She closed her eyes. "How much time do you have?"

"Any amount you need." She was affecting him so. He tried to tell himself she brought back the old, carefree days, but that didn't explain it all. He was conflicted. Right now, he neither wanted, nor needed a woman. He had expected to feel what he had felt in the past—a lighthearted, friendly, sexy attraction. An emotional small car. But from the moment she opened her door, her presence was on top of him like a Mack truck. Damn! He was well trained to keep his emotions in check. Well, that training wasn't serving him.

His mind told him he could handle it, but his feelings wandered.

"Would you go through at least some of his things with me?" she asked.

"Sure."

"Have you had breakfast?"

He shook his head. "I don't usually get really hungry until later on."

"Could you down a grilled cheese?"

"I'd like that."

They didn't tarry after eating; she took him straight to Rafael's study, to the secret panel that she opened electronically. It was a small room with shelves and built-in drawers. Everything was tidily arranged. Rafael had been a neat freak. She felt cold with dread and memory. They looked at papers and money in packets, but there were no large sums from the cursory search they made.

Jim was relieved that, in the course of sifting through Rafael's things, he was a little less aware of the way Melodye drew him. His gut was still tight, but thank God for small favors. The saucy, perfume she wore wasn't helping.

"Do you see anything here that'll be helpful to you?" she asked.

"Yes. If you will, just let everything stay as it is. I'll be back with a photographer and my own trusty camera on Monday at your convenience. Will that be a problem?"

She shook her head. "No, Odessa can take over as long as you need me."

Jim glanced at his watch. It had taken them almost three hours. As if guided by something, Melodye went to a small drawer and opened it. "When the room was finished, Rafael showed me around, laughed and said this drawer was special. You know, it was so long ago I'd forgotten what he said. I didn't want to know any of his secrets. He had a dark side and I was terrified of what I'd find." She took a deep breath. "Jim, do you have any idea who shot you?" She wondered why she thought of that now.

He shrugged. "The dude was after loot. He took my wallet, my fraternity ring and watch. I was in a neighborhood it wasn't healthy to be in."

She was rummaging all the while they talked. Frowning, she drew a white envelope from the back corner of the drawer. It had been so close to the wood, she'd almost missed it. Taking it out, she found the flap was just tucked in and on the envelope there was the name of their bank with the notation "Safe-Deposit Box."

Rafael and Melodye had once made an envelope including their joint safe-deposit-box number and the legend of what was in there, but this one made her breathe harder. Looking at the key inside, she saw that it wasn't the same number of their shared box. Of course, she'd known he had an entire life outside of her and she'd learned not to wonder. She handed the envelope to Jim.

He looked at her. "I'm going to need to check this out."

"How about first thing tomorrow morning?"

"Perfect. I'll pick you up." He wanted to say something else, but he also wanted to get the hell out of there and away from her as soon as he could. She held him as a magnet holds iron filings, and it made him angry. He had grown used to being alone. Shattering hurt was something he didn't intend to go through again anytime soon.

He left then and she went to the window, watched him go down the walk and get into his dark blue sedan and drive away; her knees felt a little weak. He was a powerful man, and she wished they had been possible before Rafael. She found herself wishing she had let him get next to her when they were young, but he'd never asked. She chided herself sharply. After Rafael, she never intended to trust another man.

Standing there, she still felt the hurt of Rafael's rejection, of his telling her she was out of shape in more ways than one. Didn't she realize that bearing the twins had been a mistake? he'd asked.

He'd said, too, that she had far more hips and breasts than she needed. He'd said she was cold and didn't turn him on anymore; in fact, she turned him off. He'd been incredibly cruel, punishing her for insisting on bearing the twins. But she felt he was telling the truth, that birthing the twins had made a difference and "thin was in." Wasn't that the American way of life?

One thing about Jim Ryman, he'd always been kind, even in what was often the cruel stage of adolescence. He'd been a dark, brooding presence even as a boy, but so much of him had been mature, even then. If only they had gotten together before she met Rafael. Now it was too late. She felt angry at the attraction she felt for Jim. Rafael had savaged her beyond repair. Now she fully intended to keep men and romance out of her life forever.

Still, she shivered a little, wishing against her will that Monday were now, so she could see him again, irritated with herself for her eagerness. One thing she knew, this time around, Jim Ryman was going to spell trouble in her life.

Chapter 2

Melodye came awake the next morning, smiling. She hugged her pillow and realized she was looking forward to the day far more than she usually did. Throwing back the covers and swinging her long legs over the side of the bed, she stood up and began to do deep knee bends, flexing her five-foot-nine-inch body and feeling pure life flood her.

She had slipped into an exercise suit when her door burst open and the room was filled with the whoops of two dervishes known as Rachel and Randy, her twins. They came to her, hugged her legs and begged for kisses and hugs.

Laughing, she sat back down on the bed then lay back as they swarmed over her.

"I'm hungry," Randy declared, making a funny face.

"So what's new? When aren't you hungry?" Melodye teased him.

"I'm hungry, too," Rachel chimed in. She usually was

exactly the opposite of her twin. "Can we have cereal and hot dogs?"

"Cereal, yes. Hot dogs, no. It's too early in the day for hot dogs."

"Odessa lets us have them. We have a good time at Odessa's." Rachel pouted.

"Hmm. That's because she only has you once in a while. She can afford to spoil you. Now, trot back to your room and play while I do my exercises and we'll all have breakfast."

Randy stuck out his tongue. "Can we have that good cereal?"

Melodye shook her head. "I'm afraid not. Remember, I told you it's too sugary? I have a new one I think you'll like."

"I like the Krispies. I *want* the Krispies."

Melodye fixed her son with a steady eye. "In this world, chum, we don't always get what we want." She chucked him under the chin. "But we take what we can get with a good heart."

She got up and herded them out and they reluctantly left. Finishing her sit-ups, she reflected that next month she was having fitness equipment put in. Then she thought wistfully that she could lose a few of her one hundred and ninety-five pounds.

She lay on her side, one leg extended upward when Randy came back in. "Is Miss Belle coming for us this morning?"

"Doesn't she usually?" She sat up to face her little boy. "Is this a ploy to come back in?"

"What's a ploy, Mommy?"

Grinning, Melodye told him, "Something to get you what you want, and you're a master at it." She hugged him tightly and his reed-slender body melded into hers before he went out, sighing.

* * *

Miss Belle and Jim drew up later that morning at the same time. Melodye saw them from her front window and went out with the twins and their knapsacks. They were ready to go with Jim's mother, who usually kept them and three other small children. Miss Belle parked at the curb and got out as Randy and Rachel ran to her. She bent and hugged them tightly, then waved at her son, who waved back.

Jim sat in the car gathering the paraphernalia he'd need to assess Rafael's secret room. He felt calm and at first was deep in thought until he focused on Melodye and the day before came flooding back with all of its powerful feelings. This time, he'd been able to think about it and he felt he was ready to hold it down. *He was wrong.* He guessed he was just a man who needed a woman, any woman, but he didn't intend to let it get the best of him.

He got out, loaded with his gear and went to the group, hugging his mother. The twins demanded a hug, which he fervently gave, and his heart began to open to them. They were so precious. He had a quick flash of them as his own and was full of irritation that his mind had begun to play tricks on him. He'd kept it all in place and he'd been doing fine. For now he hated the new development that brought Melodye and the twins into his life.

Melodye tried to be calm as she looked at him, but the previous day's feelings came crashing in. All the feverish hunger was there and it was only eight in the morning.

"Oh, yes," Miss Belle told her, "a couple of weeks from now, I'm opening Jim's country house. It's too early for swimming, but the view is gorgeous and you'll enjoy being there. Say you'll come. The twins'll love it."

Melodye thought a moment. It sounded good. "I think I'll

take you up on it," she said, "but the twins will be with Odessa again for the Children's Museum."

"Then it'll be a good holiday for you. You like Ping-Pong and both Jim and I play a mean game. He'll pick you up. I'll be packing lots of goodies for us to eat, so I'll be coming later on."

Melodye glanced at Jim, who looked noncommittal, but she wondered if a look of annoyance and surprise crossed his face.

"Yeah," Jim said. "I'll pick you up around nine, or is that too early?"

Melodye shook her head. "That's fine."

Miss Belle tucked the twins in the car and they drove off with them waving until they got out of sight.

In the car, Belle Ryman looked back, too. She was very fond of Melodye and her wee ones. The young woman was like the daughter she'd always wanted and the twins were like the grandchildren she didn't have. Now, Melodye and her Jim would make a grand pair, she mused with a smile.

The matchmaker in her chortled with delight. If she couldn't get them together, she was going to have a great old time trying. She grinned with visions dancing in her head of grandchildren at her knee, along with the twins, who were like her very own.

Melodye turned to Jim. "Shall we go in?"

"Might as well."

"Let me help you with some of that stuff."

"I can handle it."

Looking at him, she felt an odd mixture of emotions. Interest. Lust. Warmth. Coolness. She wanted to get closer. She wanted to get much farther away. Sure, she'd bet he could handle just about anything. He didn't need or want *her*, that much was plain. And she sure as hell didn't need him. Once this was over, they'd go their separate ways and, God, let it be over soon.

She asked if he'd had breakfast and he said he had. He'd already had a second cup of coffee, so they got right down to business.

His minidigital camera was soon clicking as she opened drawers and put things out to be photographed. They worked silently, both tense and focused on the job at hand. "You know I'm going to need a lot of information from you, but I'm giving you time to mull it over. Try to recall everything you think may have bearing. Any bits of telephone conversations you may have overheard. Husbands and wives talk a lot."

She shook her head. "Before he was killed, we weren't talking at all."

He nodded and looked at her. She sounded bitter. He knew she'd loved this man and he'd hurt her. Her face looked vulnerable, and he felt the way he'd felt yesterday, that her body was turning him on to high heaven. She was sure giving his loins a major workout. Okay, he thought with a shred of resignation, he was due some strong feeling after so long a spell of numbness. Better with Melodye than with some woman he couldn't trust. She had her own heartbreak and he was safe. She wasn't looking for a man.

"That wraps it up here for the time being," he finally said after a couple of hours. "Let's go on to the bank."

At the bank, in the room of safe-deposit boxes, they found that the box they wanted was near the one once shared by Melodye and Rafael. Melodye found her heart pounding as she opened the box. She closed her eyes for a moment before looking in. Jim had brought a basket to hold whatever they found.

There wasn't much. A jeweler's black box she snapped open to find a tennis bracelet, expensive and glittering with gold and good-size diamonds. Then there were two large manila envelopes, one of which held hundred dollar bills. They quickly counted fifty thousand dollars.

Jim whistled. "In cold cash, yet."

"I wonder if this is the money Turk was looking for," Melodye said.

"Could be. Let's see the other envelope."

Their fingers touched and there was the high-voltage electricity between them again. This time it wasn't surprising and both held their breath. How long would this go on? They were in a closed, well-lighted room alone and they might as well have been under a moonlight- and starlight-spangled night for all the protection they had from their unwanted attraction.

Jim looked at her closely. "We're going to have to talk about what's happening between us," he said flatly. "We have to work together on this case, but we don't have to get swamped with something neither one of us wants. Right?"

She nodded, unable to speak. Her heart thumped and fluttered. If he pressed her back against the bank of safe-deposit boxes and took her, she knew she'd let him. Since when, she wondered, with no small amount of anger, had she been such easy prey? She knew a little about him as a youth, that he was wild, but she had also found him kind and assuring. She knew little more about him as a man. He had questioned her, yes, after Rafael's death and he had still seemed kind. But Jim Ryman had his ghosts and his demons and you didn't get close to him easily.

They were locked in silent closeness when he breathed deeply and said, "Let's hit the next envelope." They were both careful not to touch again.

That envelope held one hundred thousand dollars in bearer bonds, and Jim whistled again.

"The guy sure handled plenty of moolah."

"He was careless with money."

She reached into the box, got the last item and opened a heavy, cream-colored envelope. She recognized the stationery. Rafael had asked her to order it, saying he trusted her taste and that it was special. Curious, she read the scrawled note.

Baby,
This is all for you with plenty more to follow. I'm going to help your dreams come true. In a few days we'll be in Cancun, wallowing in the sand and making love like never before. I know this will surprise you, but life is full of surprises. You'll know by this how much I love you.
Forever yours,
Your Rafael

Sudden tears sprang to Melodye's eyes. Had this note been for her? They were a week away from their anniversary when he was killed. She had needed money badly for her boutique and he had said he'd see what he could do about it. And they *had* been to Cancun on their honeymoon. Were the money and the note for her? Melodye read the note twice. Or were they for someone else?

Rafael could be generous to a fault. Unbidden, her mind flooded with the first days of their marriage and his ardor. She shuddered a bit and began to cry, shedding tears of disappointment and hurt at her failed marriage, at the pain Rafael had inflicted that she hadn't cried about. Her heart felt leaden and was bursting with hurt. She was breaking and she couldn't stop herself.

Jim covered the couple of feet between them and held her soft, lush body hard against his. His heart drummed crazily. Right now, he meant to be all about comfort, nothing else. Yeah, right, he chided himself. His loins were on fire and he wished almost violently that he could take her here and now. But his role was as comforter and he damned well meant to do only that.

After long moments, an after-sob shook her and she calmed. "I'm sorry," she breathed.

"For what? Being human? Caring for a man who didn't know how to treat you?"

Ha, he told himself, *he* wasn't a good one to talk about not knowing how to treat a woman. He hadn't been great in that department, either.

"Jim, thank you, and don't ask for what. I haven't really cried since Rafael's death. It all just seemed so unreal. I guess I'll never know if this note was for me. You'll need this money and that note for evidence, won't you?"

"Yeah. If you're hard up for money, I think I can get my department to release some of it."

She shook her head. "No. I'm doing okay." She took a deep breath. "I can't think of anyone I'd rather have on this case."

They both became acutely aware at the same time that he still held her, and she laughed a little as he let his arms fall. She missed having him hold her. His body had felt like heaven against hers. Smiling at herself, she thought, *bring on another trauma, if it's going to make me feel this good.*

He looked at her quizzically. "You're sure you're all right?"

"I'm sure. I know you don't want thanks, but I do thank you. You were always kind."

He sounded bitter then. "There've been times I haven't been kind enough." But he didn't explain what he meant.

She invited him to go back to her boutique with her and he agreed, saying the more he knew about her life and Rafael's, the better. By the time they reached the big sandstone building just above Dupont Circle on Connecticut Avenue, she felt relaxed and relieved. She also thrummed with excitement, thinking she was going to have to get used to the fact that this man excited her.

Her boutique was on the second floor and was beautifully decorated in shades of burgundy, peach and pale pink with touches of jade, red and bright yellow. It was spacious and airy and she was very proud of what she'd accomplished.

"Nice," he commented. There were only a few customers and she greeted them warmly. Women began coming in in the early afternoon.

Her best friend, Odessa Holloway, a tall, heavyset woman with curly brown hair came forward. When Melodye introduced Jim, Odessa shook hands and laughed. "Just what we need at A-1 Plus Love, a fine man to brighten up our digs. Welcome and come back any old time."

Odessa was a flirt. Her style was so lighthearted that men flirted right back, and Jim was no exception. Crinkles formed around his eyes. "I'm going to have to take you up on that, at least for a while."

Melodye explained that Jim was investigating Rafael's death. Odessa expressed surprise that it was a murder, but Melodye was sure she didn't feel surprised.

"You've got company," Odessa told her.

"Don't keep it a secret."

Odessa raised her eyebrows. "The queen herself. Your

mother. Bettina. She's back in your studio, going over some of the designs for our fashion show and ruling the roost in general."

Bettina was the last person Melodye wanted to see. She had disliked Jim in the past. How did she feel now? She decided to barge right in and take Jim with her. "Remember my mother?"

"I surely do. Think she's changed about my being the devil incarnate?"

Melodye laughed. "She was just trying to protect me. You were always something else."

He grinned. "Uh-huh. That was and is you."

Oh, he was good for her ego, she thought.

They found Bettina sitting on a tall stool in front of a drawing board, poring over sketches. Her honey skin was flawless, features and makeup perfect and her brown hair was done in a shiny French twist. Her fashionably thin body was clad in her trademark Prada. She glanced up when they came in.

"Mother, remember Jim Ryman?"

"I'm afraid I do." Her mother's husky, theatrical voice was slightly acid. "How are you, Jim?"

"Well, and you?"

"I'm a tough nut to crack. I'll always do well, I think."

Jim laughed easily. The woman's eyes said she liked him no better than she'd liked him as a youth. He'd hated that she didn't want him to be friends with Melodye. Now he didn't care. Once this case was over, he was out of here. He stood there as Bettina began to talk about the sketches with Melodye. He noted that her first comments were laced with deep and none-too-kind criticism.

After just a few minutes, Melodye stopped her. "We can do this later, Mom. Jim needs to talk with me about some things…."

"Oh, yes," Bettina said. "And *we* have a lot to talk about.

I'm really working on giving your show my all and you can count your blessings. I'm not sure you could pull it off without me. I'm moving fast, and—"

"Mother." Melodye's voice was firm.

Bettina raised her brows high and gave Jim a glance. "I certainly hope you've changed. Are you just back for a visit?"

He cleared his throat. "I've *moved* back, I'm afraid." How different he felt now from the time he'd cowered inside at her coldness.

"Oh? Your wife died, didn't she?"

"Yes."

"You were a policeman."

"I still am."

"Have you made it to captain, or beyond?" She spoke as if she found anything less to be unacceptable.

"No. I'm stuck at detective lieutenant."

"Ah, dead bodies and skullduggery. Why would you want to deal with that?"

"Mother!" Melodye protested.

"Well, it's true, but that would be just your style. You were a wild one, Jim. I certainly *hope* you've changed."

Jim laughed a little, thinking, *And you're a nasty lady who never forgives.*

"Mother, Jim and I have to get started."

Bettina sat for a moment as if she hadn't heard her, then she closed her eyes and pushed herself off the stool. She looked at Jim carefully and said, "Would you leave my daughter and me alone for a minute? I just want to tell her something that can't wait. I'll only be a minute."

"Of course."

"Please wait just outside," a nettled Melodye told him, and Jim opened the door and stepped back out into the boutique.

Bettina and her daughter squared off as Melodye told her, "You were none too civil. Live in the present, Mother. A lot of water has gone over the dam."

"Not enough, I'm afraid," Bettina grated. "I see you've still got starry eyes over the Ryman boy."

"The Ryman *man*."

"You're asking for trouble if you let him into your life, Melodye. He wasn't for you then, he isn't for you now. Lucia could handle him, *you* can't."

At the mention of the svelte Lucia, her fairskinned, light-haired sister, Melodye bristled and, yes, she *hurt*. Lucia had always been Bettina's favorite. *Favorite?* Melodye thought bitterly. No, Bettina loved Lucia and *didn't* love her. It was a sharp knife that had always twisted in her heart and it never seemed to end.

Melodye drew a deep breath. "I don't think anyone handles Jim Ryman. He's very much his own man."

"How long have you been seeing him?"

Melodye glared at her mother. "I don't want to discuss this with you. It's none of your business."

Bettina's look was full of scorn as her eyes raked her daughter's body. "Very well, my girl, but do remember that Rafael was the only man who's ever truly been interested in you. He was your only chance and by some miracle he wanted to marry you. If you weren't happy, you never told me. It's unfortunate that he was killed in that robbery, but such is life. As I said, he was your last chance and I predict it won't happen again."

Bettina drew a deep breath. "A man like Jim Ryman would never be interested in the likes of you. Maybe Lucia…"

Melodye's voice was shrill. "I'm not going to listen to this. There's nothing between Jim Ryman and me. I don't think you have to worry about that. Now, there are things we have to talk about, so I have to ask you to leave."

With an exaggerated shrug, Bettina pursed her lips, picked up her Prada bag from the drawing board and began to march out. But she flung back over her shoulder, "You can be such a fool, Melodye. Sometimes I wonder how you got to be my daughter."

Melodye felt rage creep into her system, but she seemed calm as she called Jim back in.

Just inside the door, he stood looking at her quizzically. "Again I have to ask, are you okay?"

"Yeah, I'm okay. You must be getting tired of my thanking you, but you're very good at soothing me."

She had gone closer to him than she intended and the heat from their bodies was intense. She wanted to move back and couldn't, trapped by interest and aching desire.

He bit his bottom lip. "I'll try not to take too much of your time, but the more info I can get, the faster I can put the pieces together."

She smiled. "Please don't worry about my time. I want to see this solved as much as you do." Lord, she thought, her female core was doing flips. Then she sobered as she thought of what Rafael had told her about being out of shape inside and out. Now, Jim Ryman looked at her as if everything about her was in exactly the right place and he liked what he saw. But he was distant, too, and she felt he would take it no further. In Melodye's deepest heart she felt that Bettina was right—he wasn't for the likes of her. He was gorgeous and everything she wanted in a man, but Lucia would be more his speed.

She became aware that she was dreaming and she started. "You were thinking?" he said.

"About where this will end." She meant the investigation, but what lay between them was very much on her mind.

"What's it like for you tomorrow morning?" he asked

"It's always a slow day, and my time is pretty much my own. Odessa welcomes any chance to run the show. Like me, she loves this place. Why do you ask?"

"Because I need you to go with me to see Turk Hylton in the afternoon. I plan to ask him some loaded questions and I'd like you to be there to assess his reaction."

She grimaced because she didn't want to see Turk Hylton ever again, but she nodded. "Sure. I'll go with you."

They set a time and began talking about Rafael. Jim's voice was quiet and slow and she enjoyed hearing him lay it out.

"I've got twice as much intelligence as I expected to have," he told her. "This is one of the department's most important cases. The mob likes to come into a little city like this and try to take over. Police departments in small places aren't always too savvy, but Crystal Lake is different. Chief Arnold is from New York City and he's the best. We're not going to have the mob taking over."

She nodded. "I said I'd do anything to help and I mean it. When I asked you if I'm in danger, I didn't mean that that would hold me back. I've got the twins and, yes, I'm very concerned, but that won't stop me from helping you."

He looked grave. "Good. There are ways to prevent your being exposed to much danger and I intend to use all of them."

He glanced at his watch after nearly another hour of conversation. "I've gotta go. Two meetings with the chief today."

He smiled broadly then and she wondered what made his face light up. She thought he should smile more often; it made him even more of a heartbreaker. She was glad she was off the market. For a moment Melodye held her breath because she thought he was going to touch her hand and she wanted him to. She also didn't want the incendiary flash between them that always seemed to happen. But he only shrugged and went out, saying, "See you tomorrow."

After he left she sat at her desk poring over some papers, then she picked up a sketch and studied her dress for the show. A safe draped navy crepe. Lovely enough, but nothing special. Bettina had taught her well. Nothing special for no one special. The thought flashed across her mind: How did Jim Ryman see her? He called her beautiful, but he knew she didn't have enough self-esteem and he was a kind man. She dreaded the time when Lucia would blow into town and put her stamp on him.

Chapter 3

Turk Hylton was his usual suave, effusive self. His skin, oiled brown hair and London-tailored suits were just part of his man-about-town persona. He stood up as his secretary showed them into the big, luxurious room. It pleased Melodye that Jim had a couple of inches on him because Turk had once seemed so big and threatening.

Finally he said easily, "Welcome to my palace. Sweetie, you're looking like the Venus de Milo and I'm responding. Lord, *how* I'm responding."

Turk's drink-reddened eyes had narrowed and he seemed to be eating her alive. Then he shrugged. "Have a seat, of course." He indicated a big, blue, expensive sofa, then pulled up a deep chair in front of them. A confrontational setting.

"I'll need to record this conversation," Jim said. "May I have your permission?"

Turk sat, tapping his foot. "Sure. If I don't give it to you,

you'll just haul my ass into the station house and there'll be fifty recorders going. Fire away. I've got lawyers who can get me out of anything I choose to get myself into."

Jim was silent a long while and Melodye guessed it was to throw Turk off guard. Turk's breathing was loud in the room.

"How about a few drinks to ease the atmosphere?" Turk asked them.

Melodye and Jim shook their heads. Turk got up, pulled over a small table and put bowls of nuts, corn chips and candy from his desk onto it. "I'm forgetting my manners. Forgive me."

The two men were playing cat and mouse and she thought she knew who would win. Turk and Rafael had played games with each other around her. As Turk continued to slaver over her, Jim marshaled his thoughts and dug in.

"You know all about Mr. Carter's gambling habits," he began.

Turk sighed and patted his foot harder. "Well, not all. Rafael was a man who played his cards—all of them—close to his vest. Melodye here would know as much as I do." Then he rushed on, "Rafael and I used to be the best of friends. We go back a long way."

"What caused the rift?"

"Did I say there was a rift? No, we just drifted from friendship to acquaintance. I had a lot of ideas about expanding *Steeped In Joy* he didn't go along with. He had ideas I hated."

"Such as?"

Turk chuckled. "You cops are nosy bastards, aren't you? He wanted to move the club closer to Richmond. Clea Wilde's got Wilde's Wonderland a couple of miles away and she's competition with a capital *C*. He thought we'd do better down there. I wanted to expand right here, drive old Clea to the wall. I'm a vicious competitor."

You're a vicious man, Melodye thought, but said nothing. "Did you two quarrel?"

"All the time. I've got a temper. Rafael had a temper. We nearly came to blows a couple of times, but I backed off. My mama always said a fool and his fists make dangerous partners."

Jim drew a deep breath and smiled. "I like that."

"Yeah, I thought you would. My mama was something else. She thought the same about her son. My dad was a no-show." He laughed hollowly.

Melodye had sat down closer to Jim than she intended to and her flesh tingled with his presence as if they were the only two people in the room. Animals and birds strutted their stuff to impress the mates they wanted. Jim was a smoothie and he impressed her just by being on earth and she wasn't a woman who was easily impressed. *Calm down, girl,* she told herself as she felt the familiar thrum between her legs. *This is a serious affair. A man has been murdered. Your late husband, Rafael, has been murdered. Slow down.*

But she didn't slow down. Jim's voice seemed unusually authoritative and warm, as if he were questioning a friend. He was good, no doubt about it, and Turk began to seem ill at ease on his own turf. This pleased her to no end.

Jim was in control now. "Then you two never seriously fought, but you had your differences. Was there a specific time that perhaps enraged you? You said you both had tempers."

Turk recovered a little. "Man, everybody's got a temper. I'll bet you've got one of the worst. Miss Melodye here is a firesetter. I've been on the receiving end of her wrath just because I know a great body when I see one and I've always gone for what I wanted."

"Did you want Rafael's wife?"

"Hell, don't you?"

To her surprise, Jim smiled. "Did he object to your coming on to her?"

Turk beat his fist on the arm of his chair. "Rafael had his own fish to fry. He did tell me once never to come on too strong to his wife. He was territorial and he'd stand for just so much. So I kept it on an easy scale. I ogled and satisfied myself with that. But Melodye can tell you I tried to make her see that I could service her better than he could. I didn't drink as much, didn't have as many women. Remember, Melodye?"

Melodye didn't answer him and he didn't pursue it.

Jim asked a quick succession of questions then that seemed to throw Turk off guard and that he seemed to resent. Finally he said, "You're trying to pin this whole goddamned murder on *me,* aren't you? But it won't play. I didn't kill my partner."

"Or hire it done?"

"What?" Turk roared. "Hell, no. I didn't hire it done. Everybody knows Rafael went about loaded with cash. He's lucky it didn't happen long ago. Ask some of his women if they got tired of being shafted. Rafael was a married *player.*"

Melodye sat, thinking, so there was her answer after all this time. She had suspected it. Now she knew, when it no longer mattered.

When they were finished, Jim stood up. Turk sat for a moment, smiling. "Find out anything you didn't already know?" he asked.

Jim shrugged. "Enough. Thank you."

"I think you guys are overpaid and have too much time on

your hands. Come back anytime. We've got a great band playing this weekend. Bring your friend here." He leered at Melodye again and she cringed inside. Turk was such an idiot.

Then Turk winked at her slowly and lewdly, and Jim threw him a volcanic glare. Melodye's response was glacial and it cooled his ardor a bit.

Out on the highway going back to Crystal Lake, Jim seemed deep in thought. Finally he laughed a bit as his fingers tapped the wheel. "Hylton's a piece of work," he said.

"Was the visit helpful?"

"Oh, yeah. I saw firsthand the way he comes on to you and the way you dislike him."

"Choose a stronger word."

"Okay, loathe."

"Ah, right on the button."

"Nothing brings out the way a man really is like the way a woman brings it out. Turk said Rafael had warned him about you."

"Rafael didn't care. In the beginning, when they were close, he laughed about it. Joked that we should make a threesome." She shuddered a bit. "It was only after they were no longer so friendly that Rafael began to come down on him. Turk ignored him."

Again he was silent before he said, "Call Mom, will you, and tell her to have the twins ready to roll. I've got a late meeting with the chief and I have to be there early. I was by Mom's earlier and I began telling the kids a story before I had to leave on call. I promised I'd come back and finish."

"That's thoughtful of you."

"Not really. I remember how it feels to be disappointed as a kid. Your world is so narrow, so dependent...."

He was remembering how often his own policeman father had disappointed him and it still hurt.

Miss Belle had promised to have the twins ready to go. Melodye settled back in Jim's burgundy BMW and listened to the engine purr. The windows were down and it was warm for May. They were silent, both going over what they'd just been through. Melodye always felt she needed a shower when she'd been around Turk Hylton.

Later, at her house Jim helped her put the twins to bed. They'd had supper and wanted one of the sugarless cookies Miss Belle had baked for them. "Now," Randy demanded, "the rest of the story."

Jim looked at him and grinned. "Spoken like a real little man." He sat in a chair by the bed and began the old, old tale of the wolf and the three little pigs. Before he began, he said, "All good things deserve being repeated, so I'm going to start over and this time go to the end."

"Yeah!" Randy shouted.

Melodye looked at her little boy, shaking her head, envisioning him at thirteen and storming this world.

She sat in another chair and listened as Jim told the story, acting it out in his pleasant baritone voice. She focused on Jim. He seemed like a different man with her kids. No longer brooding and distant. Too bad he didn't have children. Elyssa had been pregnant when she drowned. What kind of father would he have made? And she wistfully thought that she wanted a man like him for her kids, but her grandfather, Papa France, had to be enough. For herself she *wanted* no man at all.

When the kids were finally tucked in with kisses and hugs from Melodye and Jim, they slept and she switched on a recording of Dvořák's *Cello Concerto*. The gorgeous music always lifted her spirits.

"You like classical music," he said. "It figures. It's deep and so are you."

"Do you like classical?"

"That piece is one of my favorites. There's not much in music I don't like. Gospel. Classical. R & B. Pop. I guess country's a favorite. The white man's blues."

"There's Charley Pride. He sure isn't white."

"He's one of the greats. I love him and Otis Blackwell."

It had grown dark and she was mindful that he would need to leave. "There's a meteor shower the weatherman said we could see around this time. Would you like to watch it?"

"Yeah, I would. I once thought of being an astronomer. There isn't much I haven't thought of being. My father wanted me to be anything but a race car driver."

She teased him then. "I remember the souped-up hotrods and you were hell-bent on racing. You were going to be the first great African American racer."

He laughed. "And I wind up a cop like my dad. Same level. I wanted to race to get his dander up. He hated racing and wanted me to be a doctor. By the time I finished the academy he was dead. I think he'd be proud of me—finally. I sure gave him fits growing up."

His face had gone somber and there was pain in his eyes. "If I'd known he was going to die so soon, I would've tried harder to please him."

She wanted to place her hand on his as they sat side by side on the sofa, but she was afraid of her feelings, hated and thrilled about what happened when they touched. So she simply said, "I'm sorry. Life throws us curves sometimes."

He knew he had to leave, but he really wanted to see the meteor shower. They stepped outside on her big, dimly lit patio.

"Am I smelling honeysuckle?" Jim asked.

"I got cuttings from your mom. Isn't the fragrance delightful?"

"Yep. Sure is. Hey, there're your meteors."

They watched the stunning meteors disintegrate across the heavens and it seemed to her the night had never held so much glory. The moon was waning.

"It's beautiful out tonight," she said. "And that's a great meteor shower. I always say I'm going to watch them, but I never do. It seems so lonely watching them alone."

He didn't answer, and she knew his face would have gone remote while he was lost in his thoughts.

She didn't intend to move closer to him, but she did and his arms went around her. She thought he groaned a little as he pressed her body against his, his big hands moving up and down her back. His hot tongue flicked the corners of her yielding mouth that opened enough for him to go inside the sweet hollows and linger for long moments.

She felt his big erection and his hard, muscular body dominate her soft curves. She thought she heard him whisper her name, but she was too dizzy to be certain. She began to give in and over to him, angry with herself for being so easy.

She was deep in that kiss when he stopped abruptly and held her by her shoulders, away from him.

"We have to talk, Melodye. *Now*!"

She felt so humiliated. She had responded like a giddy teenager hungry for love. But reason told her that grown-ups got hungry for love, too. "I'm sorry," she whispered, acid tears of frustration in her eyes.

He shook her a bit. "You have nothing to be sorry about. It's a romantic night and we're two lonely people. Let's talk. Sit in the glider?"

She passively let him lead her to the glider where they sat down. She didn't want to be this close to him, yet she knew she really wanted to be as close as she could get.

And sitting there Jim thought she'd be surprised if she knew how much he wanted her, but *he* knew the score, knew this had to end with this fragment of a kiss.

To her surprise he took her hand and squeezed it and no fireworks. "Melodye, we have to work together on this case so we have to be around each other. We've always liked each other, been drawn. Now we're even more deeply drawn. We both like all the same things, so it's natural."

He fell silent again, then went on. "We haven't talked about it, but we've both been hurt. You by Rafael, me by Elyssa's and my unborn baby's death. I made her a bad husband and probably would have made a bad father."

"No," she said quickly. "I don't think so."

He went on.

"My father and I never got along. We clashed horns at every turn and I always sensed that I disappointed him. I disappointed Elyssa. In due time, if she'd lived, we probably would have been divorced. She deserved more than I could give her and we both knew it."

Raw hurt permeated his voice, and Melodye reached over and squeezed his shoulder, responding to the hurt and the need to soothe him. She couldn't know that her touch sent wildfire roaring along his sinews and muscles, touched his heart and moved his soul.

"Thank you," he said softly. "You know how much I like you, but I'm guilty of so much that I can't help. I hurt people I love, Melodye. Hurt them bad and I don't intend to hurt anybody else—ever."

"Jim," she asked softly, "do you ever pray?"

He blew a harsh breath. "I do, you know, but sometimes I wonder if God hears me. I'm a cold man and I don't seem to feel things the way other people do."

That wasn't the way she remembered him. "I think you're afraid of your tender feelings, that's all."

He laughed harshly. "Mom was always tender with me. I was a sickly kid. She spoiled me and I think that's why I grew up to be such a heller, to prove I had the manly strength I didn't feel I had. That's why I raced. Why I became a detective. I've always taken the toughest cases, the most dangerous ones. Elyssa could never understand that."

She listened intently, but what she was wrapped up in was the brief and special kiss they'd just shared. Her soul sang and felt sad all at once. He was heading her off at the pass, telling her they could never be and a part of her was glad because he was right. He *could* hurt her, and she didn't intend to ever be hurt again.

Her attention drifted and she came back to him still talking. "You've been hurt badly and I will *not* hurt you again. That's the least I can do. I'm damned attracted to you as you are to me. Let's be smart and keep working together, being together as long as it's necessary, then we'll part friends. Do I make sense?"

Melodye nodded. "Perfect sense." She felt relieved, as if she'd teetered on the edge of a precipice and some wondrous force had pulled her back.

After Jim left, she sat on the patio, still looking at the heavens. He had noticed and commented on the perfume of the honeysuckle. He'd come home with them to finish reading the twins a story, and he thought he'd make a poor father. And *husband*. One day she hoped he'd find somebody because he was a good man and he was lonely. And what about herself? She had the twins and her boutique and designing. She felt her life was pretty full. Papa France was a force in her life. The twins adored him, so she wasn't doing too badly. Well, Jim had his work and he was deeply involved.

She went inside reluctantly and worked for a while on a cocktail-gown sketch. He had talked with her about her work. She felt so good making a plus-size woman beautiful. It sure didn't seem that Jim had been back only a few days. The shock of the murder had worn off quickly and she felt little, other than bitterness, but she wanted Rafael's killing avenged, and if anyone could do it, Jim could.

In bed, she tossed. She had gone to bed too early and he had not spoken of seeing her the coming day. She thought that was a good thing. Talking with him had helped. He didn't need to worry about leading her on because she didn't intend to go down any man's primrose path.

Her phone rang and she jumped. Was it Jim? It was Papa France with his deep voice.

"Hey, baby girl. Sorry to call so late, but I wanted you to know I'm back. The fishing trip was a huge success. We caught a passel of catfish and I'll be bringing some over tomorrow. We got two wild rabbits. You get one and I get some of the stew. What's going on?"

She found herself telling him that Jim was back and about the murder.

He whistled and said nothing for a moment, then, "I always liked Jim Ryman. His father and I were close. Well, as close as you could get to Paul Ryman. The boy and I talked a lot after Paul died. I always thought Jim would make you a dandy husband."

"Papa France! Bettina would have died."

He chuckled. "Your mama can't know what's best for

you. She liked Rafael well enough and look at the life he gave you. I don't like speaking ill of the dead, but I wanted to throttle him a lot of times."

"Everything ends sometime. I've got the twins."

"Yes, ma'am, you've got a whole lot. You've done well for yourself and your grandmother would be proud, but a good man would round your life out. You say you've seen Jim a couple of times already?"

"I have, but don't go making wedding plans. He's still grieving, and you know how I feel about men."

"The right man could change your mind."

"It won't be Jim Ryman."

Papa France said nothing else, but he was thinking hard and plans had already begun to spin in his brain.

Jim came awake around two o'clock. His meeting had gone swimmingly and his chief was pleased, as was his captain. He usually slept well. Had he heard groaning? Now he listened intently for noises, but the house was quiet with only the hum of electrical appliances. Then it hit him. *He* had groaned. His big shaft was rock hard. "Down, boy!" he muttered to himself and pressed it back. It sprang up again and he let it be. His heart was pounding, too. He expelled a harsh breath. Funny how the body often just wouldn't go along with the mind. He had come to know the body had a wisdom of its own. His friend, the famous gospel singer, Whit Steele, had told him that. He wished there was something he could do to make Melodye know what a beauty she was. She often looked wistful and he felt she didn't begin to know what she had.

Lying there, he thought about how much he enjoyed her company. How would she feel about being friends? He could build her ego; he was certain of that. They trusted each other and each knew the score. Romance was lacking and often not even wanted in a whole lot of lives. Yeah, he and Elyssa had had romance with a capital *R* and where had it gotten them? Their sex life had been great. His job had been the trouble spot.

"You're married to your job more than to me," she'd often protested. "Jim, you've been shot once and grazed twice. Other detectives die in bed after long lives on the force. You always want to wrestle with the truly bad guys...."

"That's because I want to take them off the streets."

She'd shaken her head. "No, it's because you've got to prove something. I don't know what, but something. I think you volunteer for the worst ones, the most dangerous ones. You can't straighten out the world all by yourself."

No, he'd thought, but he could do his part to take the worst ones off the streets. The day she'd drowned, he'd pulled a raw one. A creep had shot three women in a beauty shop and was running wild. They had a likely suspect. It was his job. He and Elyssa had been going to a fancy estate party out on Long Island and would swim in the ocean, as well as in the estate pool. Elyssa had been furious when he'd said he had to work and she'd raged, "Look at you. You're shining. Oh, you black knight, you. When are you gonna hang it up?"

She hadn't tried to understand and it infuriated him. He'd encouraged her in her work for the city as a social worker with underprivileged kids. Why couldn't she encourage him? "Never!" he'd grated. "And you'd damned well better get used to it."

He'd regretted those words bitterly when they'd called him and told him she was dead and he knew his grief was as much guilt as anything. He was the one who hadn't understood.

He'd come to feel that in her pregnancy he should have coddled her, gone along with *her* program, but he'd been macho, trying to save the world. Being a cop was all he knew, all he wanted, but his triumphs were empty now and would he ever stop missing her?

He switched on the bedside lamp and picked up a copy of the big tome, *Principles of Investigation,* a department bible. He read until his eyes got grainy and he put the book aside. Only then did he realize that Melodye's face and body were constantly in his vision. But this was one time his mind was going to win, not his hag-ridden body.

Chapter 4

The Saturday morning Jim, Miss Belle and Melodye were going to the Virginia countryside, Odessa came early to pick up the twins. Dressed in a powder-blue lounging suit, Odessa was all smiles as the twins swarmed her. "Hey, I like that Jim. I'm getting a chance to be momma to my pets."

Melodye grinned. "Welcome to the job." It was Saturday and they would return late Sunday.

"Tell you what I'd really like," Odessa said. "Could I just bring them by quickly Monday morning?"

Melodye thought a moment. "I don't see why not. Odessa, I wish you were coming with us. The twins are welcome."

Odessa shook her head vigorously. "No, this is *my* time with the twins. One day some hunk is gonna tie me down and I want to be experienced with handling his babies." She was thirty-seven with one bad marriage behind her and her attractive face was constantly aglow with dreams.

The door chimes sounded. It was Papa France who had big hugs all around as the twins both yelled, "Papa France!" and flew to him. He had M&M's for them. Melodye ate sweets, but she limited theirs. They looked at her, their big, bright eyes imploring.

"A few," she said, "but not too many," and they soon gobbled the candy Papa France measured out to them.

She and Papa France had talked about today's trip and he'd been happy for her. He and Odessa were still there when Jim drove up. Melodye swallowed hard and smoothed her hair, a gesture not lost on either Papa France or Odessa. She had done eighteen stuffed eggs and a couple dozen of her superb chocolate-chip lace cookies.

When Jim stood in the middle of the living room, his wide shoulders and narrow hips dominating the room, Melodye couldn't help salivating. Her libido and private parts felt internally linked to him but, she thought airily, *she* still controlled her heart and brain.

His police team had taken additional photos of everything and had dusted for fingerprints. He'd been by here and the boutique several times to talk more about the case. And her body had thrummed itself into a frenzy every time they'd been together. But they both congratulated themselves. He'd been in town almost three weeks, and they'd kept it together like the grown-ups they were.

Odessa looked from one to the other. "You two go ahead. I'll lock up after I've chatted a while with Papa France. Don't worry one nanosecond about the twins, and frolic enough for me. My time is coming."

Melodye looked at her and raised her eyebrows. What was there about people that they couldn't stand to see an unmarried man and woman stay free? Well, Jim and herself were différent. She could see them in the years ahead being staunch friends, never taking it further if he didn't succumb to some filly's charms.

The ten-acre farm out from Alexandria, Virginia, was a charming place with a large white farmhouse, a big red barn and other outbuildings. Jim explained that a man and his sons who lived on a neighboring farm took care of the place; and the man's wife saw after the house.

"They usually stock one fridge when we're coming down. We have two. Today mom's bringing a lot of food."

There was also a big freezer. She put the stuffed eggs in the fridge, the cookies in a big china cookie jar.

The furniture was solid, overstuffed and tasteful. The bright and sunny rooms reflected Belle Ryman's exquisite hand. He took her overnight case. "Make yourself at home. See the lake?"

She looked out the window and there was the big man-made lake shimmering in the June sunlight. "Beautiful," she said. Swans floated gracefully—one black, one white. Huge moss-draped oaks stood at the edge of the yard and in the distance, a forest stretched out.

Amused, she noticed that they were suddenly awkward with each other. When Belle came, it would be better; the older woman was a barrel of fun. She thought wistfully that the twins would have enjoyed this.

"Tell you what," he said, "I don't want you to be bored until Mom gets here. Why don't you settle in and I'll take you out in the canoe?"

Nodding, she paid attention to the spinet that sat in the corner, went over to it and ran a few chords, saying "It has good tuning."

"Yeah." He came closer and she found herself breathing shallowly. Did his body behave the way hers did when they stood near each other? She doubted it. Men were used to being turned on all the time; they accepted it as part of their nature. Driving down hadn't been too bad. He came even closer and she cringed a bit as she sat down at the spinet and began to play "Chopsticks."

He knew she did it to get away from him and he smiled. She was safe. He wasn't going to put any moves on her. "Hey, you're tense," he said, "uptight. Mom's coming, but we don't need a chaperone. Didn't the other night prove it? We're in control, baby, all the way."

She looked up at him and played on. "Thanks, Jim. Seems as if I can always depend on you. It's almost as if you're from another time and place."

He thought about that. He felt very much of *this* time and place, standing over her, inhaling her vanilla-oriented bath oil. It felt good and it bothered him that this place seemed to seal them in with each other. Like her, he'd be grateful for Belle's presence. She played a Lionel Richie tune then and he hummed it with her. She had a surprisingly good voice when she sang.

He laughed. "A frog would envy my croaking, so I won't join in," he told her.

After a while, she got up and wandered about the house, thinking the plants and the house and grounds were well tended.

He opened the windows and a sharp breeze swept through. Then he showed her his bedroom, pointing out the several pairs of binoculars on the dresser. "The ones on the right are the most powerful," he said. "Feel free to use them. There's a lot to see out there. And those are my best cameras in those two cases."

She glanced around and held her breath, suddenly imagining him and her on that indigo blue covered bed for a few seconds before she cut it off. No, don't go there, she scolded herself. But she went there again before she could stop herself and he was inside her, deep and dangerous—and thrilling.

He frowned. "What *is* it?"

She had shuddered hard. "Nothing. I guess a goose was going over my grave."

"Go away, goose!" he teased her. He began to touch her arm and the electricity was there again.

Come early, Miss Belle, she silently prayed, remembering the night on the patio when they'd handled themselves so well. They hadn't been cut off and alone the way they were here.

She went to the window and gasped with delight when she saw several peacocks with one male in his full glory. "Hey, they're wonderful!" she exclaimed.

"Yep. Got six of them, four females, two males."

"I'd like to watch them."

"Sure, but let's hit the lake first."

She changed into scarlet shorts and a black jersey halter. The cut was conservative, but her curves were very much there. He eyed her hungrily and fiercely controlled his feelings. Would she have worn this if his mother weren't coming? He didn't think so. She considered him safe, and of course, he was. He wasn't in it for the love. Or for seducing her.

The lake rippled as a soft breeze caressed it. The canoe was big and they both paddled. She looked at Jim in his ragged cutoff khaki shorts and blue tee that showed off his just-right biceps and pectorals. The leathery, rippling tan of his arms fascinated her.

His face was grave as he looked at her. He thought then that she needed to hear every complimentary phrase he knew to shore up her ego. He would do what he could, sorry that it couldn't be more.

He cleared his throat, "You know, my girl, you have a truly beautiful body." Was that too personal?

She flushed hotly, then forced herself to calm down. "Thank you. That's a double compliment coming from a hunk like yourself."

"Your feet and legs could be in a magazine ad."

"They're okay, I guess."

"Other women with half as much are twice as proud. Why do you hide your light?"

"You're just being kind."

He drew a deep breath. "Didn't Rafael ever tell you this?"

"Rafael didn't talk to me much after the first years when I got pregnant. I don't think he thought pregnant women were very pretty."

"I'd have given anything to hold my child."

He hadn't meant to say that; it revealed too much pain. She heard it in his voice and her look was warm with soothing empathy. He couldn't help the thought that flashed across his mind: what would she be like in bed? *His* bed.

"Jim, I'm sorry," she was saying softly.

"Yeah, so am I." The swans had come close then and there were multicolored water lilies in back of them. "Are you enjoying yourself?"

"Hugely. Is there a computer in the house?"

"Sure thing. I have a study here. As a matter of fact, I have some work I have to do when we go back, but you're free to use it anytime."

She saw the peacocks trailing just past the lush vegetable garden, going toward the forest. "I'd like to spend a long while by myself watching them. I used to be a bird-watcher."

"Sure. Take the large binoculars so they'll be strong enough. I'll be doing my thing while you're out. Sure you don't want company?"

She shook her head. They'd only been out a little while, but she'd be happy to get away from him for a spell and by that time, Miss Belle should be here.

He looked at her sharply as if he could read her thoughts.

Later she nestled near a clump of lilacs and watched the exquisite feathers of the male peacocks as they strutted and preened across the meadow. Imagine seeing this every day. She'd never have thought that Jim was a man who liked peacocks, but there was so much she didn't know about this man. Rafael used to laugh and say, "The only thing I like about nature is sex. The old girl can have everything else."

She lifted the binoculars that brought the birds so close. The brilliant spread of feathers, the big dots of color that sat so precisely at the upper end of each major feather. She had forgotten her camera but remembered the camera cases Jim had showed her in his bedroom. One was like one she'd bought. She needed to capture this glory. She got up and stretched a bit, thinking she'd come back and get a lot of photos. The twins loved photos.

Almost to the house she realized she'd gone farther out than she thought. She saw Jim's tall form in the back of the garden and felt suddenly shy. Why not just go on in and get a camera and be on her way? He surely wouldn't mind. She glanced at her watch. One-thirty. Miss Belle would be about an hour she had called to say. Melodye thought she'd have her fill of peacock-watching by then.

Going through the house, she paused at his bedroom door and a smile tugged at the corners of her mouth as she pushed the door open, envisioning the peacocks she would see close up. Her whole body went up in shock as she saw him standing naked, facing her. The artist in her drank him in and her breath came so fast she thought she'd faint. She wanted, needed to say something, anything, but only a whimper came.

God, the hunger in her was terrible. Small flames lit and flashed throughout her body until they were one conflagration. Her private parts were blazing, hot and wet, and her breasts were pebbling for all they were worth. Did they reach out to him, beg him to cup them?

He stared at her, mesmerized by her voluptuous form and he thought he knew what she'd be like beneath those scarlet shorts and that black halter. An ancient, purely savage instinct held him in thrall as he heard her choke out, "I'm sorry." He wanted to tell her she had nothing to be sorry for. She *belonged* here with him. He wondered at the madness in him to possess her, even as his brain protested that he mustn't go there. His big shaft was raging to thrust inside her, feel her tender walls close around it and grip it tightly. His eyes moved hungrily across those high, full breasts and he was lost in wanting.

No force could have stopped their slow dance until they were wrapped in each other's arms. His tongue plunged into her open mouth and he explored the depths of that sweet, sweet mouth with searing heat. He licked her face slowly and wantonly—her eyes, forehead, cheeks. He moved down to the hollows of her throat and planted small, hot kisses until she thought she couldn't stand it.

Fear partnered with lust in Melodye because she knew she wouldn't satisfy him if she let him inside. This kiss was a temporary thing, never meant to last. Hadn't Rafael told her how out of shape she was, how undesirable? And Rafael knew women as Jim never could. But Lord, she thought, right now she *needed* him and she would have these precious moments. If he took her, would she, *could* she stop him?

He cupped her face with his sinewy hands on either side of her head, and she felt sealed in, doomed to let him have his way, as if it wouldn't also be her way. He wanted to cup her fabulous buttocks, but he knew that would be the end of all control. *You're a fool,* he scolded himself. *You want no commitment, you need no commitment and this is not a woman you could ever take lightly. Go away,* he snapped at his saner self, *this is too good to let go.* And the words came to mind: *sow a storm and reap a whirlwind.*

She stroked his biceps and his broad shoulders as lust ate her alive. Did those soft whimpers come from her? In her entire life she had known nothing like this. Scalding blood flooded her system, made her limbs heavy with wanting him. So beautiful and so dangerous. Every cell in her body cautioned her that she had hurt from what Rafael did to her. With Jim, the hurt could kill her. *Push him away,* every nerve screamed.

But it was then that he undid the hooks of her halter and set her breasts free for his mouth to suckle hungrily, laving them fully and fondling them. He groaned aloud and sucked in his breath as he went from one lush breast to the other, sampling the chocolate flesh. His quick tongue flicked her nipples and it flashed hazily across his mind that she was a beautiful doll. It also came to him that she was his for the taking and he couldn't do this to her. She deserved all that heaven allowed and he had nothing to give her.

He stopped cold, proud of his control, and stood up, panting. For long moments they stared at each other and he kissed her again with hot tears in his eyes.

"Melodye," he whispered. "I'm sorry," still holding her.

"It's all right," she murmured. "I could have said no."

With a deep sigh, he took her by her shoulders and shook her. "Stop blaming yourself. It was me all the way. I've got more control than this, but you're so beautiful, so desirable…"

Okay, she thought, with some bitterness, if I'm so desirable, why didn't you take me? They bumped each other as both bent to pick up her halter. He got it first and she blushed as he put it on her and fastened it, his shaft still at full mast.

She had to get out of there, let him get some clothes on. She fled the room and went all the way to the small sunporch with its bright padded furniture and brighter sunlight. She sat on a sofa and hunched down the same way she hunched down inside herself. No matter that she regretted that kiss, joy filled her. *It had been so good.* Her whole body thrummed and heat lingered in every cell. How close they'd come to making love.

After a very little while, he came out and stood before her as she looked down.

"Melodye," he said softly. "Are you all right?"

She nodded, said ruefully, "Things nearly got out of hand."

"But they didn't. May I sit down?"

"Of course."

To her surprise, he took her hand. "I said I'm sorry and I am. Melodye, Mom's not coming."

Her head snapped up. "What d'you mean, she's not coming?"

He laughed shortly and shook his head, "She just called. Let me tell you what it *really* means. She let me grieve for two years and ever since, she's been throwing women at me. She wants grandchildren, or at least one. She's crazy about you. I've told you a little about where I'm coming from. Can you understand?"

"Yes."

"Good. You know Papa France wants you married."

She laughed then. Papa France was so obvious with his matchmaking and he liked Jim. "I know that, too."

"Listen, what d'you think about us linking up, although not in the way they'd like us to? I want to be friends with you because you're good company and we can protect each other. Let's just play our game while they play theirs. We know damned well we're not ready for commitment, neither of us. We may never be. This way we all win. What d'you think?"

Melodye sat forward with relief flooding her. "I think it's a win-win situation."

"Good. Mom said she asked Tina Borders to bring over food. They had a cookout last night and she's a great cook."

"That's good," Melodye said then as her face got hot again. "I came into your bedroom without knocking because I thought you were out in the garden."

He laughed. "You must have seen Dale Borders. He and I look a lot alike… I'm glad you came in. We know the score now. We understand just how attracted we are and how to stay clear of this thing between us. Do you agree?" He sounded so formal, so sincere.

"Yes," she said, wondering if she would over be able to erase the image of Jim's naked body from her head.

"I'll tell you something else. I know you're skittish about being alone in close quarters with me now, so tonight, we won't be in the house for much of the night. I'm going to take you to the other side of the lake and entertain you. We'll take the cassette player and have music. Build a bonfire and roast marshmallows. I play a mean harmonica. I'll race you to the forest and back and we'll raise hell in general. Like that?"

"Sounds interesting." She could have kissed him because she *was* dreading being in the house alone with him. "Thank you. You know, you keep saying you're a brooder, that you don't make a good companion, yet you're so thoughtful."

"That's as long as nothing gets in the way of something I feel I have to do. I'm a loner, Melodye. My dad was. I used to hate the fact that I never felt close enough to him. Now I'm the same way."

She smiled and patted his arm, suddenly feeling more at ease. "You're just an alpha male. Not everyone can be beta. Don't you know you're the stuff romance novels are made of?"

"Romance novels, yeah, but it makes for a hard reality. Elyssa certainly thought so."

Tina Borders brought the food the next hour. A tall, thin woman with russet hair, she hugged Melodye and they all carted in the food.

"Miss Belle talks about you all the time. You should've come last night," Tina said. "The cookout was scrumptious. I brought barbecued ribs and chicken, sirloin burgers, hot dogs, corn on the cob, all manner of raw veggies, baked cheese potatoes, candied yams. I get tired of naming it all. Oh, yes, the best mac and cheese."

They stored the food, leaving some out to eat, and Melodye gave her some of the devilled eggs and cookies. Tina bit into a cookie and pretended to swoon. "They're da bomb. Do you share your recipe?"

"I will with you. They *did* turn out well."

"Hey, let me in on this," Jim said, taking a cookie and biting into it. He munched a bit and rolled his eyes. "Superb. I cook, you know," he told Melodye.

"He really cooks on all burners," Tina complimented him. "Some lucky woman gets a great cook."

Jim's face went grave. "But then a really lucky woman doesn't get *me*."

Tina look at him sharply and didn't comment.

Tina didn't stay long, and after she left, Jim and Melodye sampled the delectable food. Sitting at the kitchen table, Jim smiled at her. "We're starting out early tonight. How d'you feel about sleeping bags and a night under the stars?"

She looked at him, her breath catching. He was hitting on all cylinders. "I love it."

"The weather man is cooperating, and there's even honeysuckle growing around there."

They ate slowly, savoring the food. She was sure he felt her nervousness about being alone with him in close quarters and she was grateful for his trying to do something about it. He was a pussycat, all right. Or was he?

He had a large mug of lager beer and she sipped sangria wine. Pleased that she looked more relaxed after he mentioned sleeping outside, his conversation grew warmer. They talked about his job and her designing. Then about Rafael.

"You say he was loving in the early days of your marriage."

"Yes."

"And he changed after the twins. Did either of you ever think of marriage counseling?"

"I did. He wouldn't hear of it. Rafael didn't see himself the way other people saw him. If he wasn't right, he didn't want to know about it."

"Was he ever cruel in other ways, like about your boutique and your designing?"

"In spades." She shuddered a bit. "He used to rake me over the coals as soon as he got in the house. Boutique. Designing. The way I ran the house. He knew I was a big woman when he married me, but he was determined to change me. He always admired Lucia and Bettina."

She was silent for a moment, remembering, then she went on. "My sister is a vicious flirt and she never missed an opportunity to come on to Rafael. I have to give him credit. I think any man is flattered when a woman as beautiful as Lucia pays attention to him, but he took it in stride." She stopped talking then. The memories were still more painful than she realized. Then she said, "Mom always said Rafael was my only chance. After him, I don't want another chance."

His eyes were sympathetic, she thought. A superbly trained detective's eyes. She wanted more from him and she wanted nothing at all.

"Melodye," he said softly. "You always speak of Lucia as a beautiful woman and she is. What about *you?*"

"What about me?"

He cocked his head to one side. "How many times do I have to say it? You're as beautiful as any woman needs to be. If I weren't a hopeless case, *I'd* go for you." He could have bitten his tongue. She didn't need this.

"Only until someone better came along. I'm grateful that I could attract Rafael, have the twins, but that's enough. My life is in my work and my babies."

"It doesn't have to be. You could have so much more."

"Thanks, Jim, but it's true what my mother says. And I don't want to be your charity case," she said.

"You're no charity case," he said. "I just hate to see beauty go to waste."

* * *

She lay on the sofa and he stretched out on the floor in front of her as they watched *Dreamgirls* for a couple of hours, then listened to Dvořák's *Eighth Symphony,* old Muddy Waters gutbucket blues and a few bluesy country songs.

Afterward they discussed the movie and the music.

"Smokey Robinson and Berry Gordy are pretty steamed at the movie," he said.

"Umm," she responded, "who's interested in the truth anymore? I think the people behind the movie intended to make money, get recognition and they did. An Academy Award and top money. Who cares about integrity?"

She sounded bitter, he thought. Considering her relationship with Rafael, she had every right to be bitter.

They went to the other side of the lake around eight in an ATV loaded down with food, the sleeping bags and material to build a fire. It didn't take them long to settle down. He got a good fire going and explained that it would burn all night. Honeysuckle perfume permeated the air. By then they were hungry again and held their cooked half smokes over the fire on long stainless steel rods. After a while the kosher meat was smoky and they dug in with all the trimmings. They had more of Tina's excellent potato salad, carved raw vegetables, devilled eggs and cookies until they were sated. They had no room for marshmallows.

Melodye thought food had never tasted so good as Jim looked at her from time to time, friendly, nonthreatening. She almost felt she had imagined the intense heat of their earlier hours. She found the night beautiful in extreme. Stars clustered so thickly it seemed as if some giant hand had carelessly flung too many of them across the sky. The moon was nearly full.

He put on R & B and pop tunes, stood up and held out his hand. "Give me the pleasure of this dance."

The music was lively and they both had a good sense of rhythm and flung themselves about with abandon. Then a softly sensual Smokey Robinson song came on and he said, "Let's sit this one out. No point in borrowing trouble."

His tone was brusque and his glance at her was cool. They sat and talked again as the fire flickered and an owl hooted near them. The lake was especially beautiful as it rippled in a mild wind. He talked more of Rafael and his habits before he cleared his throat. "I frightened you this morning. It won't happen again."

He had wanted to say this earlier. What had stopped him?

She didn't hesitate. "It's okay. We just got carried away in the moment. We're hungry, Jim, for life and action. Like you, I think we can keep it cool. You said we have to work together until this thing is solved. At first, you said you thought you'd have it wrapped up soon. Still think that?"

He shook his head. "We've slowed down. There're things I can't put together yet. I'll need you to see Turk with me again. I want to go there when the club is crowded and get a feel for what happened because Rafael was killed on one of their busier nights. The guy who did it might still come around. It's worth the chance."

"I'll be glad to help in any way I can."

"You've been great and I thank you." He wanted to take her hand, squeeze it, but he didn't.

She breathed deeply, said harshly, "He was my husband, although he no longer wanted to be."

"Had you discussed divorce?"

"He'd flung it in my face many times. I didn't care anymore."

And he sat thinking that Elyssa had no longer wanted to be his wife. He'd never hurt another woman the way he'd hurt her.

They talked and listened to night birds, then got into their sleeping bags a little distance from each other with the firelight on them. She lay awake for a very long time, keenly aware of him near her. Was he sleeping? And what would she dream? She was afraid she'd cry out something wild and ecstatic to him in her sleep and she smiled. He was an honorable man and he wouldn't be in her life too much longer.

Jim slept a bit at first, then came awake. He had to look out for her. His dream had been seamless, about the stars and a storm. He glanced over at her on her pillow. Her face was beautiful in the firelight and waves of soft feelings swept him. The knowledge deepened that he wanted to keep being friends. She'd said it was okay, but even that held its dangers. Friends could be hurt, too. His father had hurt everyone he'd touched, especially his mother.

He got up and stoked the fire, feeling good inside himself. He'd done all the right things, protected her, kept from hurting her in any way. The kiss took over his thoughts. It had been like the fire in front of him, incendiary. He forced it out of his mind.

In her sleep, that morning's kiss kept haunting Melodye. She stirred as he watched her and murmured something he couldn't understand. She loved the night sounds around them, the soft breeze and the scent of honeysuckle, and felt grateful that he'd thought of this.

He sat up for a long, long while and when he climbed back into his bag, it seemed he only slept a few minutes before the sun woke them up.

They decided to leave much earlier than they'd planned. At least *he* decided and she was surprised. She'd grown so relaxed she wanted to stay longer, but she acquiesced. There were a lot of things to do in Crystal Lake and in D.C. Her boutique was closed on Mondays, but she often went in.

She found him different over coffee and breakfast. He was silent, locked into the world he'd spoken of living in. "Are you all right?" she finally asked him.

"Yeah," he answered quickly. "You're seeing another side of me, I'm afraid. I've got a lot on my mind and the case is crowding me. Lots of new ideas, new angles. Then, hell, I'm just like this sometimes. I hope it doesn't vex you too much." He was glad to be off for a couple of days straight.

"No," she answered hurriedly, "I don't mind at all. You're good company, even silent."

He smiled ruefully. "Having nothing to say, I proceed to say it."

She laughed at that and out on the road she found herself still smiling. She didn't want to intrude on his thoughts, but she told him, "I had a really wonderful time. Thank you for going along with Miss Belle's invitation."

"It was my invitation, too."

He was being kind again, but his voice was brusque and he didn't talk again for the three hours it took them to traverse Sunday traffic back to Crystal Lake. A little distance from the spot where they'd turn off the highway he said, "I'll drop you off and check to see that everything's all right, then I'll be on my way."

She glanced at him. "Thank you, but you don't need to check. I'm not even going in. I'm driving in to D.C. and my boutique. I've got sketches I need to finish to take to the dressmaker's."

"Then I'll drive you in."

"I don't want to put you to that trouble."

"I said I would. It's no trouble."

But his voice was flat, dispassionate and she wondered. He continued past Crystal Lake and into D.C. and in a short while, they had parked on the street near her boutique.

"It's Monday," he said, "and your place will be closed. I know there's a guard, but I'll go up to check it out. There's been a lot happening around here I understand from a D.C cop buddy."

"Thanks. Are you sure you feel all right?"

"Next time you see my mom, ask her about my moods. I assure you, I'm as fine as I know how to be at times like this."

Inside the glass front building, the security guard greeted them. "Hey," he said, "you've got a busy shop today."

"How so?" Melodye asked. "Has my mother been here?"

"A few hours. She and your sister're still here. Also, Manny."

Melodye felt her heart hit her shoes. She'd rather have seen the devil himself than Lucia today. Running her tongue over dry lips, she turned to Jim. "I know someone's there, but I'd like you to go up with me." Her smile was weak and his heart went out to her. "If Lucia's here, I'm going to need all the moral support I can get. I've never known her to come without bringing trouble with her."

Chapter 5

Melodye's high fashion model sister, Lucia, was the first person they saw. She came to them, all smiles. "Jim, what a delight to see you again."

She kissed Jim's cheek and hugged a stiff Melodye.

Jim's smile was broad. "Lucia. You're looking very well."

It probably was far less than the compliments Lucia constantly got, but Melodye found herself looking at him obliquely with unwelcome jealousy.

Dressed in jade green silk that set off her light brown hair flowing in waves around her shoulders and flattered her light brown eyes, Lucia was on display and enjoying it. Her creamy skin and sensuous body made most men drool.

"Talk about the devil," Lucia said, "and Mom and I were just talking about you."

"Oh?"

"Yes, we—"

Bettina came into the room hurriedly. As owner and editor of "The AA Beauty," she lived up to her magazine. Her smooth, pale honey skin was pampered and perfect, her dark brown hair expertly coiffed and her figure was as thin as her younger daughter's. She stopped short of Melodye. "Jim, how are you?" She spoke, almost as an afterthought.

"I'm well, thank you. And you?"

Lucia moved about like a gorgeous tigress. "Mom, tell her now."

Bettina looked contrite. "Yes, we *were* talking about you and I'm afraid it's bad news."

Melodye sighed. "What *is* it, Mother?"

Bettina cleared her throat. "Well, we all know Lucia's attraction for men and her penchant for loving and leaving them." She laughed shortly.

Melodye's skin prickled. "Your news, please, Mother."

"It's just that Lucia needs me in New York with her off and on for a while. She's breaking up with Raoul and I'm afraid it's getting nasty. I'm not going to be able to emcee your affair in June."

Mild shock waves ran through Melodye and Jim looked at her narrowly. Hot tears sprang to her eyes, but she batted them away. All her life she had taken a backseat to Lucia. She'd been so pleased when Bettina had agreed to emcee the fashion show that was to put her on the D.C. and New York fashion map. And Bettina had taken over, made great comments and pretty much planned the whole thing. Her mother had the moxie and the pizzazz to make it go. Dammit! Melodye felt lead seeping into her veins.

Bettina pursed her mouth and touched Melodye's hand. "Well, you must admit, it's something none of us planned on, but a broken marriage is more important than a fashion show, wouldn't you say?"

"To *you* anyway," Melodye couldn't help retorting bitterly, and she thought, *You'd leave my wedding and go to Lucia for her broken fingernail.*

"Let's be grown up about this," Lucia said airily. "Raoul and I will be getting a divorce and I'll be getting some of his millions. Don't you have any sympathy for me? But did you ever?" Lucia's husband was a Brazilian diamond millionaire, a nice man that Melodye liked.

Lucia looked at her sister sharply, keenly enjoying the competition she'd always won. Melodye didn't answer.

"Please say something." Bettina looked concerned. "It isn't as if I could do anything else and there are others you can get."

"Who?" Melodye demanded.

Bettina named a New York fashion editor and a couple of women who were prominent on the D.C. and New York fashion scene.

Melodye shook her head. "Mother, you're one of the most knowledgeable and influential women in fashion and your name alone was going to make the show."

"They're not Mom's clothes, they're yours," Lucia purred. "Aren't you *good* enough?"

That barb hurt because Melodye thought she'd never felt good enough.

The front door opened and a tall young man with dark brown skin and curly brown hair came in, glanced around. "Why're the vibes so sad in here?" he asked cheerily, and Melodye sighed. Manny Willett missed nothing.

"I'd rather not discuss it," Melodye said shortly.

"Sure," was all Manny said. "I got the grub and I even brought a couple of extras."

"Good, I'm starved," Lucia chortled. She took one of the big hamburgers and began to unwrap it, wrinkling her nose at Jim. "I'm one of the lucky ones. Eat anything and never gain a pound. Hey, you look like you're one of those, too. Mom. Manny." She glanced at Melodye slyly. "I guess nature just didn't favor you there."

Jim's eyes narrowed as he glanced at Melodye. "*Au contraire,*" he said. "I think nature put it *all* on Melodye. *Fabu-lous* is all I can say."

For only a moment, Lucia looked crestfallen, then immediately recovered. "I'll bet you and your silver tongue gets everything you want from the ladies."

"You're wrong, you know," Jim said easily.

Lucia stood near him, balled up her slender fist and tapped him lightly on the arm. "You're a charmer, all right. I could use someone like you."

Him and a hundred others, Melodye thought. She knew her sister had problems beyond her shattered marriage that had been going bad for some time. At twenty-eight, Lucia had been married three times, her career as a *high-fashion model* was on the wane and she had been desperately seeking to set up her own agency. Her husband wouldn't give her the money and her credit was terrible, but she'd gotten money from somewhere and was on her way. Melodye supposed she could be forgiven her nastiness.

Jim let Lucia's remark go by without commenting. His eyes on her were accepting, noncommittal, reflecting his training. Melodye always thought it remarkable that Lucia actually glowed around a man she'd chosen to impress, and she'd chosen to impress Jim. Melodye simmered inside. Jim and she would be over before they had begun, just as soon as this case was over.

Bettina seemed thoughtful. "I'll have time to do a little more spadework with the show before I get tied up with Lucia, but not a lot of time. My girl, did you gain a few pounds in the few days since I've seen you?" She frowned.

"I hardly think so," Melodye said stiffly.

"Vive la pounds," Manny teased. "Now, me, I think you're a fine woman."

Manny had come to her from *Steeped In Joy*. He'd been one of the favorite all-around workers there and a heads-on favorite of Rafael. But Manny didn't get along too well with Turk, and when he knew she needed someone, he asked for the job.

"I can do just about anything you need doing," he'd said. "I miss Rafael and it would help to work for his wife."

So she paid him more than she could afford and as he'd said, he was worth it. Smart, eager, he'd pitched in and asked her to teach him about the business side of fashion. He'd given her a wonderful idea for skirts that flattered the A-1 plus figure. When that one took off, as she was sure it would, she and Manny were both going to have some extra cash. Manny was studying accounting nights at a local business college.

Melodye was pleased at Manny's compliment, in spite of herself. "Thank you, I think." Manny had several girlfriends and he seemed to love them all equally. Melodye shrugged now. If they were satisfied, she was satisfied.

"Well, I can't eat standing up," Bettina said. "So, shall we all sit down?"

Melodye shook her head. "We've got to be going. I'm just picking up sketches to take home," she said, thinking she had planned to work here for a while. Now she couldn't. She needed to grieve this shock of Bettina leaving her high and dry.

Bettina bit her bottom lip. "Well, I'm going to stay and do all I can because I won't be able to do much more. We'll lock up and I've finished the initial planning, which I'll leave here for you. You're going to have to work fast. Time, like so much else, isn't on your side."

Melodye thought then that all her life, Bettina had managed to forecast doom for her in some way, big and little. Thank God for Papa France and Grandma Gina, who'd died four years ago. But even they hadn't been able to completely undo the hurt Bettina and Lucia had inflicted on her.

Once they were seated, Bettina glanced at Melodye again. "Hmm," she said, "I'd swear, you're a little heavier, but let's let it ride. New York always exhilarates me."

Lucia looked up and threw Jim a little kiss, startling Melodye. "Cops always did give me a thrill. I can even overlook the fact that they don't make much money."

Jim laughed at that one, saying only, "We manage to get by."

But Lucia wasn't through. "When I get back, perhaps we could do lunch." Then she added slyly and merrily, "you and me and sister here. We'll go someplace where she can order diet food."

Jim didn't respond to that one, but glanced at Melodye sympathetically.

"Yes," Bettina said to Jim, "don't be a stranger, dear. When I return from my on-and-off trips to New York, I'll invite you over."

Ah, yes, Melodye thought with vitriol seeping into her system. *Anything Lucia wants, Mom is certain to help her get. Did it ever occur to her that I might be interested in Jim? She wouldn't care. But her darling Lucia is another story.*

"Ready?" Jim asked.

She nodded and Manny smiled. "'Bye, boss lady. See you

tomorrow. You're missing great burgers, but I'll put one in the fridge for you."

"Better put two," Lucia said, lifting her eyebrows. "Melodye's got a growing girl's appetite."

"Nothing wrong with that," Jim said, "as long as she continues to develop into the Venus that she is."

Melodye looked at him gratefully. He always came to her aid. It would be nice to have someone like him, but without commitment.

In the car he reached over and touched her hand. She was too sad for electricity right now, but a precious warmth spread through her and she felt soothed and good inside. The memory of Lucia's beauty stayed with her. In spite of all the hell Rafael had put her through, she hadn't lost him to Lucia and that was a plus. Jim was just her friend, *if* he remained her friend. Would she lose him to Lucia? And was what Bettina had said true that Rafael was her *only* chance? She didn't want to think about it.

At her home, they unloaded the food from the trip. She invited him to stay for a while, and he agreed, saying, "Let's talk a bit about what just happened."

"I'm used to it. This has been my life. You're talking about Bettina and Lucia and what they call teasing."

"Yeah. You've got backbone and I admire you for it, but as the guys say, you've got feelings and they can be hurt."

She smiled a bit. With some of the anger fading, she had begun to be keenly aware of him again. As they sat on the sofa, she moved a little away from him and her withdrawal wasn't lost on him.

Later, it began to mist outside and Melodye watched for long moments the drops of moisture on the leaves and the light haze that would be fog in the morning. Then she sat in a chair across from him and tried to think, but her mind focused only on him, on how she kept wanting to touch him. She wasn't going to think about yesterday's kiss because that had been madness, never to happen again. Trouble was she *wanted* it to happen again.

Suddenly he sat up, smiling as if he'd never been lost to her. "I've got an idea that could work."

"Oh?"

"Yeah. I've been brainstorming it the way we do at headquarters. Now, don't rule me out until you've heard the whole thing."

"I won't." She was intrigued.

"*I'll* be your emcee."

"You?"

"It's not as crazy as it seems. In New York I emceed the policeman's ball one year and a lot of people told me I did a really good job. It was a fashion show of sorts. Beautiful gowns and beautiful women strutting their stuff. I could enlist my buddies as escorts along with the male models you've got lined up. Wall-to-wall men. We've got some pretty sharp guys on the force, fit, eager to serve. You could think about it...."

Her face lit up with delight. "I'm already thinking about it and it's wonderful! Listen, I can take this ball and run with it!" Impulsively, she got up and started toward him to give him a hug, but she paused just short of him, looking down at him. She knew what would happen if she did. Instead she grinned and told him. "You're a fireball, know that? And I'm glad you're in my life."

She cautioned herself not to be too eager. He was just being his helpful self. But the Jim she had come to know wasn't Boy Scout material. He was a quiet, solid, brooding man who kept largely to himself and lived in a world he didn't often share.

"Hey, I'm glad you like my idea. I'll get on it right away. Now, let's talk about some of the details. But before we do, how long has Manny Willett been working for you?"

"Within months after Rafael died. They were really close."

"Wasn't he close to Turk?"

"Not at all. I don't think they got along. Anyway, he's been a joy to work with. I'm glad I hired him. Why do you ask?"

He shrugged. "I was impressed with him when I interviewed everybody who'd worked with Rafael. He struck me as being far above what he was doing. I asked him about that and he grinned and told me, 'Later.'"

"That's Manny. He's only twenty-two and he's led a miserable life. Alcoholic parents who beat him. Dirt poor. He laughs about it, but there're tears in his laughter. I'm going to keep encouraging him. I think he'll find himself. I *am* a bit worried about the way he plays around."

"A player?"

"Just about."

"I was a player for a while."

She looked at him and shook her head. "It doesn't fit. You're a caring person."

"A player can care. Maybe he's afraid of caring anymore. I was. There were a lot of women in my life for a short while and I took them as I found them, no commitment and no looking back—" he shrugged "—or forward."

"You speak of it in the past. What made you change your mind?"

"Papa France."

She looked at him amazement. "Papa France! Oh, I know he always liked you, but when? You were in New York."

He drew a deep breath. "Yeah. I came home one long weekend. You and the twins were in New Orleans for a few days. It was after Elyssa's death. I was hungover and sick, with a mind sicker than my body. Mom was frantic. I think she thought I was going to kill myself and I *had* considered it. Papa France took me fishing and he told me life was really a lot like fishing. You have some great catches and sometimes nothing at all, but you fish because you love to. He told me one day I'd find someone else I loved. His words quieted me and I knew I wanted to go on. But I also knew I didn't want to be committed again for a very long time—"

"If ever," she finished for him.

He looked at her gratefully. "You understand because you know how *you* feel. Melodye, you're too lovely to let anyone spoil your life. No, not Rafael, not Bettina and certainly not Lucia. I don't want to say it too often because if I do you'll just stop listening and I want you to listen."

He withdrew a bit then and she missed him.

But he was back with a twinkle in his eyes as he told her, "We've got lots of planning to do on this fashion show and I want you to go with me to see Turk again. I have more questions and the more I see him in action, the more feel I get for where he's coming from."

"You're on. The less I see of Turk Hylton the better, but I owe you so much…"

"You owe me nothing. I've enjoyed working with you and I'm going to enjoy this new gig even more."

She sat down, feeling close to him again and almost immediately began to get up. How close was too close? And what was going to be the end of this?

He asked to see her sketches for the show and she got them for him. He studied them for long moments.

"I don't know a lot about fashion, but these seem great to me. I want to see your dress."

She showed it to him and he nodded. "What color?"

Surprised, she told him, "probably taupe, a kind of grayish beige."

He shook his head. "Uh-uh."

She drew a deep breath. "Bettina trained me well. I'm big. I'm dark. Tone it down. Light and bright colored blouses sometimes. Now, I give my customers what they want, but for myself…"

Anger flashed through him. "Melodye, you're gorgeous! For God's sake, get Bettina the hell off your back. You're thirty-three, a widow with twins. Be your own woman."

She laughed shakily, surprised to find tears misting her eyes as she wondered how someone went about giving up on the love they were never going to get.

Odessa and the twins came a short while later, excited and beaming over their day at a petting zoo near Alexandria. Odessa was so pleased to find Jim there. If she wasn't getting a man, the next best thing was having her best friend find one. Curses to them both, she thought, for being so pigheaded. Only a fool swore off love. Didn't they *know* it made the world go round?

The twins threw themselves onto Jim with abandon.

"Hey, what'd you bring us?" Randy demanded. "Papa France always brings us something."

Jim threw back his head, laughing, as he hugged the boy with one arm, his sister with the other. "Can't you welcome me, kid? Did you eat all of Papa France's candy?"

"No. Mom wouldn't let us. There's some in the fridge. Want some?"

Jim shook his head. "Thanks, but I'm full up to here." His hands indicated his chin and the boy shook with laughter.

"We're full up to here, too."

Jim hugged him. "Next time, I'll be sure to bring you two something. You deserve that for being good kids."

Rachel had been quiet. Now she spoke up. "Will you read us another bedtime story? You read good."

"Thank you. I think I'll have shoved off when that time comes around, but some other time, I'd be delighted."

They all talked about Jim and Melodye's trip to the countryside and about the petting zoo.

"Next time you come with us," Randy ordered.

"Yes," Jim answered him, "it seems like something I'd enjoy."

Jim wondered at the inroads the twins were making on his heart. Whatever else, he'd always been a sucker for kids and had wanted some as long as he could remember. He'd sworn he'd be closer to his kids than his father had been to him. Papa France was his mental role model, but his late father had proved to be his heart's role model. He didn't like the way these kids affected him, but he would enjoy the feeling of having a family, if only for a little while.

Chapter 6

The night of the A-l Plus Love Fashion Show, Melodye's spirit soared with excitement. If this went off as well as it had began, it was going to be one of the high points of her life. She and Odessa stood talking in the small ballroom of one of D.C.'s most elegant Georgetown hotels. Fashion reporters and fashion writers wringed her, asking questions, expressing delight over the ten male models and fifteen policemen and detectives, who were strutting their stuff in their tuxedos.

The fashion reporter from Paris seemed especially pleased. "Ah, you Americans always come up with excellent ideas. And who is more handsome than a handsome policeman?" Blushing, the petite blond woman placed a hand on the arm of a passing cop and squeezed his bicep. She asked if he was a policeman and he answered yes. "Perhaps I shall take you back with me," she teased. "Will you arrest me now or later?" She trilled laughter at her own joke and the policeman was all smiles.

Jim had outdone himself, calling in debts from D.C., as well as Crystal Lake policemen and he had gotten only the best. Now he stood apart, looking at what he had helped create, immensely proud of himself. But his pride in his efforts was nothing compared with his pride in Melodye. Tonight, he felt like Pygmalion, the fabled sculptor who had breathed life into a statue and had fallen in love with her. *Yeah,* he told himself, *I know that's arrogant, but dammit, she's fantastic tonight.*

He went to Melodye and touched her shoulder. "Tonight," he told her, "you're every man's fantasy." His eyes moved over her easily, gently, but there was fire, too. The way there'd been the day he'd kissed her.

Her blood ran hot, remembering. In pale yellow silk jersey, off the shoulder, draped over her exquisite breasts and molding her shapely small waist and wide hips, she was a vision. She had selected long yellow diamond earrings and the sparkle radiated over her chocolate skin, making it glow like the diamonds themselves.

Jim couldn't resist telling her, "You look beautiful."

Blushing, she avoided his gaze.

"Melodye, the show is yours tonight. I hope you know it," he said.

She smiled at him, thinking he was endearing…and sexy as hell. She had never felt beautiful before, not even in the days when Rafael had said he loved her. But tonight, after what Jim had said, she did.

Manny and the other employees were busy getting the show on the road.

Manny shook his head and whistled long and low. "Now,

I've always thought you're a beauty, but tonight you've got it all together. I *love* that dress," Manny said.

She thanked him warmly and patted his arm, thinking he looked wistful.

The room was crowded with a far bigger audience than she had anticipated, and Melodye moved about, greeting, accepting vivid compliments. Was she going to faint with sheer happiness? It helped to know she could make it without Bettina. Jim had come to her rescue and she was grateful.

A hated gruff voice spoke behind her. "I came early to enjoy your show longer. I'm sure if it had been an invitation-only affair, I wouldn't have been invited. I'm lucky it's open to the public."

Turk Hylton's eyes on her were bold and insolent. He didn't so much undress her with his eyes as ripped her clothes from her back and savored her nakedness without knowing how to appreciate it.

"Good evening, Turk," was all she could manage.

He rocked a little on his heels. "I used to wonder why I spent so much time chasing you." His voice was guttural. "Tonight, I see what you can be like. One day, I'm going to get you in my bed and—"

"Good evening, Mr. Hylton," Jim's drawl cut through.

"Ryman." Turk barely acknowledged Jim, still staring at Melodye.

Jim's big hand cupped Melodye's elbow. "They're asking for you over by the stage," he said, and guided her away.

As they moved off, an angry Turk said, "You can take her away this time, but I'll get what I want one day."

"When hell freezes," Jim muttered in a low voice.

Melodye laughed then. "Thank you. You're a detective after my own heart."

He grinned, hugely enjoying himself.

He really did look wonderful in his tuxedo, she thought.

Jim Ryman was a complicated man, yet he noticed all the little things. She found a part of herself wishing she had someone like him. The other part of her reminded her why she'd sworn off men.

She moved with easy grace, pulling the program together. This was a night honoring the big woman, the *A-l Plus woman.* Her models and the clothes she'd designed were beautiful. Perfect makeup. Perfect fit. Glowing. Hot. Enchanted happiness. And she, Melodye, was the most enchanting of all. Whoever said Cinderella was a fairy tale.

Photographers roamed the room, cameras on the ready, and the photographer who'd photographed Rafael's papers came to her, smiling. "Lady, I've got to hand it to you. You're the old fashioned 'It' woman tonight. Save me a dance, will you? There *will* be dancing?"

"Definitely, and yes, I will."

He posed her by an iridescent fountain and fussed with the lighting to make it just so. He reflected that his buddy, Jim Ryman, seemed interested in this woman and Jim usually paid women little attention except to be courteous and kind. Too bad about his wife.

The lighting in the big room was just right to display the gowns and the gorgeous flesh on display. The tuxedo'd men provided just the right backdrop and Melodye wondered how Jim had found such wondrous creatures. You just knew that the tuxes covered pecs and abs and biceps that were to die for. Tall and stalwart, they all looked as if they were headed for Muscle Beach.

The cream damask-covered tables seated groups of six with gleaming silver, china and crystal. The people in attendance were no less fashionably dressed than the models. Melodye thought it was going to be good to see Bettina and Lucia's faces when the photos came out in the *Washington Post* and later in the fashion mags. Of course, Bettina hadn't bailed on her to hurt her. She had simply done again what she had done all Melodye's life—preferred Lucia. But this almost certain success soothed her heart a little and she had Jim to thank for it.

At last they were underway and Jim was at the mike on stage. She thought he looked more splendid than all the rest.

"Ladies and gentlemen," he began, "tonight we will bring you the fashion show of shows. Tonight, we pay long overdue homage to the big and beautiful African-American woman. *The A-l Plus Love woman.* The woman who lives life on her own terms, who is healthy, brave and gorgeous. We're here to honor and support her. Let's give her a rousing cheer!"

The room erupted in laughing adulation for the women onstage with their escorts behind them. Thunderous applause filled the room with whistles and cries of "Yay! Right on!" Melodye and Odessa stood together.

Odessa wore pale blue silk, cut low. Her face was wreathed in smiles. "This is so far beyond what I expected. The men alone are worth the price of admission." She raised her eyebrows. "And I bet every one of them is taken two and three times over. But never mind, my purses are going to be bigger than Prada's."

Melodye grinned and patted her friend's shoulder. "You're right, and there's got to be at least one man available."

"Don't get my hopes up. It hurts too bad when the hoping ends."

Melodye made a little face. "Keep praying. Keep hoping. I predict one day you'll get what you want."

"And what about you? You're not even daring to hope."

Melodye drew a deep breath. "I'm different. I blossomed and wilted earlier than most."

Odessa frowned. "Some wilting. I never asked, but how come you're not all decked out in your usual navy, black and dark brown? Beautiful, but subdued."

"Like me this way?"

"*Love* you this way. Oh, you look scrumptious, girlfriend. I can't stop saying it."

"Jim insisted on this color. He thinks I look good in it."

"*Good* is too mild a word. Let me consult my thesaurus."

Melodye chuckled. "With you and Jim on my side, my ego should be up to the sky when the write-ups on this affair come through."

"About time."

Jim was strutting his stuff as he roamed the room with the models and the escorts, making the rounds of the tables of people who were charmed by the beautiful attire. One woman groaned, "Oh, if only I could order everyone one of the twenty outfits. This is as great as Eunice Johnson's *Fashion Fair.*"

"And," a table companion declared, "it's all for *us, the big sistahs!*"

About that time, Jim said, "Let's hear it again for the big sistah!" And merry applause filled the room.

Manny came to them. "Boss lady, you've done us all proud. You know, I've been thinking I'm going to go into the business side of this field in a big way."

"But that's wonderful, Manny. What made you fully decide?"

"You and how good you've been to me. I had an aunt who died young, but she was my ace, left me what little money she had and I've held on to it. I really admire you and what you stand for."

Jim passed close to them and winked at Melodye. It was a mock leer and she laughed. He was having a ball. And speaking of leers, Turk came over.

"Aren't you supposed to be seated?" Melodye asked him sharply.

Turk grinned. "I reckon. I'm just so used to patrolling the floor at *Steeped In Joy*. Melodye, you know, you and I could've made a great team with my nightclub, but you wanted to check out."

"I've got my hands full."

He looked at her hard and licked his bottom lip suggestively. "And, boy, how I'd like to have my hands full—of you."

Melodye frowned at him. "I have to insist that you go back to your party, Turk. Odessa and I have things to talk through."

"Oka-a-y," he growled. "I guess I know when I'm not wanted. But I want a dance." She saw then that he'd been drinking. "Another thing, babe, cops aren't noted these days for long lives. You shacking up with that jerk?"

Melodye's eyes flashed fire and her voice was icy. "Please go back to your seat, Turk, or I'll have to ask a security guard to escort you back."

He turned without another word and ambled back to his table, but he continued to send hot glances her way.

The softly sensuous music of Nick Redmond's combo put everyone in a relaxed mood and the room buzzed with good cheer and keen interest in the models and escorts who moved between the tables.

Melodye and Odessa walked over to the bandstand and after Nick finished playing, he greeted them. "Ladies, you're looking fabulous."

They thanked him and Odessa teased him. "You're the answer to a maiden's prayer," Odessa said to him.

"Hey, I want to congratulate you on a great show. I haven't enjoyed a gig this much in ages," Nick said.

Melodye briefly told him about Jim's input and he nodded. For a moment he looked at her sparkling eyes before he told her, "I want to meet this man."

Odessa and Melodye stood near the door when Papa France and Miss Belle came in. "We're late because our taxi had an accident and the driver had minor injuries," Papa France explained. "We couldn't leave him, but we're here."

Miss Belle looked at Melodye and threw her arms around her. "Oh, my dear, how stunning you both look." She hugged both women, thinking that Melodye's off-black hair in its new, luxuriant French twist with tendrils around her beautiful face added charm and grace. She wondered what was going on with the woman she liked so much. She had never seemed interested in men since Rafael died. Now, here was a find for her son, Jim.

"And, *you,*" Melodye told her. "Silver hair and silver silk crepe. You're lovely tonight, Miss Belle."

Odessa corroborated her compliment. With her silver hair cut short and her plump rounded figure, Belle Ryman more than held her own.

Papa France stood a little back, just looking at Melodye and Odessa. His black Italian silk suit flattered his tall, thin body and parchment-colored skin. "Well, I've had a little while to look Miss Belle over and enjoy her beauty. Now my old eyes are feasting on two young beauties. You both look beyond any compliments I could pay you, but Miss Melodye here seems to me to have something special going on."

Melodye blushed hotly. Something going on indeed.

A hostess showed the older couple to their table and they drew admiring glances from other diners. Jim broke away from his emcee duties and came to them.

"When does the dancing begin?" he asked.

"Within the hour. I'd like time for the food to settle." Melodye wondered then if sheer happiness was always a turn on. She'd known so little of it. But tonight her body seemed to belong underneath, on top of and beside Jim—naked and giving him all she had. She cautioned herself that all she had probably wouldn't be enough. Jim was a catch and he knew plenty of available, desirable women. She'd never thought much about having a brief fling, as Odessa often said, to take the edge off.

Jim couldn't stop stealing glances. He felt like a man who'd struck gold. He reminded himself that he wasn't in the market, but still, it felt good. And they were friends for the moment. When they parted, he'd know he'd left her with more than she'd possessed when he'd found her.

Manny came back, a somber look on his face. "So much luxury," he said sadly. "I just can't get used to it, or maybe I'm afraid to get used to it."

Melodye looked at him sharply. "Cheer up," she told him. "What's the worst that could happen?"

He raised his eyebrows and his attractive young face seemed even more somber. "You don't wanta know."

He was having trouble juggling his women again, Melodye thought.

After the dinner was over, people called to Melodye to stop by their tables, and she did. Nearly every attendee had an order that they'd place the following day and the compliments flowed liked the heady, expensive wine they drank.

As she passed Turk's table, he looked up at her, his attention drawn from his group. "I want to order the whole line," he chortled, "but one of the nightgowns has to have *your* body in it." Melodye gave him an icy glare and moved on as he laughed drunkenly.

Janet and the rest of Nick's and her company sat nearby. Melodye sat with them. "You've done yourself proud," Janet told her. "But my compliments don't stop with the show. *You* look more beautiful than I've ever seen you and your dress is gorgeous."

In low-cut aquamarine peau de soie and diamond ear studs, Janet was a vision herself and the sparkle of her love for Nick made some part of Melodye ache with wanting to know a love like this. But she thought bitterly that she'd been sure she *had* such a love with Rafael, and look what happened.

It was late when Manny brought Bettina and Lucia to Melodye and Melodye's heart plummeted. Bettina wore a favorite lavender Givenchy gown and diamonds. Melodye thought acidly that, no, her mother wasn't wearing Prada, but she was a devil, all the same.

It was Lucia who took Melodye's breath away. Dressed to kill, her long hair spilled in silken waves over her lovely pale shoulders. Teardrop emeralds hung from shell-like earlobes. And the dress was Vera Wang. Black silk taffeta rustled softly and swirled in rounded curves over her fashionably slender body.

"You both look lovely," Melodye said. She didn't want to speak at all. Why had they come?

Bettina pursed her lips. "We got back early and I thought you'd need me, but I see everything is going okay. I must say the men are great." Finally she gave Melodye a long appraisal. "That gown is very good, but it's really not for you. It's the kind of thing Lucia could do justice to."

Jim had come up just as Bettina spoke. His eyes on Melodye were warm and flattering. "She looks beautiful, don't you think?"

Bettina laughed shortly. "What I think is that you're being kind. Why don't you and Lucia dance while Melodye and I discuss the show?"

Jim shook his head. "Melodye and I were just getting ready to dance and I'm a possessive man. I want what I want when I want it. That kind of thing." He held out his arms to Melodye and she went into them, weak with relief.

On the floor he held her closer. "Steady," he said after a while. "Don't let it get you down. I know beauty when I see it. I've even been called a connoisseur of feminine pulchritude. C'mon, Cinderella, enjoy your ball and the coach stays a coach."

She wanted to ask if *he* could be the prince just for tonight, but she didn't. He'd rescued her again. She didn't want to ask for too much.

Out of the corner of her eye she saw that Odessa had danced with one of the policemen for the third time and it pleased her. Her friend richly deserved the love she so badly wanted. And she, Melodye, deserved only what she had already had.

Later, Lucia asked Jim and he danced with her twice, but she was surrounded by men and seemed to be having a better time than anyone else. When Bettina talked with Melodye about the show, she talked mostly about Lucia, Lucia's errant husband and how glamorous Lucia was. Now Bettina said, "You've got your boutique, your designing and your twins. Your sister has the men. She'll soon have another man. I know you miss Rafael. He was so good to you."

She had never told Bettina about the real Rafael. Bettina wouldn't have cared.

* * *

Nick's music was made for dancing. He played his popular "All I Want From You Is Everything," and Jim claimed her again. "Ever hear of the legend of Pygmalion?"

"Would you believe I have? Bettina's always been into literature. Let me see. This sculptor fashioned a woman of stone, was so enchanted he brought her to life and fell in love with her. Alive, she didn't please him and he killed her. End of story."

He was looking at her strangely and she couldn't read him. "Yeah, something like that." Funny, he thought, how the part about *loving* his model hadn't crossed his mind. Now he said, "I guess life's like that. You have something you think is perfect, but it doesn't turn out that way. If only life were simple."

"Do you ever daydream?" she asked. She would swear their bodies were moving in perfect sync as if they'd danced often together.

He expelled a harsh breath. "I'd say hardly ever. I'm not the creative one."

Did she move closer to him? "But you are. Telling me to wear pale yellow. Trying to help me gain confidence. Don't you know you're creating a new me? And, Jim, thank you."

Jim squeezed her lightly and her heart raced. *Okay, private parts,* she admonished herself, behave. *It isn't like you've never known romance. And this isn't romance. He's just a friend who likes helping someone over a rough spot.* And it wasn't as if she were looking for romance again. Not romance. Not love. Not *hurt.* Not ever again.

She thought of something then. "You know," she said, "you asked me if Rafael was close to anyone in Atlantic City and I said I didn't think so. Going to sleep last night I remembered that in the early days he talked often about a Larry

Biggs who was a bookie and who had mob ties. He was afraid of him. At one point he owed this man a lot of money. Turk got him out of that, but he might have done it again. I distinctly remember him saying that the man had threatened to kill him if he didn't pay off."

After she'd told him, Jim seemed lost in thought for a few minutes. "I've had a couple more leads from Atlantic City. I wonder if the guy is still active and alive. Did you ever meet this man?"

"I did. Twice. At *Steeped In Joy* and once he came to our house. He's a big, hulking brute. He's thoroughly frightening…or was," she said.

"Would you go to Atlantic City with me? It might help in the investigation if I can locate him and he sees you."

Remembering the man, it wasn't something she relished, but she said, "Yes, of course. But how long would we be gone?" It wasn't something she wanted to do.

"Couple of days. A long weekend. You're worried about the twins, aren't you?"

She scrunched up her shoulders. "Yes. I don't want them thinking Odessa or Miss Belle is their mother."

He hugged her, laughing. "*We'll take them with us.* I stay at an inn when I go to Atlantic City and I know the owners, Mickey and Carol Jones, well. They've got kids and they have a nursery for guests with kids. We can do our thing."

"Great. You know I'll be in touch." He realized again that he liked working with Melodye, talking with her, being with her. Her oriental-musk perfume was making his head spin and his groin throb wickedly. The jockey strap was doing its job, but his big shaft was raging to ride. He was glad then that *making* love and feeling love didn't always have to go hand in hand. He knew his body well enough to know what it wanted, but he also knew his heart and mind were at odds with his body. What one wanted with a savage need, the other two never meant to let happen.

Jim always went in with Melodye when he took her home, explaining that it was his detective's habit to check things out. She paid the babysitter who left, saying the twins had been very good, but boy they were active.

He looked in on the twins with her, but he didn't stay long. At the door when he was leaving, he stood near her. "This was your night," he told her. "Now, do you feel like the beautiful woman you are?"

She laughed a little. "I'm not certain. I think I feel a little like Cinderella waiting for her coach to turn into a pumpkin again."

"It won't and you don't need glass slippers or a prince."

"Lucia looked beautiful tonight." As if he hadn't noticed.

"*You* look beautiful tonight."

"But I'll never be in her class."

"Why do you need to be? You're in a class by yourself. You've got your own magic."

But he had danced twice with Lucia and seemed to enjoy himself.

She tried to hold herself aloof. Wasn't the ball in his court? Excited, she wanted him to kiss her as a fitting end to a great night, but he only touched her face and then he was gone.

Chapter 7

"Are you our daddy?"

Jim laughed as the question startled him. He supposed it had to come sometime. He swung Randy around again and told him, "Why don't you ask Mommy?"

But the boy wanted to be swung some more and giggled, asking no more questions.

Melodye, Jim, Randy and Rachel were on the outskirts of Atlantic City at the Dew Drop Inn, an intimate small hotel for people who wanted a home away from home. They were on the small playground out from the inn and the kids were having a ball.

Melodye came over to them. "Is he giving you trouble?" she teased Jim.

"I think I'm giving it to him." Jim set the boy down. It was a hot day and Jim was perspiring.

"More," Randy demanded. "And I need a hug."

Jim hugged him and said, "Later for the swinging."

Randy squinted and asked Melodye, "Is Jim our daddy?"

It was a question she had long expected. They asked it of any man who came around after a time or two. "No. He's not your daddy. He's our friend," she told the boy gently.

Randy craned his neck as he looked up at Jim. "D'you *love* me and Rachel?"

Jim didn't hesitate. "Yeah, I expect I do."

"Well, I love you and Rachel loves you, too. Do you love Mommy?"

Jim smiled as his stomach tightened. "We're special friends."

"Can we be special friends?"

"Yeah, we already are."

It was a tense moment and Melodye breathed a sigh of relief. So much for questions about love and loving.

Rachel, who had been playing quietly nearby with her favorite rag doll, walked over to them. Jim hugged her small frame.

Carol Jones came onto the playground. A small, slender, fiftysomething woman with jet-black hair and cinnamon skin, Carol owned the inn with her husband, Mickey. "I've got it all mapped out," she said. "You want to have an early dinner with the kids and read them a bedtime story. Then you do Atlantic City and I get to keep them until tomorrow morning at eight. That way you can sleep late. I'll give them breakfast. I can keep them until ten, if you'd like."

Melodye said she thought eight would be fine and Carol squatted to talk to the twins and to say, "Tomorrow they'll have company. Two more guests are coming in with kids. I sure miss fussing over the six I raised who fled from under our roof years ago."

They had come in the early afternoon on Friday and would leave Sunday. Atlantic City was a place Melodye had visited often with Rafael in the early years of their marriage. She had liked it then; now it reminded her too much of Rafael. But she was a water lover, so she still enjoyed vast views of the Atlantic Ocean.

"We gonna swim in the pool back there?" Rachel asked.

"Why not? I could certainly use a dip," Melodye told her, ruffling the flyaway black hair.

Randy went racing off to get on the slide, climbed up and swooped down with a war cry. Merriment was wherever Randy Carter was. She was glad that little about her twins reminded her of Rafael. It was as if they carried only her genes.

Eight o'clock found them on the way to Larry Biggs's building. It was a large redbrick structure, well built and well maintained. There were several stores on the ground floor doing brisk business. They passed the office of a private investigator and Jim looked in before they rounded a corner and were at the glass-enclosed office of Larry Biggs. There was no one in the reception area and Jim looked around for a few minutes before the big, rumpled man Melodye remembered too well came out of his office.

"I see you're right on time," Larry said. "Come in."

She noted that he still seemed as evil as ever. Dour and giving no quarter, the big man didn't tower over Jim as he did most men. Larry spread his arms, indicating that they should sit down.

"Well, what the hell can I do for you? Or do you for?"

He laughed and coughed at his joke, but Jim only smiled a little. "I'm here about Rafael Carter."

"That bum. Oh, yeah, remind me not to speak ill of the dead. If you ever find the one who did it, I want to shake his hand."

"Bad blood?"

"Damned right. He died owing me a bundle. I could've killed him myself, but he wasn't worth the death penalty."

Jim drew a deep breath. "Let me ask you, Mr. Biggs, how much *did* Mr. Carter owe you?"

Larry Biggs chewed on an unlit cigar. "Nearly a quarter million bucks. Turk had gotten his tail out of a crack a coupla times, but he couldn't quit. I dunno who else he owed big-time, but I know there were others."

"But *you* didn't kill him?"

"Now, what kinda question is that? You think I'd say if I did?" He laughed shortly. "No, I didn't. I was just left wishing I had."

"Just thought I'd ask. When was the last time you saw him?"

"The night he died. He and Turk and me stayed late at *Steeped In Joy* and, Lord, we tied one on. Must've killed a couple of quarts of Scotch. Turk and I left him there. Somebody must've been watching and knew he was alone. Or maybe he let somebody in he did or didn't know and they robbed him. We were all skunk drunk."

Jim looked at him evenly. "You didn't tell me all this when I investigated the first time. Why?"

Larry tapped his desktop and thought about it. "Turk and I decided not to. The guy was dead and you had no way of knowing. Now Turk tells me some jerk saw us all coming out of the building that night and finally decided to come forward. I'd like to punch his lights out."

"So you two left him alive?"

"Yeah."

"I see."

Larry had bad skin and he worried and scratched it endlessly. Looking at him, Melodye thought he was not a prepossessing man and wondered if he had a wife.

Jim fell silent on purpose, assessing his man, getting inside his head. After a minute, Larry seemed a little nervous, anxious for this to be over.

"This all you got to ask?"

Jim shook his head. "No, there's more I'm afraid."

Larry hunched his shoulders, turned his attention to Melodye. "Miz Carter, I wanta say, you don't seem to be grieving much."

His statement startled Melodye. "It's been over two years."

"Yeah." His voice was guttural. "I bet you didn't grieve too much at the get-go. Rafael spread it around. I don't guess he had much left over for a wife."

She didn't want to be reminded and she didn't respond.

Jim had other questions, some seemingly innocuous, some pointed. Larry Biggs answered them all.

"You're gonna find I'm cleaner'n a whistle. I'm a bookie and a gambler, although the two seldom go together. The business has been good to me. I say that to get what I want. No need to kill."

Jim chewed on that. "I'm thinking if Mr. Carter got nasty, said he didn't intend to pay you, maybe spit in your face. That would do it, wouldn't it? Rage. A falling out of old friends…"

"Whoa! Who said anything about friends?"

"Turk said the three of you were friends. Others have corroborated that."

Larry shrugged. "Maybe in a minor way. I'm a loner myself. Don't climb on my back. The bum's dead and we're all better off. Let it rest. The way things are with all the shooting going on, don't you damned detectives have enough to keep busy?"

Jim didn't answer.

The big man seemed relieved when the questions stopped and he offered them a drink, which they refused.

"Well, I'm here if you need me. Nothing I know'll help you one bit, but I've always cooperated with the law, kept my nose clean. I sure wouldn't ruin it by killing Carter."

At the end, Larry held out a hamlike hand to both of them. Only then did his eyes slide over Melodye with a lecherous gaze. "I reckon you're remembering the night I came to your house to see your husband. You heard us quarreling. You probably heard or he told you I threatened to kill him…."

Melodye nodded.

Larry went on. "I was fighting mad. I got money, but I don't like losing it. It was just—what d'they call it—heat of passion. Meant nothing. Rafael threatened to kill *me* a coupla times."

He fell silent then and Jim wondered why he'd brought this up at the end. He wasn't a man who made random moves. He was calculating and a bastard through and through.

Outside, walking to the nearest gambling casino, they moved slowly and talked.

"What do you think?" she asked him.

"That he's probably lying. The signs are all there. I've talked with Turk a couple of times lately and he finally told me Larry and he were with Rafael the night he died, after I told him what I knew. Neither of them said that when I began the investigation way back. *They* could have killed him, Melodye. God knows they had the best opportunity. In his condition, he'd be easy to gun down. A robbery to make it look real. Rafael was known to carry money."

Walking, she felt close to him, a deep part of his life and she reminded herself that she wasn't. She was a cause he'd adopted. *Make Melodye feel good about herself.* This was an era of good self-esteem and he wanted to help her get hers. It didn't explain her inflammatory response to him or the way her heart pounded and her loins melted with desire around him. It was just sex, plain and simple, and she needed to knock it off.

In the casino, they quickly found the one-arm bandits, got twenty-dollar tickets, which she put in her bag, and headed toward the machines. Memories flooded her then. She'd never won a single thin dime when Rafael had taken her to casinos. She didn't really like gambling, considered it a fool's game. It wasn't in her blood the way it had been in Rafael's.

A half hour passed while she fed several machines and Jim stood by her, breathing easily.

"Why don't you play at least once or twice?" she asked.

"Okay," he readily agreed.

He played three times, lost and declared that that was it for him.

She kept playing, got gambler's fever. If not this time, then the next. But she was tired of it and had decided to call it quits when the bell rang and she hit! Four thousand dollars and she'd spent nowhere near that amount. Keen excitement flooded her as they waited for a check to be drawn.

Dizzy with joy, she turned to Jim and flung her arms around him and he held her tightly, grinning. "I've never won anything before," she told him. "Hey, you're my lucky piece, you know. I'll split with you."

He kissed her cheek. "You'll do nothing of the sort. Blow it on clothes."

"Part of this takes us out to a fabulous dinner tomorrow night. I wish we hadn't eaten tonight."

"I could never pass up sautéed oysters and sour cream potatoes. I told you the inn food is good."

It was still early when they sat on the sand in a cove near the inn. They had changed into swimming suits. Her suit was a two piece, showing off her sharply defined waist and old-style Coca-Cola bottle hips. Her legs would make a strong man moan. His groin was killing him as they swam near shore, splashing each other and taking care not to turn each other on.

He thought that was a joke. They had only to glance at each other to turn on. Well, sex was the lay of the land these days. It was everywhere you turned. The very air oozed it. He wanted the case to be over soon because Miss Melodye had gotten to him and it didn't help that he knew very well that it was all a matter of gonads and genes. What else?

They were both hot-blooded people. Passionate people. And passionate people made love or longed to. But he thought deeply then that it wasn't going to be that way for him and Melodye. They had brains and control and they used both. They'd both been hurt and there was no way in hell they'd travel that road again.

The water was warm as it laved their bodies. He splashed her and she slipped. He caught her and her wet body felt like heaven itself in his arms. He felt his shaft rise and harden and he groaned inside. Maybe they'd better go in.

Once inside, in their suite's living room there was an ice bucket with champagne chilling and a note from management. "Double congratulations and enjoy!" Both grinned. They had told Mickey and Carol about their win before they went to the cove.

Melodye felt suddenly shy as she went to her room to take a shower and change clothes. She emerged a short while later in a very pale yellow, fitted lounging gown.

In Dockers and a blue tee shirt Jim whistled long and low. "I can't tell you how good you look in that color."

She shrugged. "I'd never have thought it if it hadn't been for you. I've had it drummed into my head. Stay with the dark colors. That way you won't look so fat."

Jim frowned at the fleeting hurt on her face. He came and stood close to her. "It's not like you're not a beauty, Melodye. Everything's in the right place in spades. You exercise, you eat healthy foods with not too much sugar and you work with your doctor. You're *healthy*." He chuckled then. "And God knows, you're really fine."

She swatted him playfully. "I think I'll have you cloned for when we no longer see you." She felt sad at the thought.

He looked at her gravely. "That could still be a while. I was moving fast on the case. Now there's a hangup, but we're very hopeful of a breakthrough. After that…" His voice drifted off and she finished for him silently. After that, their friendship would be over. They both knew the score.

Jim popped the cork in the champagne and toasted her. "To beauty and happiness. May you one day realize the wonder that is you!"

"Okay," she said softly, "you've proved your point. I haven't had you around long to bolster me, tell me I matter and how great I am. What about you? Jim, you're one of the most wonderful people I've ever known."

He bowed low. "Thank you, ma'am. I'm glad you think so."

They both liked Lionel Richie. She had brought a portable CD player and a couple of Richie albums. Now she played them and they listened, each sprawled on a sofa. In her mind's eye she saw them at the farmhouse in Virginia with her on the sofa and him sprawled on the floor. Was that before or after the kiss? No, she cautioned herself, don't think about that kiss.

The champagne was Dom Perignon and the taste said it came from an excellent year. Melodye's belly got warm, then her whole body matched it and the flames licked her again. She had always found him attractive, but had he always been this gorgeous? His muscular body talked to her in its own commanding language. His stormy hazel eyes had never been more passionate when he looked at her and the edge of danger that attracted, and at times, half frightened her lay on him like a mantle.

He got up and held out his arms as "Lady" came on and she put aside her champagne flute, got up and went into them. She shivered at the body contact, refusing to really feel the waves of passion that washed over her. His face was very close to hers and she could have cried at the tension in her aching body. They had drunk too much champagne she knew then and it was mellowing them both.

She wanted to stop dancing, go to bed, burrow beneath the covers and dream wild dreams, but she was moving in a dream. This couldn't happen. This *mustn't* happen.

But the ancient male in Jim's loins said it *would* happen. It *had* to happen and he bent her backward in a kiss that scorched her. His rock hard shaft rose mightily against her lush, soft crotch and, groaning, his big hands at last cupped her buttocks the way they'd wanted to do since the first day he'd seen her again. He didn't tell himself anything. He could only feel lost in the blinding waves of passion that held him in thrall.

The kiss seemed endless to Melodye and she held him to her with all her strength, moaning in the back of her throat.

Was it her voice that huskily begged him, "Make love to me, Jim. Please." Her breath came in snatches and this was the only reality.

He held her away from him and looked deeply into her dreamy brown eyes. He saw the fear that had made her voice quaver and he thought, yeah, his persona was of a tough and dangerous lion but where *she* was concerned, he was a total pussycat. He wished he could heal all the hurt she had suffered and his own heart hurt with sympathy. And they were lucky. Neither wanted or needed love.

He picked her up and carried her into his bedroom, kissed her again as they stood by the bed, then stripped off her lounging gown and the wisps of sheer undergarments. He flung off his own clothes and knelt before her, spreading her legs and kneading her hips. He stroked the soft pubic hairs and teased her bud until she thought she'd scream. Then his tongue found that bud and licked it gently at first, then harder, savoring the sweetness of her. She bucked beneath his tongue that darted into the opening and laved it with a vengeance.

"I don't want to come," she whispered. "I want to do the same to you."

He got up and lay on the bed and she bent over his shaft, admiring the varied coloring, the thickness and the beauty, before she took it into her mouth and licked him, gently at first, then harder as he groaned his satisfaction. His pubic hairs were coarser than hers, lighter in color. She stroked his belly and delighted in the muscular feel of him. She was lost in the glory of what she did to him, what he had done to her when he gently held her away, then pulled her up against his chest.

Cold fear assaulted her then and the hateful memory of Rafael's telling her that she was no good, stretched out of shape. Saying her precious twins had ruined her. He saw the misery on her face and coaxed her to tell him what was wrong.

When she'd briefly told him, his face was hot with sympathy. "He was blaming you for his own shortcomings. There're different positions we can try. Just relax and trust me."

As if she could ever trust a man again.

He got up and got a condom from his pants pocket and together they smoothed it on. She stroked and tweaked his shaft, delighting him as he swelled incredibly.

He hugged her tightly for long moments before he turned her over and slowly, tantalizingly ran his shaft along the folds of her, then with excruciating precision, entered her. Her soft walls closed tightly around him like a hot glove. Passion had made her firehot, wet and ready and he worked her expertly with need and maddening desire.

She clutched his buttocks as he drove into her. This was like nothing she had ever known. This surge of pure lust blended with—no, not love—but she felt so close to him. Her mouth opened as she gasped for breath and when he kissed her it sent her into orbit, opened her heart to him. It was nature's favorite dance and both knew that this was what they *needed,* even if it was not what they *wanted* to happen.

He exploded first, then waited until she finished with a wild cry, making him put the edge of his hand over her mouth as he laughed low in his throat. "Go ahead, scream. This way, no one will hear you."

Then they were both limp and wrung out, slick with sweat and laughing in each other's arms.

He hugged her tightly. "You fit me perfectly and if you were any better, my heart would stop."

"Thank you," she whispered. "You're the perfect one. I think you've given me myself."

They lay, wordlessly stroking each other for long moments.

"This wasn't supposed to happen," she told him.

"Hush. *We* wanted one thing. Mother Nature wanted something else."

"Are you sorry?" she asked him tentatively.

He was silent a long moment. "No more than I'm sorry when I watch a gorgeous sunset or sunrise. Are you?"

"No, but we can't let this happen again. We've talked about this."

He shook her a bit. "Let's talk about *this*. Are you satisfied? Had enough?"

"Have you?"

"Don't answer a question with a question."

She teased him. "Why not?"

He gripped her shoulders and playfully shook her hard. "No man bosses you around, I see. I haven't had nearly enough, my designing woman." He got serious then as he propped himself on one elbow and studied her. "Do you know what you were really designed for?"

"No. Tell me."

"*You were designed for passion,* Melodye, and there hasn't been enough of it in your life. If things were different, I'd be the one to give it to you. Sexually we're perfect together. Emotionally it's another story. It'll be a long time before either of us can love again and we're lucky to know that. Let's have this night and let it be the glory it is. Then we'll back off...."

Something in her hurt when he said it. She was sure he'd been about to say something else, but he didn't. She thought she'd like to be friends and thought they could be without repeating this. Just stack it in memory and go on.

She put the second condom on and they lost no time. Filled with relief and new confidence, she was the aggressive one then and straddled him, wondering at herself. She had never felt free to be aggressive with Rafael and she laughed a bit to herself. *Rafael who?* But she knew who Rafael was, all right, the man who had hurt her beyond bearing. The man who had caused her never to be able to love or trust again.

Looking up at Melodye as she rode him, his big shaft throbbing inside her tender gripping walls, Jim half closed his eyes. She looked like a voluptuous chocolate angel and he murmured to her, "My angel."

"I like that," she said quietly.

"You should. You are. I love the way you move. You're a natural in my bed."

"And you're not?"

"With you, any man would be."

"I've never had anything like this. You free me. I just want this to go on forever."

Her words excited him, but they chilled him, too. He didn't want to hurt her ever. He wasn't *going* to hurt her the way he'd hurt Elyssa. He told himself that sex and sexual desire had been getting people in big trouble since Adam and Eve. He promised that they wouldn't do this again after tonight. *It wasn't smart, but it felt so damned sure wonderful.*

He pulled her down and drew her face close to him, wanting her even closer. She was so open to him, so giving. She said he freed her. For what? There was no future for them. He kissed her then, going into the corners of her mouth and exploring the warm, sweet hollows and minty breath as he cupped her face in his big hands.

She stroked his biceps, thrilling at the bulky hardness of him against her own softness and he hugged her tightly.

Then on the thick carpet, he positioned her and entered her from behind. Her muscles still held him. She was so hot. So tight. So wet. He dreaded having the night end and being without her. But he fought the feeling and reminded himself that he'd been alone for almost three years and liked it that way. He concentrated on the here and right now as he worked her with fervor, stroking and kissing her buttocks, her back.

She kept feeling she'd faint with the sheer wonder of what they did to each other and suddenly without warning, a hot steam raged through her and she felt wave after wave of passion engulf her like a high tide sweeping her in to soft, sandy shores.

He heard her soft cries and his penis jerked. In all his life, he had never felt passion like this and it bothered him, but not too much because the joy was so intense it left little room for anything else.

"You thrill me," he said after a while. "It doesn't get any better than what we just had."

But his saying it unleashed a demon of fear inside her. He wouldn't want to do it, but would he hurt her, too?

Chapter 8

At *A-1 Plus Love* the next morning, Melodye went through orders from the fashion show. They had done a landslide business and Odessa was ecstatic. She came in with a cup of coffee for Melodye and looked at her friend slyly.

"I trust the trip went well. You're certainly shining."

Melodye didn't miss a beat. "All this new business and I'm *not* shining? Fat chance."

Odessa set the coffee on the desk and put her hands on her ample hips. "Now, why do I feel your glow has little or nothing to do with orders. Did you have a good time this weekend? C'mon, girlfriend, clue me in."

Melodye couldn't stop her broad smile. "I started to call you, but we got busy. I won four thousand dollars."

Odessa whistled. "I'll be waiting for my share. Somehow I never figured you for the casino type. Blackjack?"

"Plain old slots and this time *I* was the *two*-armed bandit. I wasn't going to spend more than two hundred."

Odessa pursed her lips. "Okay, babe. That covers the cost of the trip."

"The twins enjoyed themselves hugely." She told Odessa about Dew Drop Inn and the couple who owned and ran it.

"Dammit, woman, I want to hear about the real juice, like what happened between you and the fine one."

"Oh, him," Melodye teased. She had told Odessa about the kiss on her patio and the *kiss* at the farmhouse. She wanted to and she didn't want to share this with her friend. "What do you think happened?"

"Wel-l-l," Odessa drawled. "I see him knocking you down and dragging you by your long hair to his cave and ravishing you from midnight until the break of dawn. But knowing you, you probably held back, hurting for action."

"We made love, Odessa, and I still cannot believe it." Her eyes on Odessa were moist and her body still thrummed with memory. "He thinks my body is—fabulous, or said he did."

Odessa bent and hugged Melodye's shoulders, then gave a low whoop. "Hooray for you! And what in hell do you mean, he *'said.'* I'll bet he's still feeling your hot body now."

"He hasn't called."

"He's probably knocked out. He will. Listen, honeychile, I've got news of my own."

"Spill it."

"Remember Ashton Williams, one of the Crystal Lake detectives Jim whomped up for us?"

"I do. He monopolized your evening. How could I forget him?"

"He took me to dinner, and rooftop dancing yet." Her face

got somber then. "He's really nice, Melodye, and he seems to really like me."

"And of course, *you* feel nothing."

"I'm too quickly beginning to feel everything. I could go for him, but the terrain out there is rough these days and we women have to be careful. I don't mean that about Jim, though. He comes through to me as full of integrity. Oh, I know he's somewhat aloof and definitely a loner, but I see him playing fair and square."

Melodye thought a moment. "I sure hope so," was all she said.

Odessa went out and Melodye sat looking at the bright sunlight. Why hadn't he called? He had helped her put the twins to bed and they were asleep before they could ask for a story. They had stood awkwardly at the door, neither wanting to separate, but he had brushed a light kiss on her lips and left. This, after all that Friday-night passion and more of it Saturday. Was he sated? It was as good or better to her the second time as it had been the first. Did *he* have second thoughts?

She told herself he was exactly what she needed. Okay, it had been a mistake, but a grand mistake. They were grown-ups and knew where they were going.

Her phone rang and it was Bettina.

"I just wanted to tell you we've decided Lucia will stay with me while she recuperates a bit from her broken heart."

Lucia in town wasn't good news, Melodye thought. "I'm sure she'll find someone to mend it."

"You know, she seems to like Jim a lot."

Melodye's heart skipped a beat. Well, she had no claims on him.

"I think Jim Ryman goes a lot deeper than I'd thought. He could be good for her."

Melodye wondered if Bettina even considered her, Melodye, for Jim. "Doesn't *he* have anything to say about that?"

Bettina sighed, then laughed. "I've never known Lucia to fail to get whatever man she set her cap for. You're lucky she didn't get to Rafael first. Give me a little time, but I want you and Jim to come to a party I'm giving for Hunter Davis, renowned and sinfully handsome photographer. I've got excellent year of wine and an incredible champagne."

Melodye swallowed hard. She didn't want to think about champagne.

"If you'd lose some weight, start designing for the fashionably thin, you'd have *my* kind of success," Bettina said, and ended the call.

Melodye had wanted to be catty and remind her mother that most of her success had come from her settled lawsuit over a prescription drug she'd taken that had given her a stroke, but she hadn't.

Her mother never failed to get on her last nerve and this time was no exception. Talking with her made the fact that Jim hadn't called bother her more. Grow up, she admonished herself. Back off. *He gave you everything he had over the weekend,* she told herself, *and with Lucia in town, that may be all there is.*

She turned on the Bose radio system to a pop station and what should come on but Lionel Richie singing "Lady." She switched to a classical station. She refused to spend the morning mooning about Jim or any other man.

She was lost in thought, rubbing her forearms absentmindedly when he spoke from the doorway as he lounged his big frame against the jamb, looking somberly at her. She jumped and her breath caught. "You startled me," she said.

He didn't say anything for a couple of minutes. "It never amazes me that you're as gorgeous in sunlight as you are in moonlight," he said finally.

It was the last thing she expected him to say.

"Thank you, as always," she said quietly.

"I wanted to call, but there was action at the station house and I was still on call this morning."

She noticed then that his hands were behind his back. Now he brought them forward. He was holding a bunch of multicolored peonies. "How beautiful," she told him.

He walked over and thrust them at her.

She took them, smelled the heady perfume. "They're my favorites," she said.

"I remember. You see, I'm at least partially civilized."

"Oh, I think you can be well civilized."

He didn't respond, but slowly a sly, sexy grin spread across his face.

She blushed furiously and shrugged. She still felt his kisses all over her body and the hunger she felt for him threatened her very core.

"I've got a lot on my mind these days," he said. "If you don't hear from me, I beg you to forgive me in advance."

She nodded. "You don't owe me anything."

"Right now I feel as if I owe you everything," he said.

His statement surprised and pleased her even more.

She took the peonies and put them in a big crystal vase, then went to the kitchenette for water. When she came back, he was still standing.

"I bought a house near Alexandria. But then I suppose Mom's told you," he said.

"Yes," Melodye said.

"I want you to come out, give me some pointers. I'll get

a decorator, but I want your's and Mom's input, too. I'll make my special shrimp-and-crab gumbo. Your stomach will thank me," he said.

Her stomach, along with the rest of her, already was grateful to him.

She thought to herself, *a big house and us in it. Alone. I don't want what happened in Atlantic City to happen again. I may be designed for passion, but I can and I have lived without it.* "Sounds promising," she told him.

Jim was silent for a very long time, but finally sat down at Melodye's urging.

For moments he was lost in thought until she said, "Earth to Ryman. Come in, please."

He looked up, frowning. "I was thinking about the fact that I was sure Rafael had shot me because I was making such swift inroads on his and Turk's case. We were even talking to prosecutors. Money laundering, racketeering. Almost a you-name-it case. Then I was shot. My buddies didn't miss a beat. But Rafael was killed in what we thought was a robbery and we thought it was just divine justice. Then the job of a lifetime came for me in New York. I healed and left." He sighed. "And the rest, as they say, is history."

She nodded, going back to a past she didn't want to go back to. Let the evil dead bury its evil dead.

A quietly humorous voice spoke from the doorway and Melodye looked up. "Papa France!"

He came to her, hugged her, clapped Jim's shoulder. "I'm out deaconing and I thought I'd make you the first of my rounds, grandbaby. Got a invitation for both of you. Jim, I'm glad I found you here." He sat down.

Jim smiled. "I'm always open to your invitations, Papa France. What's up?"

The old man's face was wreathed in smiles. "This Sunday my church is having a gospel singing *fête*. It'll be the year's best and…"

Jim's eyes narrowed. "I'd love to be there, but I may not be able to make it. I'm sure Melodye's discussed the case we're working on, and I've got yet another one."

Papa France nodded. "She sure has and I'm wishing you luck."

"But if there's any way I can take time off…"

"Well, you try because Whit Steele's gonna be there and…"

Jim's face lit up. "*Whit?* Man, that puts a different face on it. If there's *any* way I can work it, count me in."

Papa France grinned. "Whit's a favorite, huh?"

"A *friend.* We were both in the Marines. He was a musician and I was a sergeant. When we found we were from the same neck of the woods, we became bosom buddies. Being in totally different outfits, we didn't see each other often, but we made up for lost time when we did. Yeah, if there's any way I can swing it, we'll be there."

Melodye hadn't known he was a sergeant in the armed forces. She mused that it could explain so much about his deep reticence, the edge of danger she got from him. He would've seen things that went beyond the pale. He would've lived intimately with danger and the worst life had to offer. She intended to talk with him about that.

Papa France had noted Jim's quick inclusive word *we* and was highly pleased.

He turned to his granddaughter. "Well, Miss Melodye, how've you been? And how did the trip go?"

Melodye's skin warmed and her heart beat faster. "We had a wonderful time. I'd have called you later today. I won four thousand dollars."

"Now, you didn't! Congratulations! My lunches are gonna be on you for a while."

"You bet."

"I'd guess the twins were in hog heaven."

"They were and still are."

Papa France sat musing that his granddaughter needed a man like Jim to help her. He was sure that this was the man for her. When Jim was a youth, others had said he was wild, hedonistic, but he'd found something steady and deep in the boy and had tried to be a father to Jim after his own father had died. The two men still shared a deep camaraderie and Papa France had been disappointed when Melodye had listened to her mother and passed Jim up as a date.

Well, he had plans now to rectify old mistakes.

Papa France stood up. "I've got to be shoving off. Life as a deacon for my church ain't always easy, but I've got to say it's a whole lot of fun. Church ladies are so sweet, my fellow deacons and the rest of the congregation are great and our minister is tops. Yes, life is good and God is good. I'm gonna pray you two get there Sunday. You'll enjoy yourselves, I promise."

He was gone then and Jim was still there. Suddenly he jumped a bit and shook his head. "I'm sitting here like I haven't got a thing to do and I've got a jammed day. There's a dogfight ring we're breaking up and it's not pretty."

She looked at him tentatively. "Try not to push too hard."

He smiled then, slowly and wickedly, his stormy hazel eyes narrowed. "I had a busy weekend. A great, but busy weekend and I'm still feeling the effects." He could have been inside her, her rush of pleasure was so great.

She leaned back and looked at him through partially shuttered eyes. "Poor baby," was all she said.

* * *

Papa France stopped by Miss Belle's beige brick bungalow where the children she kept climbed over him before he could get in the door.

"Well, come in, Francis," she said warmly. "What brings you by to brighten my day?"

He grinned widely. "Plotting better'n one of Shakespeare's plays. I'm just coming back from talking to your Jim and my Melodye."

Miss Belle laughed delightedly and Papa France thought as always, that she was a mighty good-looking woman. Today she had on a pale blue plush jogging suit and her short hair was a silver cap. Her eyes were like his own, brown, clear and humorous.

"You're looking charming," he told her. "Mighty nice outfit."

She smiled. "This old thing is ten years old at least. *You* always look well. How's the deaconing coming along?"

"Seems like it's what I was born for. Minister told me I was the best he's come across."

She looked at him. "So you're here to talk about Jim and Melodye."

"Yeah. Those two need to be together."

Miss Belle thought awhile. "They spent the weekend in Atlantic City with the babies. That would sound like a good sign if I didn't know better."

Papa France frowned. He'd thought it was a very good sign and he intended to push it further, faster. "What d'you mean?"

She bit her bottom lip. "Well, Jim's as stubborn as any mule and he's dead set that he didn't and won't make a good husband. He loves those twins already more than he realizes.

He comes by and he stays a while and plays with them all the time, but he insists that he and Melodye are just friends and that's all they'll ever be. He says and she's told me that Rafael fixed it for her forever, so they're soulmates in misery." She paused for a long while. "France, I never talked with you about it, but she's cried many a day talking with me about Rafael. She swears she never wants a man again. Pity."

He drew a deep breath. "Yeah, she's told me the same thing. But she and Jim are both lonely and they *need* each other. Like one swallow don't make a summer, one big hurt don't make a life. I wish I could help her see that. We have to get them to go to each other."

Her eyes grew moist. "You know I'll do anything I can. Melodye's like a daughter to me. I want grandchildren. That's why I keep children and they all help fill the gap in my life. My son knows I love him. We've always been close. He's always felt his father didn't love him and was incapable of love, but I know better. My husband was a bitter man over his parents and the setbacks he suffered. He just couldn't *show* his love for Jim and me, but I knew it was there and I told Jim so. I'll never stop thanking you for what you did for my son—and me."

Papa France looked at the woman who'd been his friend for over twenty years and there was a lump in his throat. "Anything I could do did me more good than it did you or Jim. When my wife died four years ago, you helped me more than I ever said. You were my rock then, and I don't think I've ever told you how grateful I am."

Her heart suddenly filled with good feelings. "Couldn't you do with another cup of coffee? Tea? I made good tea cakes this morning, sprinkled with coconut. I know you like coconut."

He grinned. "Never met a tea cake I wasn't partial to and I never pass up coconut. And yes, might as well take another cup of coffee. Black, please. The doctor's got me off sugar, and none'a that fancy false sugar for me."

She bustled off to the kitchen and five kids came to his knees. The twins hugged his knees hard and his heart hurt for them. The other three kids had loving, warm fathers. He knew them all. He dreamed of a father for Rachel and Randy and he'd do his level best to make that dream come true.

Chapter 9

Holy Redeemer Church was an imposing fieldstone structure that Melodye had attended as a child. In college she had
focused on another church, but still came to this one with
Papa France on occasion. Now Jim, the twins and she came
up the broad walk, admiring the flower beds, the gushing
fountain, and the well-kept shrubbery. Papa France would be
so pleased that they came.

The twins fidgeted and skipped along, bursting with
energy. "Where're we going?" Randy asked.

"We're *there,* kid," Jim answered him, brushing his hand
over Randy's hair.

The boy stared at the church as if he felt the importance
of it. Then Rachel primly gave it the once-over. "It's pretty,"
she said, then suddenly, "Mommy, you look pretty today."

"Second the motion," Jim commented.

In the vestibule, they found Miss Belle waiting for them.

She bent and hugged the twins, who were happy to see her, and she hugged Melodye.

"Did France tell you what the service is about?" Miss Belle asked.

"Just that we'd enjoy it and Whit will be here," Jim answered.

Miss Belle laughed. "There's always a method to France's madness. Well, mine, too. You'll find out once you get inside."

Randy swung on to Jim's arm and the usher registered them, then took the twins' hands to escort them to the nursery.

"Aren't *you* coming?" Rachel asked wistfully as she looked at Melodye.

Melodye bent down and took the little girl's hand. "Go with the lady and we'll see you in a very little while. You'll have fun with all the other children in the nursery," Melodye said.

Randy leaned a bit backward and patted his foot the way he'd seen Jim do. "We'll see you in a little while," Randy said to his mother.

An usher seated them in the middle section where they relaxed and looked around, focusing on a huge banner across the stage proclaiming "THE DIVINE RELATIONSHIP!" Now, what would that be? Melodye found herself wondering as Jim wondered the same thing.

It was a scene that never failed to stir Melodye's heart, the stillness at first, the rustle of programs, the expectations of fulfillment. She glanced at her own program. Whit was listed, all right, but just as part of the services. She was a little disappointed because she liked to settle down and get deep into his spirituals, with nothing to distract her.

Jim sat, thinking he hadn't been to church in quite a while. He still attended the one he attended as a child and he meant to take Melodye and the twins one Sunday. He felt an urge to take Melodye's hand, but didn't.

They sat on the end of the bench and Papa France tapped Jim on his shoulder, beaming. "Glad you could make it. You're gonna love this."

He squeezed Melodye's shoulder and whispered, "You're looking beautiful, granddaughter, as always."

The old man hurried onto the stage where he took over. "Today," he began, "we pay homage to the glory of one of God's most honorable relationships, that of a man and a woman joined in holy wedlock."

Both Jim's and Melodye's mouth opened a little. Jim shook his head. Papa France hadn't said a word about celebrating marriage, but he'd often talked with Jim about the peace and contentment of matrimony. He'd had a fifty-five-year relationship with his beloved Gina and he wanted the same for the world.

Jim expelled a harsh sigh. Well, the world had changed. Couples weren't getting married much anymore. African-American men were *fleeing* marriage in droves.

Melodye glanced at him as she heard his harsh breathing. She knew he was bothered by the same thing that bothered her—the marriage thing. Time spent in hell left you with no desire ever to go there again. Papa France and her grandmother had lived in a different era. People and conditions were kinder, gentler then.

Papa France lost little time in bringing out the man they'd all come to see and hear: Whit Steele. And the audience was on its feet cheering and applauding. Whit bowed low as he told them he'd be singing as part of the service. This wasn't a full show. "How would you like me to sing 'Amazing Grace' with you?"

The audience roared and the organist struck the chord with the white-robed choir humming on cue.

On her feet, Melodye found herself standing very close to Jim and from time to time he glanced at her. Her body felt weak with wanting him and anger that the feeling lay deep in her heart. Were they going to be a runaway train? They'd slept together once and it might as well have been a lifetime she wanted him so badly, so constantly. *Focus on the service,* she told herself. *This is gorgeous music.* But she focused on Jim and couldn't help it. She thought he seemed unruffled, but men were different. They often took sex lightly.

Jim sang the beautiful words of the hymn and felt them deeply, but he felt more—the primal urge toward being inside Melodye, and like her, he was angry. What in hell had he gotten himself into? Their bodies had been drawn together in lust and wonder and, yeah, *joy.* No question about it.

She was helping him on an important case. He had helped her make a show she'd been sure would be a failure into a success. She'd won four thousand dollars where she'd never won anything before and had come into his arms, weak with excitement and ecstasy. He shuddered with his loins hurting.

Amazing grace. Jim thought *he* was the wretch the song was written for, and at the moment, he didn't see how any grace was going to save him from his own ravening and unending hunger for the woman beside him.

The air was electric with Whit's presence, but there were other things in store. The sermon was mercifully brief and totally on the sanctity of the marriage vows as God's hope of heaven on earth. As the ushers brought around the long offering trays, Melodye was certain the offering would be one of the best of the year.

Papa France came to the podium, his face wreathed in smiles. "We're anxious, I know, to hear the great one, but the people I want to present to you are great ones, too. These are the citizens and church members who've withstood the test of time. People in the congregation who've been together more than forty years, who've stuck with each other through thick and thin, raised families, known sorrow and joy, never wavering—*together.*"

The six couples filed onstage and stood, as the pastor kissed each forehead briefly and Whit shook hands with each one. Melodye glanced at Jim, who sat a bit forward. She wondered how Jim felt about this. She knew how *she* felt: to each his own. These people had been happy, mostly for a lifetime.

She'd been happy for only a few brief years. The children that were supposed to bind her marriage had torn it apart. Melodye still wished for the deeper fulfillment that these couples shared.

The audience gave the couples prolonged applause and it seemed to Melodye that Papa France looked directly at Jim and her.

Melodye leaned over and asked Jim to let her see his program. A line on hers was blurred. As he handed it to her, their fingers touched and hot blood rushed and tingled through her body. She thought she might as well get used to it; this attraction wasn't going to stop anytime soon. They had what they had. *It was great, but how long could it last?*

In the car with the twins strapped in their safety seats in back, Jim and Melodye looked at each other.

"Blindsided!" Jim finally said.

"In spades!" Melodye agreed. She shook her head. "I'm glad you kept your cool. Only our matchmaking relatives would invite us to a church ceremony that celebrated the institution of marriage."

"The old coots," he muttered.

"The problem is they mean well," Melodye said. "They love us and they want what they consider is best for us. They just don't know our hearts the way we do. Jim, it's plain they're on a roll and they're not gonna stop. It's up to us to stop this runaway train."

"Yeah, you tell me how we do that."

She didn't hesitate. "Simple. Pretend to go along with them—up to a point. I say we stay the friends we've gotten to be and continue that. I think they'll assume we're just taking our own slow time."

"Are we?"

"You know the score on that. We've both been hurt and we're both determined not go that route again. That's our right. Agreed?"

Laughing, relieved, he held up his hand in invitation to a high five and she took it, as pleased, as relieved as he was.

Chapter 10

"Okay, we've both had a surprise we could live without. Now I have a surprise that'll please you."

They were on the highway headed away from Crystal Lake and Melodye had asked where they were going. The twins were silent, gazing out the windows, and she glanced back at them. Little pitchers didn't just have big ears, they also had incredibly busy hands.

Jim tapped the steering wheel. "You said the color you're wearing is periwinkle-blue. It does something for you and it turns me on—high."

Her mouth curved in a radiant smile. "Everything turns both of us on."

"Natural. Exciting. I like it that way. What about you?"

"I guess. It's for certain I haven't felt this way before. My life's been sort of blah before you came along."

He laughed. "I'll think of ways you can show me your appreciation."

From the backseat Randy's singsong voice chirped, "Turn me on."

Jim and Melodye looked at each other, laughing. "The world changed the day those two learned to talk," Melodye told him.

Jim pulled into the parking lot of a new restaurant on the Virginia countryside. The building was newly built redbrick and freshly landscaped. "A friend of mine just opened," Jim said, "and he's focusing on the family trade. I think we'll all like it."

Melodye thought wryly that she was beginning to like being anywhere he was.

Inside the big interior, tables were set with dark cream-colored cloths and bright floral centerpieces. The front was all glass and back walls were filled with photographs of families who had visited with their kids.

The kids were quiet. Rachel clung to Melodye and Randy to Jim. A lively, attractive hostess greeted them, explaining, "We have a special glassed-in room for the little ones where you can watch them. They'll have two hostesses of their own who're from our local college and have had training in child care. They'll love it and you can have a quiet dinner."

A young child's hostess came, talked with them a bit and took the children to their spot. Melodye was pleased that they went along with no fuss.

Seated, Jim reflected that Melodye really did look great today. The services and Whit's singing seemed to have agreed with her; she was glowing. He felt his heart thumping happily as his leg brushed hers.

"Déjà vu," she said, laughing. "The first day you came to

talk with me about Rafael, we sat at the kitchen table and the same thing happened."

He nodded. "Hey, our minds are in sync, not to mention our bodies. I was just about to mention that. Magnet to filings, come in, please."

"We do kind of magnetize each other, don't we?" she said wistfully.

He nodded with a wicked expression.

She drew a deep breath. "Getting back to our loved ones, of course, at some point they'll realize their dreams aren't coming true, but I predict by that time, we'll have schooled them on the value of friendship. We have to start doing that."

"Hopefully," he said. Then he was silent, mulling it over. "I think I'm going to have the beef Wellington. What about you?"

"Hmm, I'm going to follow your lead, except I'm sure you'll want brussel sprouts and I hate them."

"Okay, what then?"

"Asparagus."

A small, slender man with a movie-star-handsome face came to their table and Jim got up. The two men hugged and Jim introduced him.

Chef Malcolm Flowers was charming. He took Melodye's hand and kissed it. "I'd wondered why my friend is so happy lately. With your beauty, I no longer wonder," the chef said.

"You have children with you?" Malcolm asked. "We specialize in service for the whole family."

"Oh, we have children with us," Melodye told him. "They're in the kiddie room. I think this is all such a wonderful idea."

"Thank you. You'll find our food top rate, too. Our wines are superb and may I suggest the fifteen-year-old chardonnay?" He named a brand. "That is, if you favor wines as I do."

They both said they loved good wine. Malcolm left then to greet the few other customers there and the waiter in a red vest, white shirt and black trousers took their order.

Now Jim deliberately brushed Melodye's leg with his and grinned. "My imagination is killing me. If you think I'm coming on to you too strong, just tell me and I'll tone it down. My lust box runneth over with you, but that's only a part of what's in there."

She waited for him to tell her what else was there, but he didn't. After Rafael, she'd read a lot about men since she hadn't had the world of experience. She read to learn to protect her heart, and yes, her sanity. Jim expressed himself unusually well—when he wanted to. He could also be silent, even coldly so, when he wanted to. He had once told her he had Papa France as a role model, then added, "in part. I surely can't make it all the way. Too much water over the dam from my dad."

Their dinner was served under silver domes and was piping hot. The golden beef Wellington crust looked delectable and the vegetables were done just right. A big bowl of mixed salad greens completed the picture. The waiter handed them a dessert menu and Melodye looked it over.

"I can't believe this," she said. "They've got low-calorie banana pudding. This I've got to try."

"Yeah, so will I. I haven't had the dish in a long, long while."

Melodye wished for candlelight for a meal like this. One night she'd have to invite Jim over for a home-cooked dinner. *Would candlelight be too romantic?* But, they weren't in love, she thought. Even so, she'd never been happier. Although, she couldn't help wondering what it meant to him.

"Mom's been hinting," he said as he swallowed a mouthful

of the juicy beef and crisp crust of the beef Wellington.
"Yeah, been hinting, hell, saying out loud that I've got to invite you over to sample my gumbo and see my house. I spoke
with you about it before she ever got around to it, but she
doesn't trust me. Do you?"

"Trust you?"

"Uh-huh."

She dabbed at her mouth and put her napkin by her plate.
"I'm not big on trust anymore. I've told you that. I implicitly
trust Papa France. I don't distrust you. I think you've got integrity. I don't think I'd be sleeping with you if I didn't think
you had. I don't know if I trust *myself* anymore. Am I doing
the right thing? Are *we* doing the right thing?"

Jim looked at her closely. She was feeling something deep.
"I think we are. We won't hurt each other, angel, not ever.
And by the way, I could make myself sick on chocolate
again. Too much is just barely enough." He grinned. "Okay,
I'm coming on to you, but I want you to come to my house
and have dinner with me this weekend when we have more
time. You can give me your ideas on the house and I'll make
the meal. You can just prop your feet up and enjoy."

"Sounds good." She smiled. "Your mom has said several
times if I wanted to have dinner with you, she'd love to keep
the twins. Oh, yes, she and Papa France are planning our fu-
tures big-time."

"And we're planning our own."

The soft strains of "Lady" came on and Melodye shuddered a bit. She could never hear that tune without thinking
of the night they'd made love in Atlantic City. She didn't
think a moment had passed since, when she didn't want to
feel him inside her again, bringing ecstasy and joy.

They were lost in each other, courting ardently, when the

kiddie hostess brought Randy to them, explaining that he wanted to touch base. The hostess pulled out a chair, but the child went and stood beside Jim's chair.

Jim smiled down at him. "Well, did you enjoy your dinner?"

Randy nodded.

"What's in the glass?" Randy asked.

Jim explained that he was drinking cranberry juice. Randy scrambled onto his lap. "Can I have a taste?"

"Sure."

Melodye watched the interaction and held her breath. She watched as Randy's small hand swept out and the cranberry juice spilled onto the cream-colored cloth.

The alert waiter was quick and ultra efficient as he summoned a busboy. With incredible speed, the tablecloth was replaced with a fresh one.

"Don't feel bad about it," the waiter said.

"Thank you," Jim said.

For a minute or two Randy was forgotten and he stood forlornly near Jim at the edge of the table, finger in his mouth. He piped up tensely. "I'm bad, huh?"

Jim reached down and held out his arms. "C'mere! As a matter of fact, I think you're a little trooper and I need a hug."

With tears in his eyes the boy threw himself onto Jim with all his might as Jim picked him up and squeezed him tightly.

Melodye sat forward. "You know," she said, "you say you don't think you'd make a good father. I think you make a great one. And trust me, when they're your own kids, it only gets better."

It struck through Jim's mind then that these kids were beginning to feel like his own and he wasn't sure he wanted that burden. Like his father, he was basically a loner and he intended to make sure he made no one suffer for that failing.

Malcolm came then and the hostess brought Rachel back. Malcolm met and hugged the two children, and Randy excitedly told him about the accident, announcing that Jim had said he was a trooper.

"Yes, I'm certain of that," Malcolm told him. "I have six stepkids who remind me of you. They spill things all the time and its okay. They're kids and kids get awkward sometimes. It's all a part of growing up."

"Hey, I like you," Randy said cheerfully. "And I love Jim."

Malcolm grinned. "Well, I like you, too. Did you enjoy your dinner in the kiddie room?"

"Uh-huh. Mommy said I could have hot dogs." He wrinkled his nose, "but I had to eat my veggies."

"Yeah," Malcolm said, "I have to eat mine, too."

At Melodye's invitation, Malcolm sat with them for a few minutes, asking about the service and their meal. They raved over everything as Malcolm beamed. "Come often," he told them. "And this one's on the house."

"Thanks," Jim said, "but I've got to leave a big tip for the busboy and our waiter. Both were superb."

When Malcolm left them, Jim leaned forward. "Did you enjoy my surprise?"

Melodye smiled. "Oh, yes, you're full of surprises, and this is one of the best. You really *are* a nice man, you know."

He laughed. "Be sure to tell Mom. She wonders sometimes. All my life when I go into my darker moods, she's asked me, 'Where've you gone to now?' I guess, between my dad and me, she had her hands full. And she's so outgoing, so friendly."

"You're friendly. You just have your moods. You may be more creative than you know."

He shook his head. "I can't carry a tune in a knapsack and I can't think of any other creative gifts. No, I don't think so."

Her head went a little to one side and he gazed at her long, long black lashes against her cheek, wanting to kiss them. That color really did things for her smooth chocolate skin.

"Know what I think?" she said. "I believe you're creative in your living. You don't give yourself enough credit."

"Ha. And you *do?*"

She shrugged. "Oh, well, we both know I'm a hopeless case."

He looked really serious then. "No," he said adamantly, "you're *not* a hopeless case. You've got it all, Melodye. Beauty. Brains. Personality. You're a *hot* woman and you can set your world on fire."

She leaned forward. "And get badly burned in the process."

"That doesn't have to happen."

"How do I stop it from happening?"

He didn't hesitate. "By being with someone who only has your best interests at heart." He smiled a little then. "Like me."

As Melodye began to ask more questions, Lucia and a handsome escort came into the restaurant and paused with the hostess by their table.

"Well, if it isn't my beloved sister," Lucia said with saccharin sweetness. She introduced the affable man who was Lucia's type, tall, handsome and—Melodye was sure—rich.

The twins were back at the table and they both ran to her excitedly crying, "Aunt Lucia, we ate in the kiddie room!"

Lucia took a couple of steps backward because she wore a cream white minidress. "No, no!" she said quickly. "Don't touch me, sweeties! I don't want those grubby little paws on my dress. Back off!"

The twins' feelings were plainly hurt. "Rachel, Randy," Melodye said softly, "come back and sit down, darlings."

Randy pouted and looked at his hands. "My hands're clean."

Rachel put her fingers in her mouth, which meant she was upset, and Melodye was steamed at Lucia for the way she treated the children.

"Hey, kids, d'you want to see a magic trick?" Jim said to distract the little ones.

Randy brightened and Rachel put her elbow on Melodye's knee and watched as Jim took the napkin, swirled it around and made it disappear.

"How'd you *do* that?" Randy demanded.

"You can do it, too, when you grow up," Jim assured him. Both children seemed happy again.

Lucia and her man stood, watching the tableau and Lucia said sharply to the hostess, "We're not ready to be seated yet. I'll find you when we are."

The hostess nodded and Lucia moved closer to their table. "I see you're in the lighter and brighter colors again, sis." She wagged a perfectly manicured, red-tipped finger at Melodye. "I'm in the fashion world so I know what I'm talking about. You should stick to darker colors. We cover large areas with *dark* colors." She wasn't through. "Even a beginner knows that. Nature put elephants and hippos in gray."

Jim looked at Lucia long and hard. "But we *display* beauty," he said evenly, "in the most becoming colors. Melodye's kind of beauty has a choice of colors. Once people contended that darkskinned beauties shouldn't wear bright colors, and nobody looks more stunning in bright colors than a darkskinned woman. Maybe your fashion sense isn't so great after all."

Lucia brushed the barb aside, lifted her eyebrows and seemed to have forgotten her escort. "I didn't know you two were dating," she said brightly.

Melodye's beautiful bosom was held high now as she chided her sister. "Surely you don't have the time or inclination to know everything."

Lucia blew a thin stream of air. "Now, that's an evasive answer. Are you? Or aren't you?"

"Hey," Jim said, "we're here for dinner and I'm sure you are, too. Don't keep the hostess waiting. She's got others to seat."

Lucia was a beautiful woman and she was accustomed to getting her due, but her light brown, gold-washed hair, her creamy skin and model-perfect figure wasn't getting her what she wanted. "I need to have lunch with you," she told Jim, as if they were alone. "I need your help with something and I hope you'll come through. I think you will."

He looked at her without answering.

"Well, *will* you help me? May I call you at work?"

"I can't stop you." Jim sat thinking that the woman riled him and he absolutely hated what she and Bettina had done to Melodye.

Lucia was back in form. "Then I'll call you and you'll be interested. I promise. 'Bye, Melodye. 'Bye, babies." She glanced down at her dress and told her escort, "Every day I know more about why I don't have children. And I'm convinced I've made the right decision."

Lucia waved to the children but they didn't wave back. She and her date went to find the hostess.

Melodye liked the way she felt. All her life, she'd cringed after a set to with Lucia. This was different and she thought she had Jim to thank. He hadn't compared her plus-size lushness with Lucia's model slender, sylphlike figure at all, and that was new for her. She looked at herself through Jim's eyes and found herself lovely. No, not beautiful the way he said she was, but highly attractive. It was a very good feeling.

Jim looked at Melodye. "I'm proud of the way you handled her," he said.

"I'm proud, too. I don't mind telling you you're good for my ego."

"And you're good for mine."

A small sharp ache lodged in her heart then. He wasn't going to be in her life forever. Yes, they were friends now, but neither of them wanted ties, nor commitments, so it made no sense to be too close too long. And she wondered if what he'd helped her gain in the way of self-confidence would last after he was gone. At midnight, like Cinderella, would her magnificent stagecoach turn into a lowly pumpkin again?

Chapter 11

Tuesday morning Melodye had come awake on top of her world. At first she'd had the inclination to just lie there and dream, but she groaned because she'd had to get up. A quick run on her treadmill, then her stationary bike. The week before, her doctor had given her a glowing bill of health.

"This is where it's at," the doctor had said. "It's a matter of how healthy you are. The minute I see signs of deterioration, then and only then will I put you on a diet. You're a lovely Juno and I don't want to see you lose it."

The twins were still sleeping when she went under her newly installed triple-headed shower. Ooh, that really felt good. In her bedroom she slipped into a blue jogging suit. Since she'd known Jim, she had worn lovely, lacy underwear.

There! Just in time because she heard her front door slam and knew it would be Papa France, who'd called to say he'd stop by.

In the living room she hugged him and he patted her back. "I'd have come by yesterday, but a couple of my fellow deacons wanted to go fishing before daylight. Baby, we caught a mess of catfish. One of the guys cleaned them and he'll bring them by today. You get a lot of them. I know how you love catfish."

Melodye always prepared coffee the night before to drip automatically the next morning. She wasn't ready for hers, but Papa France poured himself a cup.

He cleared his throat. "Miss Belle thinks I might've been a trifle pushy in inviting you to church without telling you what it was all about. You testy with me?"

His eyes pleaded for understanding and she shook her head. "No, but you and Miss Belle have both got to understand that Jim and I have our own lives to live. Papa France, the world is moving away from marriage. You have to know that."

He sighed. "Guess I haven't wanted to notice. You were happy with Rafael at first, but he was never the man for you. Don't let one rotten apple spoil your whole life. Jim's a good man and you're a good woman. You need a husband and the twins could use a dad."

"We're friends," she said, and didn't add that even that would end. "I think we'll always be fond of each other, but that's all." She went to where he sat at the table finishing his coffee, sat on his lap and hugged him.

"I'll be fine," she said, "and he'll be fine. I don't trust any man but you any longer, and Jim thinks he was a lousy husband and would make a lousy father."

"You believe that?"

"I don't know. He knows himself better than I do." She glanced at her watch. "I've got to get the twins and myself ready. Miss Belle will be by any minute. Will you let her in?"

"Sure will."

* * *

The twins were in a good mood so she was able to get them into their clothes and ready to go in record time.

Downstairs Papa France and Miss Belle talked over cups of coffee. He looked at her thinking she had held her own. Why hadn't some man grabbed her? Now he said, "Would you like to go to the movies?"

Miss Belle smiled. "I'd love to go."

Melodye was early at the boutique. Odessa hadn't come in. A customer waited, one of the models for the fashion show. She hugged Melodye and did a little dance.

"So much excitement so early. Explain yourself." The woman's joy was infectious and Melodye already had her own store of excitement.

"It's my husband," the woman said. "He's been courting me ever since I began wearing the underwear you designed, not to mention the clothes. We've been married seven years and we're on a honeymoon. I think your scrumptious clothes get a lot of the credit."

"And you're here for more."

"I sure am. This time I'm going to do what I see you doing, try some lighter colors. He's loving me and I'm loving it."

Melodye turned on the coffee urn and set out refreshments for the day. The customer wanted only a 7-Up and Melodye fixed it for her. *A-1 Plus Love* clientele deserved china, crystal and silverware, Melodye felt.

Odessa came in with a tall, handsome man she introduced as Ashton Williams.

"I remember you, Ashton," Melodye said. "You're a Crystal Lake detective and you were one of the models at the fashion show."

He grinned. "Yep. And you were knocking 'em dead in that gorgeous yellow gown. D'you mind seeing a lot of me? I'll try not to get in the way. Odessa and I seem to have found each other." He was all smiles, handsome, spice brown with a cleft chin.

"I'd love seeing a lot of you."

Melodye was in her studio and behind her desk when Jim spoke from the doorway.

"Morning, angel." His voice sounded sexy.

Her mouth opened a little and she didn't look up for a moment because she needed to get herself together.

Finally she said, "Good morning, yourself. How *are* you?"

"Now that I've seen you…" he began, and chided himself. No, that's what men said to a woman they're crazy about, not to a friend. But he knew very well that she had quickly become much more than a friend, a fact he wasn't wild about.

She brushed the remark aside. "What brings you by?"

"I wanted to come by yesterday, but I was overloaded." Then he said without further preliminary. "Lucia came to see me."

"And you had lunch?"

"No, there wasn't time. We talked in my office."

She wanted to ask him what they talked about, but she didn't. That was his business.

He went into a customary silence and she didn't interrupt that silence. He blew a stream of air and moved closer to her desk. "You know you could be wrong about Lucia. She might be fonder of you than it seems."

"Ah, yes," she said heatedly, "and pigs might fly one day. Spare me Lucia, Jim. I can't take her."

"Well, she didn't say one unkind word about you and she paid you a couple of compliments."

"Earth to Jim. You know how she performed at the restaurant Sunday."

"Yeah, but you have to give people a chance."

She sounded a little bitter then. "She's hired you as her new publicity man. Congratulations! You're doing a fine job."

He shook his head, laughing. "You're something when your temper rises. I'd love to see you in a real snit."

Hot tears came to her eyes. It was a joke to him, the tension and the hostility between Lucia and her. Damn them both! Didn't he have sense enough to realize that Lucia knew how to play the game with men, always had known. Maybe it was a gift.

But Jim wasn't the dunderhead she'd thought him. He came around the desk to stand in back of her and placed a hand on the side of each shoulder. "Sorry, honey. I know how you feel. I didn't take Lucia to lunch because I knew you wouldn't like it. We're friends, Melodye, at least until we can't take it anymore and run scared. I could've gotten out of it somehow, but I didn't and I just told you why. Okay?"

"Yes. Thank you."

"You're welcome. Is Manny in?"

"I'm sure he is. He'll stick his head in the door any minute."

"I need to talk with him. He'll make a good candidate for the force, I think."

"He's going to be overjoyed."

His voice went lower. "Hey, come sit down across from me."

"Why?"

"Because I like looking at the drumsticks you call legs."

Melodye couldn't help laughing as she slowly got up and walked around the desk.

"Damn and damn again!" he said mildly. "You've got *pants* on. I think I'll outlaw them for you."

"Oh, no, you don't," she scoffed. "We're independent people, both of us, and we like it that way."

They sat down in tub chairs opposite one another and he sighed. "Well, at least I see beautiful ankles and long, perfect feet. I'm looking forward to our dinner Saturday night."

She drew a deep breath. "So am I." She had the urge to tease him then and she asked, "Am I safe alone with you?"

She looked at him from under incredibly long black lashes and his shaft gave a powerful lunge as heat rose between them.

He breathed hard then, wanting to throw her onto the desk and take her and take her some more. His voice was husky, low. "D'you *want* to be safe from me?"

Her body grew still and heavy with desire, her voice was little more than a whisper when she told him, "Not really."

Manny knocked and came in then, looked from one to the other barely suppressing a grin. "Morning, Melodye, Jim. I got the material you sent and I really thank you."

Jim stood up. "I want to talk with you." He turned to Melodye. "Can you spare him? This'll take a half hour or so."

"Take all the time you need. The beginning of the week is slow."

Jim turned around and looked at her again when he reached the door. He winked, slowly, provocatively. It was hot. It was conspiratorial. He wasn't making it easy for her, she thought with heat radiating.

In a small room, Jim and Manny sat at a small table. "I keep the material you sent me both here and at home. Man, no way can I tell you how much I thank you."

"Glad to help. I think you can be very useful to us. You're bright. Willing. Eager. We need your kind."

"How soon can I get started?"

Jim breathed easily. "I'd like to orient you first. Tell you what to expect and you tell me what you expect. Have a physical before we give you one. That way you can correct little things that come up. Watch all the cop shows you can. No, they're not always right, but they give you a feel for police work."

"Hey, man, it sounds great and I can't wait to get started."

Jim nodded. "I'm going to want to talk with you a lot. We do background checks and I'm going to want to know about your background. Things like how long you worked at *Steeped In Joy* and how you got along with Rafael and Turk."

Manny shrugged. "I liked it sometimes. Sometimes it was the pits."

"Yeah, well, we haven't got time to go into it now, but could you arrange to be free to talk with me often this week?"

"Sure. Anytime. Anyplace. You just tell me when."

Chapter 12

"This gumbo is the best I've ever eaten and I'm a gumbo connoisseur."

Jim smiled across the rose candlelit table. "You inspire me and that's a fact."

Melodye drew a deep breath. "The whole setting is wonderful and I'm glad I inspire you. You certainly inspire me."

"Miss Belle helped plan the whole thing, even to suggesting you wear that shade of blue. It looks really good on you."

"Thank you." She savored the shrimp-and-crab gumbo over brown rice as the flavor buds burst on her tongue. The soft, hot French bread slices were spread with garlic butter. She loved good food and wasn't far from a gourmet cook herself.

"Speaking of mothers," she said. "We're invited to Bettina's for a party she's throwing for Hunter Davis, the celebrity photographer."

"Yeah, I know. I got an invitation both formally and via Lucia."

"I see. Bettina said she supposed I'd want to bring you. I said 'damned right.' You know, she's helping Lucia rope you in."

He laughed. "Honey, I'm not a steer. I'm interested in Lucia's sister—you. Do you have trouble with that?"

Jim's eyes met hers and she looked down. His glances at her always caused heat to flood her body. He was so intense.

Her heart swelled and danced with joy. She dreamed of this night since he'd asked her.

He thought about rich, warm chocolate every time he looked at her and that chocolate melted on his tongue. His loins were on fire and it was just eight o'clock. The night stretched before them, he thought, like a blessing.

He brushed her leg with his on purpose and felt a thrill shoot through him as she smiled. "I think I'll ask you to do my vegetables every day," he said. "This salad and dressing are da bomb. What's in the dressing?"

She told him and he nodded, memorizing the recipe.

The table was set with crystal, silver and china. When she admired the peony and maidenhair fern centerpiece, he smiled. "I have mom to thank for that. She masterminded this whole show."

"She did a superb job."

They lingered over dinner, and he poured thick Turkish coffee, adding light cream. He suggested that they have dessert in the living room, and she helped him carry trays that held crystal dishes of ice cream made with real vanilla beans, with thick chocolate-raspberry syrup over it and slices of orange-rum pound cake. They sat on his big curved sofa, and he asked about her preference in music.

"I think I'd like classical. Do you have Beethoven?"

"Most of the symphonies. I've got William Grant Still, too, the noted African-American composer."

"I'd like to hear those sometime, but Beethoven's *Sixth* keeps running through my mind. Pastoral and gorgeous. I shiver every time I hear it."

He laughed. "That'll give me a chance to hold and warm you."

Her breath came quickly then as she envisioned him covering her. "If I get any warmer, I'm going up in flames."

He laughed at that. "We're both going into one big ball of fire."

Savoring the dessert, as she had the rest of the meal, she closed her eyes. "Now, I don't have to ask about the cake. I have this recipe from your mom."

"Yeah. Most of my recipes come from her."

"She's got some great ones. I want you to have dinner with us one weekend when the twins can enjoy it, too."

"Anytime."

Strange, she sat thinking, how he hadn't had one meal at her house. Refreshments, drinks, yes, but they'd both been so busy working on the case.

She apologized for that now. "The twins know you better than I do. Your mom tells me you're often there in the late afternoon and you play with them, bring them presents...."

His eyes on her were lazy and focused as he grinned. "You and I know each other in the biblical sense and thank God for that."

"I have to agree with you." But some part of her didn't altogether agree.

He took the trays back to the kitchen and came back. "Do you mind if I'm in a talkative mood tonight?"

She looked up at him standing. "I'd welcome it. You're not often in a talkative mood."

He lowered himself to sit close to her as the wondrous strains of the Beethoven's *Pastoral Symphony* washed over them. He pondered how to talk about what he needed to talk about. They were getting closer and he was beginning to run scared. He could feel his gut tightening. No way was he ever going to hurt her, but maybe it was best if they cut free before he got the chance. If he could tell her where he was coming from, let her know something of his heart…

He began. "I've told you before that Elyssa and I often quarreled and it always seemed to be about my work and my silence." He cleared his throat. "I love being a cop, Melodye, and I find it hard to share what's on my mind and in my heart. When I was young, I was hell-bent on being a race car driver and my dad was hell-bent aginst it. He used to take me with him to the station house when I was a little kid. But he didn't talk to me or listen when I tried to talk to him. When I got older, I stopped going with him and it hurt him. I *wanted* to hurt him the way his aloofness was hurting me.

"Then after he died, I found myself more and more attracted to police work, especially to being a detective. He always admired detectives and I guess that was my way of linking to him. He was a lieutenant. I've never made it past lieutenant, although I could have. That ought to tell you something."

He was silent for a long time and his eyes were full of pain, his wide shoulders slightly hunched. She wanted to comfort him, but she wanted him to go on.

"I loved my dad, Melodye. I love Mom, too, but I guess I took her for granted. She was always there for me. It seemed to me Dad seldom was. He seemed to hate racing as much as I loved it. Mom was afraid for me, but she backed me. If it hadn't been for Papa France, I don't know what I would've done. I wasn't close to any other man. He always encouraged me to be what I wanted to be."

He laughed shortly then, a bark of hurt. "Hell, I've come to understand Dad a lot better since I've grown up. *I* have trouble being close to people. Something keeps me from getting up close and personal. Am I so afraid of being hurt? You tell me. When I found Elyssa, I thought I had it made, but she wanted what I couldn't deliver. 'Talk to me' she used to say. 'Tell me what's in your heart.'

"But I was afraid that, like him, if she knew what was in my heart, she'd leave. Dad's first wife, his childhood sweetheart, left him. My dad was shot apprehending one of the worst criminals on the streets. He took five bullet, but managed to kill the thug. Got his man. Lost his life. He was one of my heroes. Papa France is the other one."

He paused and sighed deeply before he continued. "So much hurt, so much anger. My work was my life instead of Elyssa. I never gave her what I should have and on the day she died we were quarreling over my hours. We'd been invited out on Long Island and she wanted me to go with her. I said I couldn't. She was really furious. 'Other detectives keep decent hours. Why can't you?' she asked me. Then she summed up my life. 'You're in love with danger, Jim. You always pick the roughest cases, go after the worst criminals. You want to die a *hero*.'"

Jim stopped talking then and tears stood in his eyes as his big body slumped. "Then she told me something I'll never forget after she said I wanted to die a hero. She said, 'Or maybe you just want to die. I can't get close to you. You seem to me to want something you don't have, that you're never going to have. You're running scared. What in hell are you so afraid of?'"

He sighed again. "I wish I knew. I only know Elyssa went to Long Island, and that afternoon the host called me, told me she'd drowned. She was so hurt and angry when she left. She said maybe we were all wrong for each other, that she didn't want the baby she was carrying to grow up like me." He seemed strangled then. "She said maybe we should talk about divorce while she still had time to learn how to be alone before the baby came...."

He was crying then and his big body heaved in terrible sobs that shook him to his core.

Melodye moved over to him and took him in her arms, pulled his head onto her aching breasts and simply held him as the dam broke and he sobbed brokenly, wetting her dress with his tears.

Pillowed on her breasts, he felt her steady soothing heart-beats and Jim knew he wept for all the times he'd tried to reach his dad and failed. He wept for his failed marriage that failed because he couldn't be a giving husband to a woman he loved, a woman who carried the precious child he wanted so badly.

"You did the best you could," she told him gently. "That *has* to be enough."

Melodye stroked his back as tears of sympathy stood in her eyes. She thought she understood him then and felt so close to him as she stroked him gently. The CD changer cut off and the room was silent. Some night bird sang outside and a high wind whipped tall shrubbery against the front window. They sat there for a very long time until she kissed his face and he stirred and sat up.

"I want to sleep with you," he said softly. "Just sleep, not make love at first. I felt so good in Atlantic City and I want to feel that way again."

"Okay." She kissed his face again and her fingers moved lightly over his lips as he shuddered with pleasure.

He put his face close to hers, but didn't kiss her. Her vanilla perfume soothed him and her soft, gentle voice filled him with flaming desire.

In the bedroom, he turned back the covers of the king-size bed and they lay down. Soon, they were fast asleep. In his dreams he was deep inside her and he groaned in his sleep.

She dreamed of carrying his child and being happy with him, then she was crying as Elyssa had cried, that she couldn't reach him, that he wasn't there for her and her child.

She came awake more than an hour later with him bending over her, tracing her jawline with his finger. The rose light in the room shadowed her face and reflected a maternal beauty that radiated from within.

Looking at her, he smiled, closer to her and to himself than he could ever remember being to anyone. He raised himself to one elbow. "You were sleeping so peacefully I hated to wake you, but I've got big plans. I want to repay you for what you've given me the best way I know how."

He placed her hand on his swollen pant-clad penis, and she stroked it, causing it to twitch wildly. "You're so beautiful. You don't know how much I wish things could be different, that *I* could be different."

She pulled him down to her. "Your life isn't over yet. Change is what life is all about. If *I* could trust again. If *you* could believe in yourself. Life is about life, Jim, not death."

"Yeah," he said softly. "Elyssa was a social worker with a minor in psychology. She knew a lot about psychology. At John Jay I had a few courses in it. I guess I'm what's called schizoid. Unable to be really close to anyone, even myself.

It's thought to be caused by fear of being hurt. I've been there, done that, in spades."

"I'm sorry," was all she could say. She wanted so badly to help him, but what could she give him when she no longer trusted herself to know what was best for her, what was safe for her?

He smiled then. "You like my surprises. I have another one. Come on and I'll show you."

They went to his blue and stainless steel kitchen where an ice bucket in a small pantry held a bottle of champagne. "Bringing back Atlantic City," he told her, "and going beyond." Then he showed her a jeroboam of champagne behind the door.

She laughed. "Are you trying to get me really drunk?"

He grinned. "Nothing so simple as that. I'm going to blow your mind. I'm gonna make this a night neither of us will ever forget."

She knew very well she wouldn't be forgetting this or any other night with him. Her heart pounded as he pressed her back against the pantry door and his hard, muscular body bored into her soft flesh.

"Baby," he whispered. "Tonight, you're gonna get it all. Everything I've got to give."

He forced himself away from her long enough to pop the champagne cork and poured them flutes of champagne. Dom Perignon, as in Atlantic City, her favorite brand. She sipped it slowly. The coldness caused her to shiver and the bubbles made her nose tingle. He kissed her again, his tongue vividly exploring her mouth. Champagne kisses. Heady. Incredible. He licked around her lips, put his tongue in the corners of her mouth and it thrilled her, made her core burn with a rage to take him into her body.

The kitchen lights were bright and unromantic, but he unzipped her dress and slid it from her shoulders, letting it pool around her ankles before she picked it up and flung it onto the kitchen table. Before she could straighten up he was pressed to her buttocks, his rigid penis hard against her, his big hands pulling her back onto him. She stood for a minute as he bent and kissed her back and her buttocks, running his tongue over them. He got a condom from his pocket and she helped him smooth it on before he grabbed and kissed her again.

She leaned back in his arms. "Drive me crazy, will you? Well, I can play that game." She turned and flung her arms around his neck grinding herself into his body in voluptuous, wanton grinds until he thought he'd lose it. He sprang stone hard.

They drained that round of champagne and he poured more, but this time he poured a little into his palms and spread it over her heavy breasts. Then he bent and suckled them softly at first, then harder as she cried out his name, holding him against her.

Somehow they managed to finish undressing, clothes flung everywhere, and stood in the kitchen in each other's arms. He clutched her buttocks and lifted her, carried her to the table straddled around his waist.

On the table she moved in rhythm with him as he suckled her breasts and groaned in the back of his throat. He thought if he lived to be a hundred, he'd remember these incredible feelings of flying when he was inside her. She fit him like a snug glove, and she scorched him as he expertly played her. He placed a hand on either side of her face and kissed her with nearly savage ardor.

She spread her fingers over his at first, then moved them down his back and to his hard buttocks where she pulled him until he was completely inside her. In ecstasy, she threw her legs around his back and pressed her soft feet against his spine, moving her toes slowly up and down the ridge.

It fascinated him that the liquid of her inner walls was like heavy peach syrup that soothed his every nerve. *He wanted her* with an ache in his groin. He didn't want to want her the way he did and he knew there had to be a stopping point, but he couldn't focus on that now.

The explosion in his body rocked them both as his loins quaked and poured his seed, causing him to hold her so tightly she could hardly breathe.

She was right behind him, shaking like a rag doll until she was limp.

They were silent then as he held her. "We need to rest," he finally said, "but I don't want to let you go." And it was minutes later before he did.

Later they lounged on the bed and he held her close to him. "Passion flower," he said huskily, breathing in her perfume. Slowly and lazily he began to lick and kiss her from her scalp, down her throat, breasts, stopping to suckle the nipples, then moving on to her tender belly and to her core.

By the time he reached her feet, she was on fire again, moaning softly and threading her fingers through his hair. She writhed in ecstasy and lured him on. "Jumping your bones," he told her, "is the best exercise I ever had."

"Best I've ever had, too," she murmured. Had she actually spent time feeling she was no good sexually or sensually? A failure as a woman? Jim certainly seemed to think she was wonderful in bed, and a worthwhile woman. He fed her ego, lifted her spirits to high heaven. When he turned her over, her every muscle seemed relaxed, yet intent on calling him in to her. He began the kisses again on her scalp, then down her back to her buttocks where he kneaded and squeezed gently, then stroked. When he reached her feet, she thought he'd come back up and inside her again.

But he sat up on the side of the bed and spread a hand over her hip. "You wanted to know what I'm—what *we're*—going to do with that jeroboam of champagne."

"Yes."

"Hey, come with me. I can show you better than I can tell you."

In his big bathroom with the salmon-colored sunken tub and the pearl-gray plush rug, he asked her to get in and sit down in the tub. Excited, she knew what he was going to do and she laughed as he popped the cork and poured champagne over her body from the shoulders down. The cool liquid felt so good and the smell was heady as it ran over her body. She saw then that there was a bottle of champagne in the ice bucket. He popped that cork and poured them flutes of champagne and she felt drunk with pleasure, even before she drank the champagne.

"Like that?" he asked.

"Love it. Now it's your turn."

"What do you plan to do?"

She stood up and stepped out of the tub. "Hush and get in the tub. Mama's got plans for Papa and she doesn't like to be kept waiting."

"Yes, ma'am." He got in the tub, sat down, and she gleefully lifted the heavy bottle and dumped the rest of the champagne over the top of his head.

"Hey!" he sputtered. "You don't play fair!" But it was plain he was loving every second of it. He licked the champagne from around his mouth as it ran down his face. "You know, you're gonna pay for this."

"Hmm," she murmured. "I'm ready for any torture you want to put me through."

Dripping champagne, he got up and stepped from the tub, caught her to him fiercely. "What if I bring you on at least five times?" His eyes on her were wickedly lustful and he felt that tonight he could deliver what he threatened.

She grinned naughtily. "Make it six and you're on."

Their wet bodies locked together, and Jim thought that on her champagne had never tasted so good. He got a condom from the cabinet and rolled it on. Kneeling behind her, he went in slowly, bit by bit as he stroked her buttocks and licked the liquid from her back. "Never knew my tongue to be so useful," he said huskily.

How could anything be this good? she wondered as he throbbed mightily inside her. She felt half crazy with lust and glory. Her breath came in gasps and she was falling, falling into an abyss of glorious colors and feelings. *Danger went with this territory.* She didn't think of her fear of being too close to him because she couldn't think of anything except his body, his throbbing penis and what he did to her.

His big shaft was hell-bent on the maximum pleasure he was getting and giving her in spades. He worked near her womb and it thrilled him that he was caught and held. Listening to her soft moans he was overcome with ecstatic feelings that blotted out everything except the woman moving under him in a rage to fulfill them both.

They came together and to both it seemed too short a time as their blood surged. And each had moments of glory when sweetness seemed to be in their very veins and life seemed everything it ought to be.

He carried her into the bedroom then. "I don't know how I've got the strength to do this," he told her. "God knows, I'm knocked out, but I just want to stay with you, inside you. Do you mind?"

She laughed throatily and answered, "What do you think?" as he laid her on the bed.

Lying there, she said, "We had no music to make love by."

He lay beside her breathing deeply. "Baby, tonight, we *are* the music. I never missed it."

The winds were high outside, whistling along the eaves and it sent wildness whistling into their bloodstream. Lying there, he thought, *I'm as hungry for her now as I was the first time.* And fear seeped into him then. He didn't *like* wanting and needing anybody too much. Hurt came when you needed people. He knew *how* he could come to need Melodye and it scared hell out of him. But he would run later because he wasn't about to run now.

Light rain began to strike the windowpanes. "Perfect weather for making love," she murmured.

"Any weather's perfect for making love with you."

"You say all the right things, do all the right things…"

His voice was suddenly harsh. "No, baby, not always. Sometimes I couldn't be more wrong."

She listened carefully, said nothing. After a very long time of silence, he began to stroke her again. He had talked more tonight than he could remember talking in his life. She was so easy to talk to. He liked action better though, and he began to stroke her again, taking and placing her hand on his penis where she stroked him, squeezed him until he was jumping and throbbing.

He pulled her on top of him and she straddled him lightly for a while until she began to ride him aggressively. He loved that and lay back letting her do her thing.

Melodye moved back and down and he was halfway out

as she licked his flat nipples in circles, teasing him. She suckled his nipples and was rewarded by his swelling inside her until she couldn't believe it, and reaching down, encircled his penis with her fingers. "Know what? I think you like what I'm doing. You're even bigger."

He laughed. "Now, I wonder what makes you say that. If I'm bigger, use it and stop talking. It won't last forever."

For one brief minute she thought that he didn't need to be big. He could be any size and with his expertise he'd thrill her. She began to ride him hard, writhing and grinding as she had done earlier and he gave a hoarse yell of intense pleasure. She was easier then, her breasts over his face as he raised up to suckle them. The wings of her hair brushed him and she was all over him like a goddess certain of her power over him. He was glad he had been the one who made her realize that power.

This time she came first with all the passion she had ever had in her heart for this man. She was caught up as he was caught up shortly after and together they knew moments in time that they both wanted to last forever.

When they woke the next morning, it was gray, overcast and late. Melodye woke first. The digital clock on the night table registered nine o'clock.

"I've got to get going," she said in mild panic.

Jim rolled over lazily. "Why? Odessa's got your back at *A-1 Plus Love*. Mom's got the twins, so if you spend the day, you're covered."

He could be so precious. "Odessa's a courting woman now and can't always cover for me. The twins will want me there. Oh, yes, I'm sure Miss Belle will be tickled pink. She'll look at my face and know what went down. No, I've got to get going."

"What d'you want for breakfast?"

"I don't think I have time."

He grinned as he kissed her nose. "Hey, you've got time. I put a bee in Odessa's bonnet and she's cool. You know the score about Mom. She'd keep the twins for a week and be happy when we're together. How do pancakes hit you? I make sourdough pancakes with yeast and I've got blueberry syrup." He kissed her throat, ran his tongue over her collarbone. "That is, I've got all that after you make me know you're grateful."

The way he was looking at her made her dizzy. "Let me go to the bathroom and I'll give you my answer."

She used the bathroom they had been in the night before. Looking at herself in the mirror, blushing with memory of the champagne, she felt as beautiful as Jim said she was.

They met again in the middle of the bedroom where he took her naked body in his arms. "It doesn't take moonlight to turn me on," he told her. "I want to be inside you with brilliant sunshine heating us outside the way we burn inside. Do you know what you do to me, angel?"

She sighed. "I know what you do to me."

They weren't long this time and afterward they slept again for over an hour.

The breakfast he made was almost as good as the dinner had been. Sitting across from him, she felt contentment she'd never known before.

He knew he hated to take her home and felt fear gnawing at his gut as he wondered where they were headed and what was going to be the price of getting there.

Chapter 13

"Boy, am I absentminded."

Jim slapped the side of his hand to his forehead as he and Melodye pulled in and parked at the underground lot of Bettina's luxury condo on the D.C. waterfront.

"So what else is new?" Melodye twitted him. "You were preoccupied the last few times I've seen you."

He sighed. "Yeah, this case is keeping my feet to the fire. New leads are suddenly coming in fast. I can't discuss it, but it's mostly good."

He reached across her and unlocked the glove compartment, took out a white bag containing a small, flat package done in shades of rose organza.

"This is one fancy package," she told him.

"Open it."

She did as he asked, hating to disturb the beautiful wrapping. There was a rose velvet case, and snapping it open, she gasped to find a gorgeous small crystal ball about an inch in diameter filled with suspended red rose petals. The chain was gold herringbone and gleamed in the light.

"Oh, Jim, it's beautiful and it's a Lalique."

He grinned. "Like it?"

She threw her arms around his neck. "I love it. Lalique's one of my favorite designers. Both Bettina and Lucia are wild about those designs."

He held her close to him, his tongue lightly outlining her lips. "I don't want to take all your lipstick off, although I'd love that."

"Umm, go ahead. There's more where that came from."

He kissed her then, long and hard and her arms stole around his neck, drew him harder against her.

"We'd better go in before we get arrested for making out in a public place," he said huskily.

"Where did you get the pendant?"

"At a jewelry shop in Georgetown a friend owns. I saw it in his window and it just seemed to be you."

She pulled away and turned her back to him. "Please unfasten the one I'm wearing and I'll wear this one. My earrings are gold and match anything."

He did as she requested and she turned to face him. His loins got heavy and throbbed as he looked at her with his pendant suspended over the valley between her breasts. Tweaking a nipple under the fabric of her silk gown, he told her, "Did I even remember to tell you how great you look? Absolutely edible."

He kissed her again, and she murmured against his mouth, "You look pretty edible yourself, Mister Man."

He laughed and placed her hand on his trousered swollen shaft. Speaking to that unruly organ, he cautioned, "Brother, this is neither the time nor the place."

She laughed, then grew sober. "Jim, I love what you've

done for me. I never thought I'd feel the self-confidence I'm feeling these days. I know it can't last, but it's been so great while it does."

"It's not over yet," he said gruffly. "I'd like for us to stay friends, and I don't see our lovemaking being over for a while. It's just that we decided if either of us gets in too deep, we'll cut—"

"And run," she finished for him. "I think we've been really good for each other. You're more open, more forthcoming and God knows, I feel so much better about myself."

He took her face in his hands and kissed the sides of her mouth. "Put more lipstick on," he told her. "I've wrecked what you had on."

She shook her head. "Uh-uh. I want everyone to guess you've kissed it all off. I guess we'd better go in."

"Yeah, before I turn the car around, take you home and ravish you, or better yet, take you to my house."

She laughed. "Please don't talk about your house. My body catches fire when I think about it."

His forefinger traced her jawline. "And I've got a whole lot of other things that catch fire when I think about it."

Bettina greeted them at the door. Melodye always felt a twinge of envy when she stepped into the sunken living room with the luxurious handmade furnishings and the deep piled white rugs of her mother's three-bedroom condo.

"Darlings," Bettina said, "you're a bit early and I'm grateful. I don't like stragglers. The guest of honor and his wife are due any minute and my angel Lucia is getting even more beautiful." She rolled her eyes. "She's well aware that Hunter Davis is a beefcake *and* famous and she means to flirt. I hope his wife understands."

"Lucia could always not do it," Melodye pointed out. "One day she'll run into a jealous wife and there'll be hell to pay."

Bettina shrugged. "Lucia can take care of herself. Besides, I think she's growing fonder of Jim. What's with you two, anyway?"

Melodye smiled sweetly. "Mom, I'm sure you have lots of business you could mind."

Bettina looked from one to the other with narrowed eyes. "I ask for a reason, my dear. Lucia likes Jim more than I can say and my daughter takes no prisoners." She looked Jim over. "I must say I like her choice. You're more her type than Melodye's. And to think, once I didn't like you."

Jim looked at Bettina, amused and noncommittal, thinking that he had always picked his own women.

Melodye was grateful that Bettina said nothing about the color of her dress, but suddenly Bettina exclaimed, "I'm getting senile early. I didn't notice. That's a fabulous Lalique, Melodye. When and from where did you get it?"

"Jim," Melodye said proudly. "Isn't it beautiful?"

Lucia came up behind Jim and placed her slender fingers over his eyes. "Guess who, and if you're right, you get a kiss," she said in a stage whisper.

Jim gently removed her hands from his face, smiling. "It's Lucia and I'll pass on the kiss for now."

Lucia pouted. "Well, anyway, you add 'for now,' and that gives me hope. Um, you *do* look good, Jim."

A good cross-section of D.C. luminaries were at this party. The mayor, many on the city council, business owners, a couple of fashion editors from New York. Some of Melodye's customers were here and they greeted her warmly. The waitstaff wore scarlet jackets, ruffled white shirts and black pants.

Melodye murmured to Jim. "Trust Bettina to give the extra touch."

"The old girl throws a fabulous party," Jim said in agreement.

The buffet was loaded early with every type of food. Sushi, hors d'oeuvres, stuffed shrimp, artistically carved vegetables and down-home foods like macaroni and cheese. A smaller table held a mouth-watering array of desserts. Polished fruit was there for those who wanted lighter fare.

Melodye served her plate and Jim's with a sampling of many foods. More stuffed shrimp and devilled eggs for Jim because he was so fond of both. Huge black olives for both of them. Lots of salad greens.

They sat on a white curved sofa, savoring the food. "I shudder to think what her cleanup bill is going to be for this," Melodye said.

"Umm," was Jim's only comment.

They both saw Lucia coming before she stood in front of them. "I get first dibs on your first dance," she told Jim, all but ignoring Melodye.

Melodye looked up, her mouth pursed. "I thought that's what the man tells the woman."

Lucia shook her head saucily. "New day, my sister. My day," Lucia said.

Jim put his free arm around Melodye's shoulders. "Melodye makes my day every day," Jim said.

Melodye basked in his compliment and had the satisfaction of seeing Lucia's face cloud.

But Lucia's negative expression was fleeting and she quickly said, "Jim, I *do* need to talk with you about what we talked about last week. I have lots of ideas that you can either accept or not."

Jim looked uncomfortable and cleared his throat. "Sure thing," he said.

Lucia seemed stuck to them like glue. "Maybe we'll get a chance to go over some of it tonight. This party goes on forever."

"Tonight's not the best time," Jim said. "I haven't had as much time as I'd like to mull it over."

"Okay then, whenever." Lucia unglued herself from them and flounced away, throwing them—or *him*—a flirtatious kiss as she left.

Melodye felt apprehension creep into her body. Should she ask him what he and Lucia had talked about? She wasn't sure. But he turned to her. "We've been talking over—some things, Lucia and I…"

"Secret?" she asked archly. Years of competing with Lucia and losing had taken its toll.

"Not really. One day soon I'll tell you about it."

One day. When she takes you over? Melodye thought glumly. *And she is interested, Jim, make no mistake about it. Bettina will give her all the help she can.* Because *he* seemed to be becoming more interested in Lucia. How *much* more interested? she wondered.

"Earth to Melodye," Jim finally said.

She ate the last of a black olive. "I'm here."

He said nothing further about Lucia, but took her tray and stacked it with his. "I'll be back in a minute, and I want to dance with you."

On the dance floor, Melodye was always struck by how well they danced together. Her deep curves seemed to meld intimately with his sinewy frame, her lushness against his rock-hard strength. Jim's face was close to Melodye's and he kissed her cheek lightly as they swayed to the slow music.

"You're not leaving any doubt about what's going on with us?" she teased him.

"I don't believe in doubts. Be clear about it." He pressed her waistline.

Lucia danced by with a handsome partner and gave Jim a provocative long wink.

"You're under siege," Melodye said.

"Your sister's a tease. I don't think she can help it, but sometimes she means well."

Melodye's eyes narrowed. He had defended Lucia often lately. Her heart constricted a little. He was the one who'd said if either of them found him or herself in too deep it was best to cut and run. No, *she* had finished that sentence for him.

"I'm going to request a samba," he told her. "Give us a chance to shake our booties."

"I'm not very good at Latin dances, but Lucia's a master. She can swivel hips with the best."

"I'll teach you."

They passed the buffet and Melodye saw that slices of various melons had been put out. She wanted honeydew and they stopped for it. The melon was sugar-sweet and crisply cold. "Oh, this is wonderful. I don't think I've ever had a better one," she said.

"Yeah, it *is* good." His eyes caressed her gently as if he were dreaming. She forgot about Lucia as they finished the melon and resumed dancing, going over to the bandstand where Jim made his request.

With the change in music, Jim began to instruct her in the art of the samba. "If you give yourself over to it, the movements are easy. Never resist the music. Think about that music flowing in your bloodstream. It's a dance of pure passion, a blend of Africa and South America, and what a blend. Steady at the top and wicked at the bottom. Let the hips take over."

His voice mesmerized her as he talked and she found herself following him effortlessly. He was very good at this, she thought. He'd told her he'd traveled extensively in South America and had lived for a while in the Canary Islands.

"Did you learn to samba in the Canary Islands?" she asked him.

"Yeah," he said.

The samba rhythm really spoke to Melodye as she glided with Jim, her supple body learning the intricate movements with ease. A few of the dancers had stopped and were watching them as Jim strutted his stuff. "You're a natural for any kind of dancing, Melodye. I read somewhere that a woman who dances well makes the best lover."

She looked at him archly. "And do I measure up?"

"What do you think?"

She laughed. "Never answer a question with a question."

He borrowed a page from her book and asked, "Why?"

"Do I?" she asked quietly, trying to hide the anxiety she felt.

He squeezed her. "No one does it better," he said quietly.

At that moment, Lucia danced near them and winked again at Jim, spoke with her partner and broke free. Laughing merrily, Lucia tapped Melodye on the shoulder and asked, "May I cut in?"

Jim looked at Lucia and smiled. "I don't think so. I'm teaching Melodye to samba. She's proving to be a great pupil and I don't want to stop her progress."

Lucia's mouth opened a little as she ran her tongue over her bottom lip. "Then later," she said urgently. "You and I have things to talk about."

Jim saw the concern in Melodye's eyes and moved to reassure her. "You're gonna laugh when you find out what this is all about. Wiggle those beautiful hips for Papa. The samba was made for you to dance—with me."

He went into the rhythm of the dance and led her expertly as Lucia quickly found another partner. Then it was Lucia and her partner who took the floor as she flung herself into the samba with abandon, commanding everyone's attention.

Jim and Melodye stood on the sidelines, watching like the others as Lucia danced the truly sensuous samba with her partner. Head thrown back and slender, perfect hips gyrating, she was both jungle queen and highly sophisticated society beauty. She was Lucia and she had and always would have it all.

Bettina came over and introduced a New York fashion editor who told Melodye she'd be in town a couple of days and wanted to talk with her about a new line for the plus-size woman they wanted to do. They made an appointment.

"Mom, where'd the honeydew come from?" Melodye asked Bettina.

Bettina smiled. "Oh, you noticed, did you? It's a Chilean import. I buy them all the time." She gave her the name of the grocery store, then said to Jim, "When they were children, Melodye noticed the food. Lucia noticed the boys. And, oh, did they ever notice her. Doesn't she look ravishing tonight?"

"Yes, she does. You have *two* ravishing daughters."

"And you haven't danced with her once."

"I will, later."

"See that you do. Lucia's quite taken with you."

Melodye felt the start of anger then. She couldn't remember her mother ever campaigning for a man for Lucia quite so hard.

* * *

Just then another gentleman came up and claimed Melodye for a dance. She accepted the invitation and moved onto the dance floor.

Jim's eyes lingered on her as he turned and left.

From the dance floor Melodye watched as Jim went over and asked Lucia to dance. Lucia cozied up to him as if he were what she'd wanted all her life.

When the set ended, Melodye glanced at her watch. It was a little after midnight and she felt thirsty, she supposed from all the dancing she'd done. Excusing herself, she went toward the kitchen. There was ice water in silver Thermos pitchers, but she only drank tap water.

Passing the library, she heard merry voices and laughter through the partly open door. A wave of dizziness took her as she saw Lucia's arms go around Jim's neck and he placed his hand on her bare flesh. They kissed with Jim's back to Melodye. She couldn't be sure of anything as the room slowly spun, but she thought she saw Lucia look directly at her through the small opening. She didn't think she only imagined the hateful triumph in Lucia's eyes.

Water forgotten, Melodye leaned against the doorjamb of the other side of the door and fought to get her breath. *She had to get out of here.* Turning and moving swiftly on legs she wasn't sure would carry her, she snatched her evening coat from the hall closet, got her purse, then rode the elevator down to the lobby.

A young security guard was on duty as she began to pass through. "You're not going out there alone, are you?" he asked.

She said she was. She had to have air, lots of air, because she wasn't breathing very well.

He shook his head. "It's not safe, ma'am. We've had several robberies in this area in the last two weeks. Let me call you a taxi."

"No. It's okay," she assured him. I'll be all right. M Street is a short distance away and there're always taxis passing."

"Sorry, ma'am. I can't let you do that." He saw that she was in some kind of shock and it moved him. He went toward her, saw the panic flare in her eyes.

"I've got to get outside, I tell you."

"Look, I can radio my supervisor and walk you over to M Street, hail you a taxi. I can't let you go out there alone."

They stood outside where she gulped fresh, cool air and he called his supervisor, then they were on their way to M Street and a taxi. She thought then she'd *wanted* to walk that distance, had *welcomed* the danger. The chance of being robbed was nothing compared to seeing her life go down the drain again.

And she thought, it was past midnight, so it had taken a little longer, but the nightmare she had feared had come true. Her fantasy of a splendid coach to take her to the ball had happened, all right, complete with the handsome prince. Now that same coach had turned back into a pumpkin and if the prince came looking for her with her other glass slipper, she might kill him for the pain he'd caused her.

Chapter 14

When Melodye reached home, still dazed, she let herself in with trembling fingers. The babysitter rose from the sofa, a look of alarm on her face.

"Melodye, what's wrong?"

Melodye shook her head. "Just something I can't talk about."

"Let me fix you a cup of valerian tea or some coffee. You look like you're about to pass out."

Hot tears lodged just behind Melodye's eyelids and her heart felt like lead in her breast. "I'll be all right. Please don't worry and I don't need tea or coffee. I couldn't drink it. Did the twins behave?"

Continuing to look at her closely, the older woman said, "They were as good as gold. Being with them tonight was like being on holiday. They wanted two bedtime stories and I read them. They're precious children, Melodye, and I'm glad they've got a mother who appreciates them."

The babysitter smiled a little then. "Only thing is every time I read them a story, little Randy always talks about how *Jim* reads them stories. I think Mr. Ryman's got a fan."

Melodye clenched her teeth. Right now she didn't want to hear Jim Ryman's name.

"Now, my husband will pick me up as soon as I call him, but I can stay a while longer. You don't look like you need to be alone."

"No, please," Melodye managed to choke out, "you go on home. It's late and I'll be all right. Really, I will."

Turning aside reluctantly, the babysitter called her husband and very soon he picked her up.

Melodye realized then she hadn't taken off her evening wrap. Going into the twins' room, she left the door open and looked at them sleeping like dolls. They had been all over her when she and Jim were leaving. "You look pretty, Mommy," Rachel had said. "You look happy."

Randy had stood back, appraising her before he finally said, "Yeah, pretty."

She stooped and kissed each velvet face and a tear fell on Randy who stirred, turned and slept on, a chubby fist under his chin. She thought then that he would miss Jim even more than Rachel, because she knew then what she was going to do. Jim would want to know what happened to her, why she'd left the party. He'd call, she was certain, but she'd just plead a vicious headache and say she hadn't wanted to bother him. He never had to know she'd seen him and Lucia. Later they'd talk and she'd let him go.

Funny how the one thing that kept her from hating Rafael had been the fact that he had paid Lucia little attention. But then Lucia had never come on to him the way she was coming on to Jim. She thought then that even a saint would find it hard to resist Lucia and her wiles. She was beautiful, sexy, the right size—thin. *Thin was in.* She felt the cruel desire to laugh at herself hysterically.

She'd left this house tonight on top of the world. Full of Jim's lovemaking, his encouragement and his compliments, she had believed him completely. She thought bitterly then that she'd been a fool. He hadn't misled her on purpose; he simply hadn't known his own heart.

In her bedroom, she undressed slowly, removing the Lalique pendant last. How beautiful it was, but she wanted to fling it far away from her. Taking time to put the vanilla crepe dress and evening wrap on padded hangers, she stripped off her lacy bra and thong, threw them aside. Full of misery she turned on the light and studied herself in the triple mirror. Mirrors lied, she told herself. She'd never again look at herself in one through someone else's eyes.

She wasn't crazy about her deep curves now. Venus. Angel. Passion flower. All the tender names came to haunt her. Her heart felt shattered, but she wouldn't let herself cry. She'd always held herself together for her twins and this would be no different.

Slipping into a cream-colored long nylon tricot gown and robe, she stood again and looked in the mirror. What was she looking for? The fool who'd glowed with happiness thinking she could win after all, even against Lucia?

She froze when she heard her front door open. Only three others had keys: Jim, Odessa and Papa France. Going quickly into the living room, she knew who it was even before she saw him and they looked at each other across the room.

"Why'd you leave?" he asked her in a low, husky voice.

"I had a terrible headache. I didn't want to bother you."

He crossed the room to stand before her and sucked in a

deep breath. She looked hurt, but God, she looked beautiful, sexy as hell. A few flames crawled up his belly and flickered there. He wanted to hold her, but there was something he had to say.

"The only reason I can think of for you to leave like that is—you saw Lucia kiss me, didn't you?"

"What do you think?"

He nodded. "It wasn't what it seemed, Melodye. She flung her arms around me in a moment of excitement and kissed me. We were discussing something special. I don't think Lucia knows how to kiss a man except on the mouth. She almost knocked me off balance and I put my hand on her back to steady myself. That *had* to be what you saw. Oh, baby…"

He moved a little closer, his gaze tender and warm on her. She stepped back. "No, don't touch me!" Her voice was half strangled.

"Don't you believe me?"

Her chin went out defiantly. "It all adds up now. Your defending Lucia. Her flirting with you so much lately. Bettina's helping her, liking you where she never liked you before. *She* could see what was going on."

He shook his head. "There's nothing between Lucia and me. There're reasons why I *have* to talk with her, be friendly…"

Her breath was coming too fast and she was sick with hurt. "I don't want to hear what those reasons are because I don't believe you. My sister's a neat piece of meat and you fell like men always fall for her." God, she thought, why did he have to be more gorgeous than ever with deep concern in his eyes?

He moved forward again. "Melodye, please!" Close now, he gripped her shoulders, shook her lightly. "Snap out of it. We've always been able to talk…"

But the hurt went too deep and old hurts twisted the knife in the wound. For such a little while she had thought she mattered to this man. It was too much like what she'd known with Rafael. First, the rollicking good times and the good sex. Then Rafael had said she was no good to him. Well, she'd be damned if she'd stick around to hear Jim repeat those words and shatter her heart again.

"You're wrong," he said huskily, "and I know where you're coming from, but I'm not Rafael and I've meant and mean everything I've told you. You're a beautiful, desirable woman, Melodye, and I'll keep saying it until my last breath."

She wanted so badly to believe him then and against her will, she relented and his mouth came down on hers, bruising it for long moments. She began to respond, then pushed him away, fighting the fire in her own belly more than him. He pulled her hard against him, kissed her again. His tongue traced the outlines of her lips as she shuddered with desire like wildfire in her veins.

Holding her, he thought he had to make her know he wanted her, that he'd never found a more desirable woman than she was. Rock hard and throbbing, he found himself fighting to be inside her again, to try to assuage the bitter hurt he knew she was feeling. Again he traced the outlines of her lips with his tongue, knowing this had always turned her on sky-high. And she *was* coming around—

But she pushed him away violently. "No! I want you to leave!"

He reeled from the fury in her voice, but, feeling defeated, he steeled himself. "All right," he said quietly, "I'm not going to force myself on you. I'd never do that to you. I'll leave if you want me to, but, baby, we *need* to talk and I'm so sorry…"

She was coming apart. She saw the hurt on his face, heard it in his voice and her heart melted then with memory of what they'd known. Not quite of her own volition, she flung her arms around his neck and drew him to her, feeling the rippling muscles of his neck and back. She lost herself in the passion of his fire-hot kiss as he clutched her buttocks and held her against his swollen shaft.

He stood thinking with her lush body melting into his, that he had to reach her, comfort her, make her know he spoke truth, and always had.

They had known stunning passion before, but this was even deeper. She wouldn't, she *couldn't* think about what had happened tonight. She'd live in this moment, go with this feeling, blot out everything else.

She led him to her bedroom where he stripped her garments from her and hastily took off his clothes. She snapped on the rose nightlights as he lifted her and placed her on the bed. Pulling her legs apart, he bent and kissed her inner thighs. He tongued the tender flesh before his tongue flicked in circles up to her core and she thought she'd lose it. Her fingers gripped the short strands of his hair and she kneaded his scalp with her fingertips as he groaned aloud.

She was crying then, tears of joy and frustration. How had she ever thought she could do without him? "I want you inside me," she whispered.

"In a little while."

"No. Now. I want you now."

He got a condom from her night table and she smoothed it on as he looked at her precious, curvy body. She gave his shaft a long, gentle squeeze.

"Like that?" she whispered.

"Love that."

Laughing a little, he moved to give her what she wanted. Lifting her legs, he slipped into the syrupy, hot, tight path she made for him. Resting a minute, he felt her deliberately grip his penis and release it with the muscles of her inner walls and he shuddered. "You want to bring me on in a hurry, don't you?" She was so damned hot. So tight. So wet.

She laughed a little then. "We can always start all over."

His mouth found her full chocolate breasts and he suckled hungrily, then rested. He imagined snow and ice and it slowed him so he could lick her breasts with a tantalizing slowness that brought her to the brink of madness.

They were both wild with the pain of nearly having lost each other and finding their way back again. She moved under him in a perfect frenzy and his thrusts were deliciously hard. The night's champagne was in their bloodstream, the remembered samba. For moments she forgot how the party had ended for her. She had this and this was what mattered.

They were so good together, she thought. Reaching over, she snapped on the CD changer and the wondrous strains of Borodin's *Nocturne* poured over them. This was the melody that a pop tune had been taken from. She remembered too late that the song was "This Is My Beloved." Love didn't enter into this relationship. There was too much fear to let it through but that was all right, she thought. They had this.

He worked feverishly, expertly, his mind on what he did with her. He felt as if they'd been trapped on the edge of a precipice and kind hands had pulled them back. He wished he was different, that he could be close with his heart, as well as his body. But right now, his body was performing at its peak.

Neither could get enough of the other. They moved in delirium and the heat from each body radiated to the other until both were scorching.

He told her then, "Let's stand up. I want to do something to you."

She smiled and told him archly, "There're a few things I want to do to you, too."

They stood in front of the mirrors, reflected three ways, and exhilaration filled them as his big hands spread across her buttocks and pulled her in to him. He was rock hard, throbbing and jerking in her walls, and thrills were dancing through them both like spilled silver mercury that couldn't be caught or contained.

Bending, he kissed her full breasts, licked, then hungrily suckled them hard. It was like eating the best chocolate, only tastier. Standing seemed to him to add something special. He stroked her back and sides, then suddenly gripped her buttocks again, pulling her in to him, kneading her hard.

This time she wriggled frantically against him, working with the rhythm of his hands and both came together. Rockets hit his body with lightning speed and power, exploding fireworks that shook him to his core as he gasped for breath.

With Melodye, ancient seas surged in her body as tidal waves rocked her and finally swept her onto a familiar shore—languid, thrilling, completely spent.

Lying on the bed, physically exhausted, but emotionally exhilarated by what they'd just known, Melodye felt a wave of sadness wash over her. As Jim rolled over to embrace her, she murmured, "We have to talk."

"Yeah, I said we did. You want to do it now?"

"Jim, I'm not going to see you again."

He sat up, his breath coming faster, feeling like he'd been

sucker punched. "What d'you mean, you're not going to see me again? Melodye, I thought you understood."

She expelled a harsh breath. "I *do* understand. I don't think *you* understand. I'll never let myself go through again what I went through with Rafael. It almost took me under and I've never fully recovered. Yes, you've helped me a lot and I thank you, but Lucia is always going to be a thorn in my side."

His voice was quiet and he had never looked so precious to her when he told her, "You can't spend the rest of your life running from Lucia. You have to fight her and you can. You just don't know how you've blossomed."

He propped himself on one elbow, bending over her and she could have cried. She still wanted him, all the more because she wasn't going to have him any longer.

"That's the hell of it," she told him. "I *do* know and I'm more grateful than I can tell you. We've said if we ever got in too deeply, we'd back off, end it…."

"Do you really want to end it?"

"Yes. I want to end it now. I'm *going* to end it now."

He was silent for a long while. "I don't want this to end. I want us to go on being friends. Take a while to think about it."

She shook her head vehemently. "I *have* thought about it. I've been afraid of this. Seeing the two of you brought back all the heartbreak of growing up. Lucia's determined to have you, Jim, and I've never known her not to get what she wanted."

"Her husband is divorcing her. He's had enough. So she *does* lose."

"Lucia's call, I'm sure. He told Mom he didn't want the divorce. It's the way she operates. Dump the old and take on the new."

"I'm not available to her."

"You *think* you're not."

"I know I'm not, and I wish you'd understand that."

Inside she started crying, wondering. *Then why didn't you back away? You could have, you know.*

"Can't you just think about it for a while longer?"

"No. My mind's made up."

He heard the finality in her voice and it struck him that just a few minutes ago they'd been locked into some of the most glorious lovemaking he ever hoped to have. Now she was telling him it was over.

"Why'd you make love to me?"

She didn't hesitate. "I wanted you. I know now I'll want you for a very long time. Maybe for the rest of my life. But the better it gets, the more I know I can be hurt...."

What she said made sense, he thought, because it was like that for him, too.

He threw a wild card. "I've bonded with the twins, Melodye. I never really thought about it, but I have. They need me and I need them."

She was silent for a few minutes. "They'll survive. They have Papa France as a male in their lives."

"And he's a wonderful male to have, but they have me, too. You know how easily children are hurt by separations. They feel abandoned."

"They have me. They won't feel abandoned. I think you'd better go now."

Jim clenched his teeth. Blindsided, his heart hurt as he reached for her. It had worked once tonight. He knew she still cared. But she held herself rigid in his arms and closed her mouth against his. His tongue on her lips made no difference this time. He could have been a stranger trying to get to her.

"Baby, please," he whispered, and hugged her.

Struggling out of his grasp, she sat on the edge of the bed, then stood up. "Please leave now. It's early morning and I'd like to get some sleep. I have a hard Saturday ahead."

"Okay," he said wearily, "I'll call you later today."

"No, please don't. I want a clean break. Be kind to us both."

He didn't get up immediately. He'd been the one who'd said if they got in too deep, end it. Now that statement was biting him on the ass. He knew he'd call again because he couldn't help it. He had had few friends in his life and he considered her one he meant to keep if he could.

"We don't have to sleep together. We can just be good friends…."

She laughed then with tears in her laughter. Fat chance. For her, it was all or nothing.

"Jim, I mean what I said."

"Yeah, I'm beginning to see that. I hate this like hell."

"So do I, but it has to be. Would you please leave now?"

He tried to gauge what lay in her voice and couldn't. He was trained to read voices and stances, but his training failed him. "Okay, I'll leave, but may I look in on the twins, kiss them…" He started to say "kiss them goodbye" and couldn't.

"Of course."

He dressed slowly, heavily, thinking that putting on his clothes was far different than the excitement he'd known pulling them off. In the twins' room, he stood looking down at the children in their twin beds, sleeping peacefully. Three rips from his heart and it was bleeding. He told himself he'd make her change her mind, but the fire she'd branded him with was cold in her now.

He bent and kissed Rachel first and lingered, then did the same to Randy. He had known the joy of being a father after all and, Lord, it had felt good. Then his old sense of independence asserted itself and he suddenly told himself that it was for the best. This way he wouldn't hurt Melodye the way he'd hurt Elyssa.

The trouble was he didn't believe his own thoughts. He'd never hurt Melodye because he had said he wouldn't get too close, wouldn't get too deeply involved and hadn't. At the front door, he paused, not thinking to give up his key and she didn't ask him to.

"Take care of yourself and the twins," he said huskily. "And I *will* call, whether you want me to or not. You're my friend and I care. I can't help caring. I wish I could be different, then *this* could be different."

She wanted to kiss his cheek then, but she didn't. "We're not different, neither of us, so we have to settle for what we have. You take care and, Jim, it really would make it easier if you didn't call. Please understand."

He nodded and she thought she saw tears in his eyes; hers were dry and burning.

Because he couldn't help it, he went close and took her in his arms with a gentle hug and kissed her on her cheek. Who was it who said this was the way the world ended, not with a bang but a whimper? He was leaving and his heart was crying, "Don't do this to me."

After he left, Melodye watched him go down the walk and thought about how different his going had been from his coming in. She turned and stood with her back against the door. It was useless to try to blot out the memory of the past night and this early morning. Useless to try to stanch the pain of his leaving. At least she'd had the courage to send him away before he left after telling her she no longer satisfied him.

Chapter 15

Melodye slept for just a little while before she came awake, alone in the darkened room. Knowing she'd sleep no more, she padded over and closed the window she'd opened after Jim left. A sharp breeze blew in, cool for July. She stood for a long while looking out at her side yard, at stars that still clustered and a waning moon. She hadn't cried. She wouldn't cry.

Just after dawn, she called Papa France. "I know I said I was coming to pick up the tomatoes and okra from your garden, but I wonder if you could bring them in early?"

"Don't see any reason why I couldn't," he rumbled in his hoarse early-morning voice. "Baby, you sound like you don't feel so good."

A few hot tears sprang to her eyes. "You're really perceptive. Can we talk about it when you get here?"

"Sure thing. I won't be long. I'm bringing pork sausages.

My neighbor and I butchered a hog yesterday and the sausage is the best I've done in a while."

"That's really saying something. I'll expect you and I'll have coffee ready."

She drank a cup of coffee, then went and sat in a chair in the twins' room watching them sleep. Jim was right, she thought, they *would* miss him. But *she* was right, too, they had Papa France and they had her. Growing up, she'd had few friends, no male friends at all because Jim wasn't the only boy Bettina hadn't liked. But Bettina'd always approved of Lucia's male friends. Well, Jim had told her often enough that she wasn't in that time or that place anymore.

It had seemed like a miracle when handsome, wealthy Rafael Carter had come along and swept her off her feet. He'd been ardent and flattering in the days before they were married. Then he'd continued being ardent, but he took her life over early, even as he made love to her. He suggested this or the other hairstyle, clothes he liked her in that weren't always what she liked. But he never failed to tell her how much he loved her and she would have done anything to please him. Jim was different. He hadn't taken over, just made mild suggestions.

Rafael backed her in her boutique and her designing, took her to Cancun and to Egypt, to Saudi Arabia's fabled resorts. She lived in a brand-new world that quite took her breath away and the icing on the cake was that Bettina approved of and liked her new son-in-law. Lucia had been newly married to the Brazilian jeweler and was in love.

Then Melodye's pregnancy and Rafael's fury that she wouldn't get an abortion. His cruel words that stung her still. Yes, she thought, she'd been right to break off with Jim. It *was* a new world. Women lived and were happy, successful and contented without a man. She was determined to be that way, too.

Rachel came awake first, rubbing her eyes and sitting up. "Mommy, did you sleep in here with Randy and me?"

"No, sweetheart." She held out her arms as Rachel climbed out of bed and onto her lap. "Quick squeeze," she told the child as she hugged her.

"I dreamed Jim took us to the zoo. Will he take us?"

The simple question wrung her heart dry. No, Jim wouldn't be taking them anywhere anymore.

"We'll see," she said as she kissed Rachel's downy cheek.

Randy sat up with a start, jumped out of bed and ran to them. "Hey, you woke up before me."

"Sure did," Rachel said saucily. "Sleepyhead. Sleepyhead. Are you gonna stay in bed?" It was what Melodye often told them.

She took them to the bathroom where they showered and went through their morning ritual. They dressed themselves and sat down with their toys while Melodye went to prepare breakfast.

They were eating by the time Papa France came in, loaded down with vegetables and three long, thick stalks of sugar cane. The twins whooped when they saw him, got up and fell on his neck with avid hugs and kisses.

Papa France laughed delightedly as he looked at them all. "These kids remind me of the old, old Longfellow poem about his children almost devouring him with kisses." His eyes twinkled. "Whatta way to go!"

"Your tomatoes are fabulous this year," Melodye told him, handling the big, juicy fruit.

"Yeah, they did turn out right well. Now, I shelled a mess of butter beans for you and there's a plastic bag of peeled and cut up sugar cane for all of you. I know how much you like the stuff. I've had my fill. Got to bring Miss Belle some. She likes it, too."

"And *you* like Miss Belle, don't you?" Melodye teased him.

He thought a moment. "Now that you ask, I'd reckon I do. She's a mighty nice woman, gentle and kind. Lovely. I could do worse and she could do better'n me."

"Umm, you're in luck. From what I can see, she likes you, too."

As Randy reached for the bag of sugar cane pieces, Melodye told him he couldn't have any until he finished breakfast and his mouth puckered in a pout.

"*I'm* not pouting," Rachel bragged.

"And it isn't going to do him any good. Finish your breakfast."

Randy raced through his breakfast and got his several pieces of sugar cane, then went with his twin to their room to play.

Melodye sat at the table with Papa France, who looked at her sharply. "All right, now, what's going on? Tell me why you're looking so sad."

"Do I?"

"Don't play games with me, young lady. I know your moods. You and Jim have a tiff? It's natural. The path of true love never did run smooth."

She lifted her hands in exasperation. "We were never in love. We never would have been. We were friends, absolutely nothing more."

His eyes narrowed. "Why're you talking in the past. *Were. Would've been.* What's happened?" He looked alarmed.

She shook her head. "I'm not going to see Jim anymore."

He looked as if she'd struck him. "But why? What happened?" he repeated.

"It's a long story…."

"And I want to hear it all. You put up with a lot from Rafael, but you can be hotheaded when you feel you're right."

"I *know* I was right."

She didn't want to talk about it, but Papa France was special. He'd always been in her corner and he needed to know. Telling him the bare minimum, it angered her to have hot tears clog her throat and sting her eyes.

He got up and came around the table, bent and put his arms around her shoulders. "I know you think you're right, but he told you why it happened. Why don't you believe him? Jim's a straight shooter, always was, even when everybody said he was a no-good heller."

She spoke slowly then, feeling her way among possible words to explain herself. "If it had been anybody else but Lucia… Papa France, when Lucia makes up her mind to go after a man, I've never known her not to get him. And she's after Jim. Whether to hurt me, or because she really wants him, I don't know."

He went back to his side of the table and sat down. "Don't you believe you can *win* where Lucia's concerned?"

"I never have. Lucia's beautiful." She didn't mean to say it, but it slipped out, "And she's the right size."

Papa France huffed then. "Dammit, woman, *you're* the right size! When're you going to realize how beautiful you are? Rafael's dead, and let the dead bury the dead. Are you going to live forever bleeding over what he told you about yourself?"

"I don't know," she said miserably. "I don't want to, but it's a memory I can't get rid of and it goes back to even before Rafael."

He nodded. "How well I know that. Your mama and your sister and their swivel-hipped shapes and the things they told you about yourself. Your grandmama and I did our best to cushion their evil, but I see we didn't succeed as well as I thought we did. When Rafael fell in love with you, you were happy and we were happy for you. Then he pulled the stunts he pulled… It's a fact of life, baby, that mothers don't always love the children they bring into this world. If you could get past Rafael and that…"

The doorbell sounded then and Melodye nodded. "That'll be Miss Belle. Please let her in."

She sat at the table thinking about what he'd just said, but it made no difference. For once in her life, she was certain she had done the right thing.

Miss Belle stood in the doorway looking at her pensively. "I imagine you're busy today," she said, "but I wonder if I could ask you to follow me home, either in your car or with Papa France. I want to talk with you and I need to get back home as quickly as I can."

"I'll do that," Melodye said, wondering what Miss Belle needed to talk about. Jim would probably have told her about the breakup, but maybe not. Melodye thought the woman looked as sad and forlorn as she herself must have looked.

"Good. Are the twins ready?"

"Wouldn't you like coffee and a bagel or a Danish?"

"No time, dear. I see they've had breakfast."

Melodye said they had, were ready and got them and their knapsacks.

Once they were gone, Papa France and she sat at the table again. "I'm not going to lecture you," he said. "You're a grown woman and you ought to know your mind. But we're all kids sometimes when it comes to our emotions. Don't make a mistake you'll regret for the rest of your life."

She wasn't sure she should tell him. "Jim and I were

friends. We were never in love and we didn't delude ourselves." She hesitated, then said in a low voice, "We were lovers…."

A beatific smile spread across her grandfather's face. "I knew it all along, and a good thing it's been. Intimacy between a loving man and a woman is a gift from God. You've glowed like all the stars in heaven. And Jim looked like he had the world on a string. Lovemaking's a wonderful thing between two people who care about each other. Nothing better. Nothing more important. Your grandmama and I had that."

She hunched her shoulders. "It takes two to tango, Papa France," she said. "I have fears and Jim has fears. We're like east is east and west is west and never the twain shall meet."

He sighed. "A saying that may or may not apply to you two. You two *did* meet and from the looks of you, it went smashingly. You need to give it a chance."

Melodye said more sharply than she knew, "And *you* need to give it a rest."

"All right. I'll take you to Miss Belle's and bring you back, and I'd like to take you to work. Do you have to go in today?"

"It's Saturday and one of our busy days so I have to go in. I'm okay."

He shook his head. "No, you're not okay. You look like death warmed over and you and I both know you've been looking like a million bucks. Will you think about what I've said?"

There was pleading in his voice and she knew he felt he was right and always wanted what was best for her. But only she could know what was best for her.

It took her a while to dress in a periwinkle dress Jim had liked so much. Leaving the man didn't mean she'd leave what she'd learned from him. She made up her face carefully. Melodye did look woebegone and Odessa was going to have questions she had to answer. She made up her face carefully as if she were going on a date with Jim, but she told herself she had customers to face and she had to shine for them.

A few minutes later at Miss Belle's house, Jim opened the door to them and Melodye's heart lurched and raced. He looked so haggard, she wanted to hold him, soothe him. He'd probably come here instead of going to his house.

"Morning, Jim," she said stiffly.

"Melodye." His eyes on her were calm, hiding his feelings, but she had never looked more precious and in fantasy he crushed her to him as champagne memories poured over his body and his shaft twitched wildly with newly minted heat. She hadn't slept and there were dark circles under her eyes. They should be in each other's arms, he thought, not standing here like strangers.

"Well, come on in, you two," Miss Belle twittered. "Have another cup of coffee."

In the kitchen, Melodye demurred, but Papa France settled back with his coffee.

"You wanted to talk with me," Melodye told the older woman. "Unfortunately I don't have a lot of time."

Miss Belle put a beef roast in the oven. "Oh, honey, I know that. I just have a few things to say. Let me finish this and we can go in the sunroom."

Melodye went back to the living room and looked at an early TV show, seeing nothing at all. She was so conscious of Jim, even when she wasn't in the room with him. Again she wondered what Miss Belle wanted to talk about.

Miss Belle came in, an anxious look on her face, but she

smiled brightly at Melodye. She smiled until she faced Melodye in the room with the sun pouring in. Such a sunny day; such glum people, Melodye thought.

"Jim told me you don't want to see him again. He's crushed, Melodye."

Melodye drew a deep breath. "He won't be when he realizes that this is for the best."

"You two belong together."

"No, that was never the case." She even smiled a little. "We were two ships that passed in the night and we were with each other for just a while. It was never meant to last. We knew that from the beginning. I think we both told you, but you and Papa France saw what didn't exist."

Miss Belle sighed. "I know I saw my son look the way he hasn't looked since Elyssa died, and even better than he's *ever* looked before. I think you two were having an affair and it did glorious things for both of you."

"Nothing lasts forever."

They sat side by side on the sofa and Miss Belle's plump hand covered hers. "I know how bitter and hurt you've been over your bad marriage, dear...."

"That doesn't begin to describe it."

"I don't think Jim would ever hurt you intentionally."

Melodye shook her head. "It isn't just Jim. It's both of us. You can be hurt beyond repair, Miss Belle, so that you never trust again. Don't let anybody tell you you can't. We both said at the outset that if we got in too deep, we'd stop. Like I've told Papa France, this is a different world from the one you two came up in."

"Do you believe in marriage?"

"For some people, yes. For me, no way."

"Couldn't you just stay friends?"

Melodye found herself getting restive, a bit angry. "No, we could only do what we did."

"But Jim said *you* were the one who wanted to end it…."

Melodye took Miss Belle's hand. "Please. I don't want to discuss this any further. You know your son is a wonderful man and our friendship has been a blessing, but…" She shrugged then and closed herself against Miss Belle.

In the hallway going back, Miss Belle was disconsolate. She was so close to Melodye and she'd felt that she could talk some sense into her. Lord, Melodye was as bad as Jim when she'd tried to talk with him.

Jim and the twins played horsey on the floor where the children squealed with delight. First Rachel rode, then Randy, but Randy didn't want to relinquish his horse for Rachel's next turn and Jim had to intercede.

"See here, sport, we can't have what we want all the time. You're going to have to understand that."

Randy pouted again, but got off Jim's back. Melodye stood, thinking and frowning. Her little boy had been pouting more lately. What was bringing it on? She felt a shudder go through her. Was he getting to be like Rafael who could pout, unspeaking, for days? She certainly hoped he wasn't. Jim was so good with her kids.

"Okay, that's it for now," Jim told Rachel. He stood up and told Melodye, "I'd like to talk with you for a few minutes."

"Of course," she said, finding her voice didn't go above a whisper. She didn't want to talk with him, to be near him at all.

They went to the sunroom where he lowered the blinds against the sunlight. The gesture took her breath because in quick fantasy he came back to her and took her in his arms, kissed her, squeezed her and she stood filled with ecstasy at what he was doing to her and what was to come. Predictably, small flames lit in her belly and crotch. She shouldn't have come.

"Melodye?" Jim had said something and she had missed it.

"I'm—I'm sorry," she stammered. "What were you saying?"

"That I'm sorry about everything. But maybe it really *is* for the best." He couldn't help adding that last because it was true. Wasn't it?

It stung having him say it like that. "What did you want to talk about?"

"Two things. First, I'm going to have to come to your boutique to see Manny."

It flustered her because she didn't want to see him again, hadn't wanted to see him this morning and wouldn't have come if she'd known he'd be here. "Couldn't you see him at the station house?" She felt cornered and her voice was sharp. She needed time away from him, beginning now.

He expelled a harsh breath and shook his head. "Manny and I need to talk about his coming into the department and he wants you around when we talk. He thinks the world of you. He was sure it would be okay if I came in. Of course, that was before…"

"I understand. I'll expect you."

"It's going to be afternoon before I can make it. I'm swamped with paperwork, and Melodye?"

"Yes." She didn't dare look at him. Her stupid heart kept reaching for him, pulling him to her.

"I'll be going away for a while, maybe for good."

"Away?" Did she have to sound so desperate?

He breathed shallowly, needing to get it all said in a hurry. "I'm going back to Manhattan for a little while and my old chief has offered me a new job there. I'll probably take it."

"But what about Miss Belle? You came back to be with her."

"I'll be asking her to move there. She likes cities, shows, that kind of thing."

It came unbidden then. "Did you *ask* to be assigned to New York?" *Because Lucia lived in Manhattan.*

"I had been asked and was considering turning it down. My chief called me again early this morning and I accepted. I'll be leaving tomorrow on assignment from here."

Why was she crying inside? she wondered. Wasn't this what she wanted? A clean break, then him away to make it easier to get over him? All right, already. Get it over with! She felt flat then to counteract the sharp pain. What *did* she want?

"I wish you all the best," she said very calmly.

"Yeah, me, too, and I'll see you this afternoon."

They both tried to smile and neither could make it. She felt his quiet strength behind her as they left the room. He went into the family room where the twins climbed on his lap demanding a game of Ride 'Em, Horsey as they each sat on a knee.

Miss Belle and Papa France sat at the kitchen table. "I'm ready to go now," Melodye told him.

She saw that both of them searched her face, probably for signs of a reconciliation.

"Uh, just a minute, honey. There're a coupla things I need to tell Miss Belle."

The two old people moved to the sunroom and tears stood in Miss Belle's eyes.

"They're both stubborn as mules!" she said vehemently.

"Yep."

"I'm never going to know how it feels to have grandkids."

She looked so sad and Papa France's heart hurt for her.

"We did the best we could. You raised a fine son, Belle." On impulse, he hugged her and she felt good in his arms. Even sad, she drew him like a magnet.

She relaxed in his arms. "And you raised a wonderful granddaughter. I'm glad you at least know the joy of being a grandfather."

He had to reassure her. "One day. We'll just keep praying. Praying big. Praying huge. That's my motto these days. My prayers've been answered many a time and I'll keep the faith. You do it, too." He took a clean handkerchief from his pocket and dabbed her eyes.

"Thank you. I never thought about praying your way, but I'm going to try it and hope it works."

Chapter 16

Later at *A-1 Plus Love*, Melodye could smell coffee brewing as she let herself in. Odessa stood halfway across the room, glowing, with her hands behind her back.

She danced over to Melodye, then looked subdued. "Why're you looking so down, girlfriend? Are you okay? The twins? Jim?"

"All fine," Melodye said shortly.

Odessa's expression changed to one of deep concern. "But *you're* not fine. Wassup?"

"You don't want to know. Why are *you* so happy? Did Ashton give you a new BMW?"

"I'll tell you if you'll tell me."

Melodye nodded. "Let me get my third cup of coffee and I'll tell you, and you know I'm a one-cup-a-day woman. Out with it. I need all of anybody's happy news I can get today."

Odessa held out her hand, displaying a large white diamond ring.

"Beautiful," Melodye told her, forcing a weak grin. "Ashton, I presume."

"Who else? Denzel doesn't come around anymore. Okay, let's ride. What's with you?"

Melodye poured herself more black coffee and they went into Melodye's studio and sat in tub chairs. "Jim and I broke up last night."

Odessa looked at her in disbelief. "But *why?* God, you two really had something going on."

"*Had* is the operative word here."

Holding herself tight, she told her friend about seeing Jim kiss Lucia. Or was it the other way around? No, he'd said she kissed *him.* Something about excitement. Oh, yes, Lucia was nothing if not exciting.

"Don't you believe him?"

Melodye drew a deep breath. "The hell of it is I do. Jim has a lot of integrity. I don't think he'd lie, but I do think he's in over his head. You've heard Bettina brag that her beloved daughter takes no prisoners where men are concerned. Jim Ryman's a sophisticated man, but he's no match for Lucia. She'll eat him for breakfast."

Odessa was silent for a long while. "Lucia's always hurt you, hasn't she? Don't you think she just may be after him to hurt you?"

"Probably, but I think she really does go for him. I've watched her with other men. Lately she's been different with Jim, more subdued, more serious."

"And what about *him?* How does he respond to her?"

Melodye pondered this one. "He seems interested to me. He studies her and Jim isn't a flirt. I get all his attention when we're out together and he isn't into every woman who comes in view. I've liked that. You know Rafael would flirt with a lamppost...."

Odessa looked at her intently. "So you showed Jim to the gate. How'd he take it?"

"He wanted us to talk more about it. He even said he thinks Lucia's friendlier to me than she lets on, that she hides her feelings the way he does—a lot."

"So they're soul mates in that?"

Melodye sighed. "I really hadn't thought of it that way."

Now Melodye realized that talking about it was bringing it all back more vividly and she hurt bad. Her head throbbed. Her stomach hurt. She had to cut this short. "He's coming by this afternoon to talk with Manny about Manny's going into the department."

"Couldn't Manny go to the station house?"

"I'm sure he could, but he said Manny wants to talk with me about it, too."

"I think Jim's looking for another chance to see you."

Melodye knew then what was hurting her even worse. "He's been assigned to New York for a while. Lucia will be leaving soon for New York, too."

"Bummer! If he were here, I think he'd change your mind. I know you don't want commitment and he doesn't want commitment, but anger and disappointment and striking back are pretty cold bedmates."

Melodye lifted her shoulders in an exaggerated shrug. "It's *over,* girlfriend. I know you like him, but get used to it." She knew very well she talked to herself, as well as Odessa.

Manny knocked and stuck his head in the door. "I'll come back. I picked up the bagels, cream cheese, Danishes and cinnamon rolls. We're set for the rush." He hesitated, nodding at Melodye. "I need to talk with you about Jim."

Odessa got up. "I'm through here for a while." She looked at Melodye. "Do you want to talk with Manny now?"

Melodye said she did. Odessa left as Manny came in and stood, shifting from one foot to the other. "This'll only take a minute. I told Jim we could talk about the department here. I want you in on it. I'm turning over a new leaf and I want you as witness. Melodye, you know how much I think of you and how you've helped me, giving me a job and all?" He seemed so uncomfortable.

"I think I do, Manny. You've done a great job. How're your studies coming along?"

"Fine, but I'm really not into accounting that much anymore. Jim told me to continue, that everything I learn'll be useful. Well, that's about it."

She cupped her hand under her chin. "He'll be in this afternoon."

No doubt about it, she thought, as Manny left, Jim was his hero. He'd been one of her heroes, too. Her stomach and her head coalesced into one big ache and she wondered how she'd make it through the day. Dear old aspirin. Whoever perfected it deserved a presidential award.

A few customers had come in and asked for Melodye. They stood with Odessa and the other saleswomen, drinking coffee and tea, chatting and munching on the goodies. Big bowls of almonds and walnuts were on the credenza. Melodye thought it was a great scene and one of the reasons she'd survive.

"Oh, I love this place," one very attractive plus-size woman said. "I don't feel this much at home in my home. How did I spend my days before you set up shop, Melodye?"

Melodye laughed, beginning to feel better. "I don't know, but I'm glad you're here now."

Soothing pop music played in the background and for a moment she nearly panicked because Lionel Richie was singing "Lady." She was in Atlantic City, then in Jim's house, in his bed and they...

Stop it! she told herself sharply. She listened to herself and stopped. It was plain this was going to be worse than she'd thought.

The woman with her asked if she were all right and she nodded. "I'm fine."

The woman looked at her closely. "Well, my husband's surely delighted with your designs. He says he's falling in love with me all over again. My friends say I've never looked better and I owe it all to you."

Effusively hugging Melodye, she kept raving about the designs. "I want that slinky green one in three colors."

At noon she sat at the drawing board in her studio building strength for the rush that would come in a couple of hours.

Odessa stuck her head in the door. "What'd you do in your past life to deserve this? The princess of hell would like to see you. I'm surprised she didn't fly in on her broomstick."

Melodye's head snapped up. "Lucia?" Her voice was a croak.

"No more, no less. Shall I send her in or lethally dispatch her the way I'd like to."

"Dispatch her, then send her in," Melodye said, laughing in spite of herself.

When her sister came in, Melodye couldn't help reflecting that Lucia never looked less than perfect and she kept that illusion. Lucia never let you see her at her worst, if she had a worst. Even growing up, she'd race to the bathroom when she got up in the morning, lock the door and come out looking fabulous.

Lucia stood in the doorway in an ivory silk pantsuit. No Saturday jeans and big shirt for her. "Well," she drawled, "what car hit you? You look terrible. And you certainly left the party in a hurry. Mom and I were quite worried. What happened?"

Melodye drew a deep breath. "So many questions and I have no answers, Lucia. Not for you anyway."

"Jim disappeared, too, without saying a word," she purred. "We'd been having quite a chat. Interesting. Satisfying." She half closed her eyes.

Melodye shook herself to clear cobwebs from her brain. "I really don't have time for this, Lucia. What do you want?"

Lucia licked the proverbial canary feathers from her mouth and smiled narrowly. "You and Jim are going deep, aren't you? Or you *were* anyway?"

"How can that possibly matter to you?"

"I *like* Jim, Melodye. I'm interested in him and you know my track record. I'm going to take him from you."

"He's not mine for you to take." There. She certainly was being cool enough.

Lucia still stood and Melodye thought she'd be damned if she'd ask her to sit down. Let her say what was on her mind and get out.

Lucia's stance gave her the edge and she used it. She was up and Melodye was down. "Oh, Melodye, you're such a fool. Didn't you ever guess that Rafael and I were lovers?"

Melodye's breath came too fast. She stiffened. "You're lying. You'd say *anything* to hurt me."

"*Am* I lying?" Lucia recited the words on the note they'd found in the safe-deposit box. As best Melodye could remember, it was verbatim. "You see, I remembered because it was so precious to me. The money—fifty thousand in cash and one hundred thousand in bearer bonds—was a beginning sum to set me up. Rafael described a tennis bracelet he bought me.

"That cash was in part for me to meet Rafael in Cancun. He didn't want your stupid questions about charges on a credit card. We were lovers, all right. God, were we lovers. We lit up New York and the Cancun beaches where you two went on honeymoon. There were times when I lay in his arms and your picture floated before me, and I laughed in your face.

"He was going to divorce you, but you found you were pregnant and he decided to wait. If he'd lived a little longer, we would have married." Her smile was mocking, vicious. "Why would he want you when he could have me?"

For a few seconds Melodye couldn't breathe as she waited for the shattering pain to begin the way it would have happened in the past. But she felt nothing. It was simply another blow on flesh and spirit that already felt dead.

Then the last nail in the coffin. "Jim and I are going up on the same flight to New York tomorrow. Wish me luck, sweetie. And I wish you luck because you're going to need it."

Lucia was laughing when she left and Melodye felt a rush of anger that energized her. She thought she knew then what murderers feel just before they kill.

She found it hard to go back to putting the finishing strokes on the design she worked on. It was for a woman who'd be in this afternoon and she sighed. Mrs. Parkins was a very demanding woman and one of her best customers. She tried not to think about Lucia and Jim in New York, but she gritted her teeth as visions of them together closed in on her.

The more she thought about it the more she felt breaking off was the right thing to do. It would have been far easier if she didn't have to see him at all, but if that weren't possible, she was good at steeling herself against emotions she didn't want to feel. She'd had a whole lot of practice at that with Rafael. So far, it wasn't working as well with Jim.

She got up and went to the windows, surprised to see it was raining because only a thirty percent chance had been forecast. In fact, this was more like a squall. Well, there went her crush of customers for the afternoon. Rainy days were always slow.

Manny knocked and came in. "Boss lady, I know you usually eat around this time and I know you don't feel well, so I fixed a little of your favorite soup, crackers and whomped up a salad. You need something. Odessa agreed with me."

She turned, nodding. "Thank you and I *am* a little hungry."

"While I was out I got that great chocolate-chip ice cream you like so much, and it's waiting."

"Okay, but just a little bit. Manny, you're a love."

He flushed and set the tray on her desk. "Okay, I'll leave you alone to eat." He had set a pretty tray with a rose in a bud vase.

"Manny."

"Uh-huh."

"You're really into becoming a detective, aren't you?"

His smile was suddenly wide and effervescent. "More serious than I've ever been about anything. You know I had dreams as a kid of getting a hold of a lot of money any way I could. To be honest, I even considered dealing drugs. But I've been running scared all my life. The whole time I worked for Rafael I didn't like the looks of a lot of people I saw come by and I wanted to leave a long time before I did." He looked really bothered, paused, then continued. "Yeah, I'm really into it."

"And you like Jim a lot."

"*Love* the guy. He's a straight shooter. I'd rather be like him than anyone I know."

She sat down to her lunch and he went out, still radiating happiness.

The New England clam chowder he'd brought her and the saltines were all delicious. He'd put together a good salad with blue-cheese dressing. She shook her head. She'd be a lot better off if she didn't love food so much.

The phone rang and it was Rachel. "Randy's acting like a bad boy again, Mommy."

"Why do you say that, sweetie?"

"He's pouting again. He won't behave."

"And are you behaving?"

"Yes. Miss Belle wants to speak to you."

Miss Belle got on the phone. "I think the wee ones are having a tiff. Rachel wants to play with a toy he's monopolizing. I wouldn't exactly say he's misbehaving. In fact, he's a replica of Jim when he was that age. Oh, Melodye, your children are wonderful and I'm so happy to keep them. Has Jim come by? He said he was."

Melodye felt a small thrill go through her when Miss Belle said his name and it irritated her no end.

"No, he said it would be later."

"You're still adamant about breaking off?"

"Afraid I am. I'm sorry, but we can only go the clear way to go. I think you'll know that in the end...."

Miss Belle sounded sad. "My dear, I hope *you'll* know in the end what's best for you both. You're so beautiful together."

Melodye thought sharply, *We're so much better off apart.*

When she and Miss Belle had finished talking and she'd spoken with Randy, who was a little testy with her, she ate the rest of her lunch and Manny brought the ice cream in. She tasted a bit and shivered. She wasn't hungry today the way she usually was. Somehow food reminded her of Jim. He loved good food.

She asked Manny to stay a bit and he sat down. "You know," she said, "I'm working through a raise for you. You've really been so much help. When we get those skirts made up and on the market, I think you'll have a lot of extra change."

"Hey—" he got up, bent and kissed her cheek "—boss lady, you're the best."

Finished eating, Melodye took her tray out and put her dishes in the dishwasher. There were only two customers in the shop and she greeted and chatted with each one. They were still talking about the fashion show.

Back in her office, she finished the sketch and began going through some bills that would go to her accountant Monday morning. Odessa came in looking exasperated, her hands on her hips. "You're not gonna believe what the storm washed up. The devil must be on vacation because all the inmates of hell are escaping."

"Bettina?" She groaned inside.

"Worse. Would you believe Turk Hylton?"

"Turk?"

"Yeah. Odd name for an odd character. I told him you were busy because I know you don't want to see him, but he says it's about Manny and a couple of things you'd told him you want to talk about."

Melodye leaned back, expelling air from lungs, which

hadn't breathed well in the past hours. "He's not telling the truth. I haven't talked with him since the fashion show. Send him in and I'll make short work of him."

"Hmmph. Other people don't tell the truth. The Turk is a big liar."

Melodye couldn't help smiling. "Among other things."

Turk came in with a flourish, pulling off his expensive raincoat. "Good thing I keep this in the car," he said, indicating his coat.

"I'm pretty busy," she said. "Please tell me what you want."

He looked at her slyly, his eyes half closed. "Doesn't look too busy out there to me. And it's an ideal time to make my proposition to you. May I sit down?"

Melodye frowned. She sat behind her desk and had forgotten to offer him a seat. "You may," she said coolly, indicating a chair opposite her.

"Thanks. Now I'll get right down to brass tacks." He leaned forward, his long, well-manicured fingers playing with his big diamond ring. Oh, Turk Hylton was your elegant hood, she thought sourly.

"Melodye, I want you to help me lean on Manny to come back and work for me."

She coughed and she sputtered. "What? Why would he want to? No! No way!"

He had thrown her off balance and he laughed happily. "Listen," he said, "I never realized until he left that the kid's worth his weight in gold to me. I'm sure he's talked to you about his hellish life as a child. Not a pot to piss in and no window to throw it out of. The kid had dreams when he worked for us, dreams of making it big and getting rich. And Rafael was in his corner."

He paused and Melodye thought about the conversation she'd had with Manny just a little while before Turk came.

Turk sighed, a rare thing for him. "Well, he and Rafael were as thick as thieves!"

"Yes, and I remember you didn't get along with Manny."

"Well, that was just because he wanted to do everything Rafael wanted him to do and nothing I needed him to do. The truth is, I haven't been able to find anyone like him to do our errands and handiwork. He's smart and willing to work. Listen, Rafael intended to train him to go to the top at *Steeped In Joy,* make him manager because Rafael was cutting back. He had other fish to fry." He winked slyly at her.

"I can't do what you ask. Besides, I don't think he'll ever go back to you."

"He might, if you leaned on him, along with me."

She shook her head. "I'm not going to draw this out, Turk. I won't do it and that's my final answer."

Turk's eyes narrowed. "He'll be back, with or without your help. Count on it."

She was quick with her response. "I don't think so. Besides, if you're so certain, why're you here?"

He changed the subject abruptly. "Any news about who killed Rafael?"

"Not that I've heard."

He raised his eyebrows. "Just thought with you sleeping with the cop, he might be telling you his secrets."

She didn't intend to honor his barb with a comment. "Is that all?" she responded icily.

He laughed. "Not quite, lady. The other thing is you and me."

"I beg your pardon?"

"Melodye, I've never made any secret of the way I feel

about you. If you married me, you'd get half of *Steeped In Joy* back without paying a cent. All you'd have to do is roll those hips under me in my bed a coupla times a day and do the little things I like done when I make love."

Melodye stood up. "If you're not finished talking, Turk, I am. This conversation is over."

She glanced at her watch. Jim would be coming along at any time.

Turk still sat. "Not so fast," he said. "I've followed you around town, Melodye, here in D.C. and in Crystal Lake."

She wasn't surprised at anything he said. "There're laws against stalking, Turk." She hoped her voice was as cold as she felt.

"You can't call it stalking. I haven't threatened you, but I could." His eyes got as cold as her own and she wondered why now at this late date.

"I don't think that would be wise," she told him.

"Many a man's lost his head when a woman he wanted turned him down. Women have been shot, beaten, doused with gasoline and set on fire…." He looked at her narrowly, his smile evil and sinister. "Do I need to paint you a picture?"

"I'm not afraid of you."

"And I don't want you to be. I admire spunk in a woman. If you checked the front of my pants, you'd find me ready to roll."

He laughed then, and with fury, Melodye walked from behind the desk, picked up his coat and threw it onto his lap. "Either you leave or I'll have security escort you out."

He rose slowly, his eyes still disrobing her. "Miss Melodye, queen of the haughty broads. One day, baby, I'm gonna bring you lower than you ever thought you could go. And you're gonna be wallowing and loving it. Okay, I'm going. I've done all the damage I can do here."

In a perfect rage, she felt she was breathing fire. As he got up, he told her, "Watch your back, Mrs. Carter, because I sure as hell will be."

Chapter 17

Later, it was still raining heavily as Melodye worked. Instinct made her look up from her project to see Jim lounging against her partially open door. Her breath caught and she put a hand to her bosom.

"You startled me," she breathed, her face somber.

"Sorry. I didn't mean to interrupt," he said.

"No, please, come on in. Did you see Manny outside?"

"Odessa said he's on an errand for her and should be back any minute," Jim said.

Melodye looked at him and wrinkled her nose. "Why don't you take off that wet coat?"

She picked up the intercom and asked Odessa to please send Manny in as soon as he returned. Drawing a few deep breaths to right herself, she told him, "Why don't you sit down and rest your feet?" she said.

Melodye realized that she couldn't control her body around Jim, but she had to try.

"Could I get you anything? We've got tons of food. We had prepared for a big crowd, but the rain washed out the event," she said, trying to make small talk.

He shook his head. "I saw it. Quite a spread." He noted the dark circles had deepened under her eyes and she looked restive. He thought she still looked beautiful—and cold. His eyes went to her breasts and lingered, flustering her. Looking into her eyes, he saw clearly then that she meant what she'd said last night.

All the little things they'd shared pressed in on her, beginning with champagne kisses. Memory could be such a bitch, she thought bitterly. He was a gorgeous man, no question about it, but did she have to slaver over him? With a lump in her throat she wished they could have at least gone on being friends. But with Lucia in the picture, that wasn't possible. She thought with a wry smile if she found Lucia in Heaven, she'd choose hell.

He was silent, but attentive. An odd smile played about his mouth. He had his memories, too, and they were sizzling. He ran a quick tongue over his dry lips and studied her, knowing it made her uncomfortable and getting a strange, somewhat sadistic charge from knowing.

"Turk was by earlier."

"I thought he might have been. I talked with him on the street near here."

"Oh?"

There was no question about whether she should tell him what Turk said, so she did, surprised to see the sharp look of concern on his face as she finished.

"Did he talk with Manny as far as you know?"

She shook her head. "If he did, Manny said nothing about it. You looked bothered when I told you. What's going on?"

"A hell of a lot and it's coming in faster than we can sort it out. Manny won't be going back to Turk."

"No, he hates Turk, I think." She laughed then, her voice breaking. "Oh, yes, I'm forgetting. Turk talked about stalking me...."

He shook his head. "He's not that big a fool. Are you scared of him?"

"A little, I guess. Should I be?"

"You've got more protection than you're aware of. I told you before."

"But you're still saying I should be careful."

"Yeah, definitely, but Turk won't be bothering you or coming around again. We're putting him out of circulation a bit before we'd intended to. He took his own freedom away."

She breathed a sigh of relief as Manny knocked and came in, beaming when he saw Jim. "You say I'm in on this?" she said to them.

"It's Manny's show."

"Yeah," Manny said, "I want you here." He cleared his throat and sat down. "I want it written in stone that I'm beginning a new life. I'm gonna try like hell and if I get through the academy, I'm on my way. I wouldn't mind settling in Crystal Lake and a long time from now being police chief...."

Melodye threw her head back, laughing. "You don't dream small."

Manny began to talk then of his hopes and dreams. Finally he said, "Out with the old, in with the new. I swear, my new life is gonna be a completely different story."

They had talked before; now Jim told him additional informal things about the Crystal Lake Police Department. And there was always D.C.'s police department nearby.

Manny shook his head. "I like small cities best." It hit him then that he was actually on his way to a different life and acute anxiety followed. "You really think I can make it?"

"If you want to," Jim said quietly, "and work at it."

Both men were subdued, seemed close and Melodye envied that closeness. She thought of a happy Odessa outside, showing off her diamond. Melodye neither had, nor wanted that symbol of commitment again. Jim had done wonders for her self-esteem. But Rafael couldn't praise her enough in the beginning. In her life, happiness had been fleeting, pain a dependable companion.

After an hour or so of talk, Manny hunched his shoulder. "Well, here's to trying hard," he said.

"And making it," Jim told him.

Manny looked at Jim intently. "Man, I'm really grateful to you. I owe you my life and I'll repay you in every way I can."

Jim looked somber then, even sad, Melodye thought as he said, "You already have in more ways than you know."

Manny left and Jim got up and paced the floor and tried to make further conversation, which Melodye didn't follow through on. She wanted him to leave. *And she wanted him to stay.*

Reluctantly, she decided she'd mention it. "Lucia came by today." She really didn't want to talk about her sister.

"Oh?"

She sighed then. "She told me Rafael and she were having an affair. The money, the bracelet and the note were for her. You found that out, didn't you?"

"Yeah. We did."

"Why didn't you tell me?"

"I didn't want to hurt you. I figured she'd wash your face in it some day, but I hoped she wouldn't."

So he was protecting her. But he couldn't protect her from Lucia and himself.

"You're both taking the same flight tomorrow."

"Yeah."

Just that and nothing more. A day ago he would have rushed to reassure her that it didn't mean a thing, that Lucia didn't matter and she, Melodye, did. Now some part of her cried at the loss. Was she going to lose it all inside herself? Okay, if he wasn't going to take it further, she certainly wasn't. Her body got stiffer and her mind closed against him with the mention of Lucia's name. Would he have said anything about their flight tomorrow?

Listen, Melodye, she told herself, *what do you expect? You shafted him, without the option of friendship. Please don't whine that he's finally seeing the light and playing it cool. It's his prerogative. What do you want from him?* And the answer was silence because she no longer had a clue as to *what* she wanted from him.

Jim sat down, then got up and paced again. He felt so frustrated. They were worse than strangers, he thought. There was always hope that strangers might become friends, and so strangers left that avenue open. Melodye had completely closed herself to him. The phrase "as cold as yesterday's boiled potatoes" was something he thought fit the situation. Memories didn't help anymore and it made him angry. He was chopped liver, no doubt about it.

He sat down and leaned forward, his legs spread, his big hands laced in front of him. "I still think you're wrong about my not telling the twins I'm leaving."

She shook her head. "No. It'll be all right. They're so young…"

"And besides, they have Papa France—and you." He sounded mocking, derisive and it made her angry, but she tamped it down.

"That's right." The words nearly stuck in her throat.

Odessa knocked lightly and came in. She looked from one to the other and it made her sad. The tension was so thick you could cut it with the proverbial knife. "I hate bothering you, Melodye, but Mrs. Waring has a problem she insists you handle. She says she won't take up much of your time. Can you see her?"

"I will. Do you know what it's about?"

"No, I don't. She refuses to say."

Melodye stood up and Jim studied her languidly graceful body. She didn't want him here; that much was certain. Well, he had more to say and he intended to say it. He'd be waiting.

"This may take a while," Melodye coolly informed him.

"I've got time." He bit off the words. Did she intend to push him aside like some boy toy she'd picked up? Well, he had other plans.

Once she was gone, his mind actively went back to that first Sunday when he'd knocked on her door, saying he needed help with Rafael's cold case. And after a while, it ended with their last night's violent kisses and more violent lovemaking. The way she'd responded to him still took his breath and it made him hot thinking about it.

Okay, so they couldn't make it as a committed couple. They'd long agreed on that. Too much baggage. Too many broken dreams. And, yeah, too much *fear.* But they'd had something rich and precious. They'd been true to their hungry bodies and had enjoyed more than they'd ever dreamed they could.

The customer's problem was quickly settled and Melodye walked back to her office on trembling legs. Why did he insist on staying when she felt she'd made it plain she didn't want him to stay? Her hand lingered on the doorknob a long time before she opened it.

He looked up as she came in. He'd thought she looked good when he'd seen her that morning. Now he could have had her for dessert.

"All finished, so soon?" he asked sardonically.

She said nothing, only looked at him, and that was a mistake because he'd had more experience with silence than she had. Silence was his turf.

He sat, with her still standing. "So you're sure you don't want me to say anything to the twins."

"I *said* I was sure." He could be so exasperating.

"Melodye." Why was he speaking so softly?

"The last time I looked that's still who I am."

To his surprise, her flippancy made his blood boil. He wasn't used to losing his temper, whatever else his faults. "Be serious."

"Would that matter? Are you listening, Jim?"

"Your heart isn't agreeing with your mind."

His saying it angered her because she knew it was true. Did he know, couldn't he *feel* how hard this was for her, how close to the edge she was? He was flying to New York with Lucia tomorrow morning. Lucia, who'd always had so much Melodye had wanted—even Rafael.

Leave, her mind screamed at Jim, then her heart humbly begged him to stay.

He stood up then and his big body drew her even before he moved toward her. "Can't you be a little more than barely civil?" he asked her. "It's not like we don't *know* each other very well." His grin was wicked, taunting.

His saying it brought it all down hard and her heart lurched crazily. Her private parts were tingling and hot, wet and aching with desire.

She intended to hit him where it hurt, make him back off for good. She smiled a little as she told him, "There *are* things I'm gonna forget in a hurry."

She was between him and the door when he grabbed her. Half carrying her, he pressed her back against the door and locked it. Ancient male dominance surged in his loins and he stood, looking down at her upturned face wishing he were free to love her. But why, when she obviously no longer wanted him? In a flash, he decided he'd leave his emotional brand on her—or die trying.

He studied her, his mind racing with God knows what violent thoughts. Cave men dragged women to take their pleasure. Did he intend to do this? He wasn't sure.

Placing a flattened hand on each side of her head, he put his head close to hers and licked the corners of her mouth as she shuddered.

His stormy hazel eyes imprisoned her, and she whimpered as her blood scorched her, turning to molten gold in her veins.

"Don't!" she whispered.

But he slowly ran his tongue lightly around her mouth, outlining her lips. Her mouth opened at the onslaught of his tongue and her response was as wild as his own. His big hands cupped her face, sealing her in with him.

What did he plan to do? she wondered, as his big body pressed her back against the door? He kissed her ruthlessly, hurting and bruising her mouth. His erection was stone hard against her as he moved against her crotch, setting up fever so scalding she thought she'd die from it.

She couldn't take it when he kissed her cloth-covered breasts. His mouth was like hot coals on the tinder of those swollen mounds of flesh. She fought to keep herself from moaning.

All conscious will had left her. She *belonged* to him completely and it infuriated her.

"Damn you!" she told him in a strangled whisper. But she wanted him to do with her what he would.

He exulted then, his loins on fire. *She wanted him. She still wanted him.* His heart exploded with lust and other feelings he refused to acknowledge. Her coldness seemed like a facade and he *had* to find out if it was. This was not the time, nor the place to take her, he thought, as he relaxed a bit, breathing hard.

"Damn you," she said again, but her voice was slurred and sweet the way it had been before, and there were tears in her eyes.

"Bless you," he told her softly, "and I wish you all the best."

It was the hardest thing he'd ever done, but he got his raincoat, unlocked the door, then kissed her on the mouth again, savoring the lushness of her bruised lips.

After he was gone, she stood unmoving, then walked on unsteady legs to a chair, plopped down and wept with her head in her hands.

Odessa knocked and came in a little later, pausing in the doorway. "Are you okay?"

Melodye couldn't look at her. "I'll be fine." A dry sob took her.

Her friend thought it best to give Melodye space, but she said sadly. "Jim came through, looking as if his world had ended and here you are. Melodye, I hope you two can work it out somehow, because apart, neither one of you is going to make it."

* * *

Outside, getting into his car, Jim noted that the rain had slackened to a drizzle and it matched his spirit. He'd had to know she wanted him because it meant she still cared. There was no question of dominance; they were in thrall to each other—equals. There was so much between them now that had to be worked through, both inside and outside of them. He wondered if they could work things through in time for them to ever be friends again.

Chapter 18

In the days ahead, Melodye congratulated herself on keeping it together. Oh, yes, she dreamed about Jim, vivid, painful dreams. His kiss still burned her soul. But waking, she was calm.

Then it was two weeks since he'd left. She was doing fine, she thought, and Rachel was taking it well. Randy was another story. Every day, her little boy asked about Jim, even in his sleep. When Melodye and the twins were around, Miss Belle always rolled her eyes and lifted them toward heaven when he asked.

After a few days, Miss Belle frowned. "Why hasn't Jim called them?"

Melodye told her then that she'd asked him to make a clean break. Miss Belle sighed. "I'm not too sure that's wise, Melodye. Some children take separations so hard. I think it would be best if you asked him to call them."

Melodye was sure she was right and it simply didn't occur

to her that she was protecting herself. She told herself she didn't care if she never saw Jim Ryman again.

That morning, Randy was pouting and Rachel was being the little mother. "He's a ba-a-ad boy," she teased her twin.

As Randy glared at his sister, Melodye picked him up and hugged him, concerned. "He doesn't seem to be feeling too well," she told Miss Belle.

The older woman made a funny face at Randy, putting her hand on his forehead. "He seems a bit hot. I'll take his temperature."

"I did. It's up a little. The pediatrician has long told me children get high fevers that would mean trouble in an adult, but fade quickly in a child."

"Well, I'll take his temperature frequently and keep you posted. You say you're rushing." She looked wistful. "I thought you could stay and chat a while. Jim's been gone two weeks."

Melodye felt spiteful. "Yes, he went up on the same flight with Lucia."

Miss Belle looked surprised. She knew nothing of that development. "You *have* forgiven him for that harmless kiss with Lucia?"

Melodye felt the start of exasperation. Even Miss Belle didn't always seem to truly understand the bad blood between Lucia and Melodye.

Raising her eyebrows, Melodye murmured, "Miss Belle, I really have to rush."

Miss Belle nodded. "Well, I've got to say, you're looking better. Not as drained. I'll be checking with Jim often, and I'll keep you posted."

Melodye blew a stream of air. "It's over between us, Miss Belle. Please get used to it. I have."

Miss Belle's heart hurt with regret. The other woman's

words sounded final, and as Papa France and she often said, both Melodye and Jim were stubborn. The twins were asking for their toys then and Miss Belle went to get them. While she was gone, Melodye quickly kissed the twins and left, calling goodbye to Miss Belle.

Outside, she had some trouble starting her car. She really needed to take it in for its regular tune-up, she thought.

After the motor purred, she put her head down on the steering wheel. She didn't want to talk with Miss Belle about Jim, but she knew the older woman gently nudged her again and again. Hunching her shoulders, she thought about that last day. She'd known she'd dream about Jim and she had, night after night. Touching her face, her lips, she relived that cruel kiss that still burned her. He knew he could always get to her, turn her knees to jelly and set her body aflame. She had responded well to Rafael, but always felt in control.

She felt ashamed then of how she went out of control with Jim, then thought firmly that it was a good thing she had a mind. He couldn't get to her mind; that was still clear. Their affair really hadn't gone on too long; she was happy about that. She wondered how *he* felt about the way she melted when he touched her, stroked her. Did some little part of him despise her for being so wanton with him? She felt a moment of panic. She wanted him to think well of her and she wanted to think well of herself.

Getting into her seat belt, she reminded herself sharply to keep her wits about her. It was a crapshoot driving into D.C. on a Monday morning. She offered up a prayer that Randy was okay and that she'd get in safely.

The day at *A-1 Plus Love* had passed uneventfully with Melodye grateful business was slow. Odessa and Manny did everything they could to be supportive. Melodye hadn't cried again and she was glad about that. Tears weren't welcome. What was needed here was backbone and she felt she had that in spades. Neither Odessa nor Manny mentioned Jim at all.

Miss Belle called a couple of times to say that Randy still had a slight fever, but it had gone no higher. Melodye decided she'd take him in to his doctor and check in late the next morning unless the fever had cooled. By quitting time, she was feeling a whole lot better.

Late that afternoon, she sharply reminded herself that her thoughts and her eyes had strayed to her door again and again. Her mouth opened a little when she thought about it and she could still feel Jim's hot mouth on her face. If he'd unbuttoned her blouse, she would have been undone.

Angrily snapping to, she began to breathe deeply, for common sense to prevail, she told herself sharply. But one thing would end this nonsense: thoughts about Jim and Lucia on the way to New York. She couldn't help wondering what time the flight had arrived. Had he seen her to her hotel?

She clenched her teeth. She was torturing herself and this wouldn't do. Maybe it *was* Lucia's kiss, but he hadn't backed away. Only thinking of that kiss stopped her thoughts, brought cold reality. She got up and began to get her things together for the long ride home.

That night, Randy came to her bed around midnight. "My head's hot," he told her.

Melodye got the thermometer and felt panic. The child had a fever of one hundred and five degrees. She gave him baby aspirin as the doctor had told her to do, then took his temperature again a half hour later. Was that time enough? He'd had no fever when they got home.

But the fever didn't cool this time. She called the doctor who told her to take him to Crystal Lake Hospital emergency.

With the children bundled in their car seats and Randy moaning and crying, she managed to get to the hospital and was grateful to be processed so quickly. The doctor had called ahead.

Doctor Monica Adams was there in record time, checking and consoling. One of the staff found a bed for Rachel and put her in it. There was also a bed for Melodye, but she knew she'd get no more sleep this night.

She anxiously watched her small twin as he tossed, his breathing labored, his little body burning up. The doctor ordered more medication, but the fever didn't break.

Frowning, the doctor pulled up a chair by Randy's bedside as he slept in fits and starts. "I'm puzzled," she said. "This has all the earmarks of something like leukemia. You know I've said Randy's white-blood-cell count is somewhat too high, but children can have that. I've sent blood to the lab on special and it'll be back tomorrow morning. *That* should tell us what we need to know."

She paused, frowning. "Has he been upset about anything? He keeps calling for Jim. Is Jim his father?" Dr. Adams was new to them.

Melodye's heart plummeted. She didn't tell the doctor he called for Jim in his sleep at home. Instead she muttered, "No, remember I told you his father's dead…."

"Oh, yes, I remember now. Then who is Jim? Because he's important to Randy."

Melodye looked down. "Jim's a…friend both the twins were fond of, Randy even more than Rachel."

Dr. Adams looked at her sharply, her kind, middle-aged

face sympathetic. "You say 'were', my dear. Randy still *is* very fond of this man. Can you get him here? Because I don't like Randy's vital signs and I don't think the lab tests are going to prove anything better. But he *can* very well be suffering emotional shock. Will you get him here?"

The doctor looked at Melodye carefully as Melodye began to shake her head no.

"I'm going to have to insist that you do everything possible to get this man here because your little boy is suffering and he may be in grave danger, Melodye. It may mean the difference between…"

"Life and death?" Melodye said suddenly as the full import of the doctor's words hit her.

"Yes, *now,* if at all possible. Move heaven and earth. I'll stay with him while you make that call."

In the hallway by the windows, Melodye prayed and dialed Jim who didn't answer. She left a frantic message, her heart at rock bottom. How could this have happened so suddenly? Did children so small grieve this deeply? Rachel had taken Jim's leaving well. Melodye didn't *want* to see Jim Ryman again, but Randy needed him and that was all that mattered. Had she been wrong not to let Jim say goodbye to the twins? God, where *was* he? She didn't let herself think he might be on a mission, didn't let herself think he and Lucia might be in bed… *No, don't go there.*

She had walked the length of the hallway three times when her cell phone rang and it was Jim. She was crying as she told him what happened. He said immediately he would be there as soon as human effort allowed. The lump in her throat almost choked her as she prepared to wait.

When she told the doctor, the woman nodded. "Tell Randy

Jim's coming," she said softly. "Tell him again and again and hold him as you've been doing. And, Melodye, pray as you've never prayed before. Even with the lab tests, we can't be certain right away, but this is a crisis and we've got to get on top of it."

Melodye sat on the bed, held Randy and began saying it immediately. "Jim's coming, darling. Just hang in there. Jim's coming." After a while it became her mantra.

Jim was there by one that afternoon and he went straight to Randy's bedside, held the child tightly in his arms. "It's Jim, Randy. I'm here."

He said it several times as he hugged the little body close to his heart. After a few times, Randy's eyes flew open, but he quickly closed them again, tight.

"Open up, tiger," Jim said gently. "I want to talk to you."

"Jim!" Randy whispered, opening his eyes. His arms went around the man and hung on for dear life.

Hot tears stood in Jim's eyes. "I'm here, Randy. I came back to see you."

Randy cried then. "You'll go away again," with a thin edge of hysteria.

"No. No, I'll be here until you get better, then you know what?"

Randy couldn't take his eyes off Jim, fearing he'd disappear again.

"Tell you what. You get well and I'll come and get you or someone can bring you to New York to spend some time with me."

Randy rallied with superhuman speed. "You mean that? New York? Oh, boy!" His voice was hoarse and weak, but his eyes brightened.

Jim hugged him again. "But you have to get well first. Will you do that for me?"

"You won't leave me again?"

"Not until you're much, much better, and then you'll be coming to be with me."

Randy could barely contain his happiness. Now all he had to do was get well and his little body was fighting to do just that.

Melodye's throat was choked with feeling. The doctor had known best after all.

The nurse came in. "I can't believe this is the same little boy who came to us early this morning. Hey, you're getting there."

"I'm going to New York with Jim!" Randy excitedly told her.

"You're going to go a lot of places, young man," the nurse responded.

She turned to Melodye. "I have to take him to have some tests run. He'll be out more than an hour."

The nurse took his temperature, looking pleased. "Ah yes," she said. "We're *really* getting there."

Dr. Adams came in just after the nurse had taken Randy. She had talked with the nurse and turned to Melodye expressing pleasure at Randy's progress.

"I was wrong," Melodye said. "I thought Papa France would be man enough in his life."

Dr. Adams touched Melodye's shoulder. "You know the old African saying: It takes a village to raise a child." Then she offered her hand to Jim. "I'm so happy to meet you."

Alone with Jim, Melodye felt ashamed of the cold way she'd treated him, no matter what the cause.

"Thank you so much," she said simply.

He reached out and patted her shoulder. "I had to come. Your kids and you are special to me. Melodye, could we go some place and talk? Please?"

"Oh, yes," she told him. "Let me make calls to your mom and Papa France and Odessa. How about the waiting room?"

"All right, then we need to hit the cafeteria. I'll bet you've had nothing to eat."

She shook her head. "I couldn't eat. And we have to get back to see what the test results are."

She called all three people and was rewarded with cries of pleasure. No one blamed her for not letting Jim tell the twins, but she blamed herself.

Seated near windows that brought in the afternoon sunlight, they sat side by side on a sofa. They were awkward with each other at first before he began, "There's so much to be said."

She nodded. "But first, how did you get here so fast?"

"Privilege," he said, smiling a bit. "Our chief has ties all the way to the top. There're ways for police to go anywhere in the world on very short notice. Luck figured in a little. A taxi driver from National Airport was particularly helpful."

"Thank you again." She looked deep into his eyes then and saw herself reflected there. "You were right, you know. I should've let you talk to them about your leaving. He's so little and he paid the price for my narrow-mindedness. I was just so angry. Can you forgive me?"

He patted her hand, held it. "There's nothing to forgive. I want to tell you some things about Lucia, but, unfortunately, I can't tell you all."

She held her breath then, aware of her hand in his, aware of his nearness and his big, protective body. "Okay."

He cleared his throat. "Lucia came to me and said she

wanted to give you a huge birthday party in December. She asked me to help her plan and keep it a secret. Of course I agreed, gave her all the ideas I had. It was then she flung her arms around my neck and kissed me. It meant nothing to me. She said she'd always been mean to you, that she was sorry and wanted to make amends."

"I think she suckered you," Melodye said quietly. "I told you she told me about Rafael and her. I don't think she'd have done that if she'd been sincere."

"Yeah, I think you're right. I've thought about that."

"You said you couldn't tell me everything…."

"That's right. I know you have a hard time trusting, but I have to ask you to trust me on this."

Right now, she thought, she'd forgive him anything. She'd even try to trust him.

Reluctant to talk about it further, she changed the subject. "You came straight here. Your mom and Papa France have been here much of the morning. They went home to take care of some things. She glanced at her watch. "They should be coming back anytime now."

He studied her with a slight smile playing about his mouth. "You've got to get some sleep, too."

"Later. I'm wired, but I'm feeling better all the time."

"I'll be coming back next week to take care of some police business."

"Oh?" How to say it. "Jim, do you still want to be friends with me?"

He hesitated, no question about it. "I do, but I don't think you really want to be friends with *me* again."

It cost her to say it. "I want to continue being friends. How can we do it otherwise with you so necessary in Randy's life? We don't have to sleep together. Do you want us to be friends?"

He didn't hesitate then. "Always. We were good for each other, on the same wavelength. And you're right, we don't have to sleep together, although I truly value that."

"I think we understand each other, most of the time."

He played with her fingers. "We got off on the wrong track. I wanted to tell you about the surprise party, but I was so pleased for you and I didn't want to spoil it."

"I understand. It's just that this thing between Lucia and me goes so deep and has gone on all our lives. I've told you you helped me."

"I'm proud of that. You've helped me more than you know."

He'd just said he couldn't tell her everything about Lucia. He'd also said the kiss meant nothing to him. Would he have said that if he were falling for Lucia? He could have meant the kiss meant nothing at that time. The suspense was killing her. She wanted to ask him when he'd tell her more about what he was talking about. But she didn't want to crowd him. Let him take his time. She was too grateful to him to press him any further.

"Another thing," he said earnestly. "When I grabbed you and kissed you that day at your boutique—"

"Yes, what about it?" She still dreamed of that kiss.

"It was sadistic, a bastardly thing to do. But I was furious that you were so cold. We'd just made love the night before and it seemed like you no longer gave a damn."

"I'm a good actress." She grinned then.

"You bet you are. Am I forgiven?"

"What do you think?"

"What I'm thinking is I'd like to go there again, but I know that's not possible. I'll just be grateful for what we had."

She smiled a little, thinking Papa France and Miss Belle

would be so happy to know that Jim and she were at least friends again.

"It's going to be a strain on you taking Randy to New York. Did you mean it?"

"You bet I mean it. And it's no strain. The station house has a nearby nursery and I can check on him easily."

"You're so—" She was lost for words, shaking her head.

"Wonderful," he teased her.

"Oh, yes."

The familiar voice came from behind them. "They said I'd find you here. Hello, Jim."

Jim stood up. It was Bettina and she bore down on them in full splendor. "Melodye, could I talk with you for a very few minutes? I'm so sorry about Randy. Why didn't you call me?"

"There wasn't time. Everything's been so crazy. Randy's doing much better since Jim came."

"Well, that's certainly a relief." She turned to Jim. "Have you seen Lucia lately? But then I'm sure you have."

"I've seen her," he said shortly. He didn't seem inclined to talk about it, and Bettina didn't follow through.

Jim excused himself, saying he'd go back to Randy's room and wait for him. Melodye said she'd join him in a few minutes.

Once they were alone, Bettina seemed shaken. "So he is better."

"Yes, but it's not over. He could have leukemia. They're running more tests."

"Poor child. Melodye, I can't ask you to forgive me for what I'm going to tell you. You certainly never learned forgiveness from me."

She paused for long moments, then swept on. "Lucia is

your half sister and I've loved her because I loved the man who was her father. Your father and I had to get married because I was pregnant with you. He never loved me and never let me forget that he'd had to marry me."

Her eyes were distant then. "After so many years, I met a man and we fell in love. I was going to get a divorce and marry him, but he died of a heart attack on the golf course. I didn't know I was carrying Lucia, so he never knew he had a daughter. The next year, your father died and I was left with two little girls to raise—alone. Fortunately, there was money enough and I've been very successful in fashion with the money I won in the medical lawsuit."

It took a while to digest, then Melodye said stiffly, "Thank you for telling me."

"It doesn't make up for the shabby way I've treated you. But your father hurt me so badly. I took it out on you and I'm sorry. I never knew before now that I love your children. I never wanted to be a grandmother, never wanted to be old…."

Melodye smiled a little. "Thank you for telling me, Mother. Old age happens to everyone and you're living in a fortunate time when we don't age so fast."

She thought then that she was commiserating with Bettina on *her* problems. But it was all right because this new information made her feel better, explained to a large degree why her mother had always seemed to almost hate her.

"Can you find it in your heart to forgive me?" Bettina pleaded.

Melodye nodded without hesitation. "I can."

Bettina looked relieved. "And, darling, if Lucia takes Jim over, please don't hold it against her. I'm afraid I've spoiled her. She's fond of him and he does seem to like her."

She wasn't about to talk with Bettina about Jim and Lucia.

It seemed to her he might be harboring tender feelings he was fighting for her sister. Jim had great common sense and he had to know that Lucia was trouble for any man. Was she worth it to him? And why couldn't he say what he had to say about her?

Melodye saw then that Bettina hadn't changed. Lucia was still who she loved, not Melodye, but she'd cared enough to unburden herself and Melodye told herself it was enough.

Bettina didn't stay long enough to see Randy, saying she had an appointment she had to keep and she'd send him lots of balloons.

He still hadn't come back when Melodye went back to Randy's room. "I made a quick call while I waited," Jim said.

"Oh?"

"Yeah. I called a toy shop over in Georgetown a friend owns and he's sending over some toys for Randy and Rachel," he said.

She shook her head. "You do think of everything that matters." She looked at him and smiled. "I've said it before. You really are good people." It felt so good to be friends again, but it scared her, too.

Randy was wheeled back in, lively enough that they had trouble keeping him in place.

Dr. Adam's face was wreathed in smiles. "He doesn't have leukemia. It's an infection, all right, and I'll watch him carefully for a couple of weeks."

The big-eared little pitcher was listening and he piped up, "Can Jim come get me and take me to New York with him soon?"

The doctor shook her head as the nurse settled Randy in bed. "You bet he can. In a few weeks, I'll have you flying to the moon."

With his head to one side, Randy told her, "You talk funny, doc. I can't fly, but I wish I could."

The toys came in record time and Randy was overjoyed. "What do you say to Jim?" Melodye asked Randy.

"I love you," Randy shouted hoarsely. "Do you love me?"

"Oh, yes," Jim assured him, "until the end of time."

Papa France and Miss Belle came then with Rachel, who jumped on the bed.

"Our prayers've been answered," Papa France told them as they all nodded elatedly.

"I'm going to New York with Jim," Randy piped up to all concerned.

"This kid's a whole lot better, that's for certain," Papa France said.

Jim hugged his mother and Papa France. "How long'll you be here?" Papa France asked.

"Until he's much better. I have all kinds of leave."

"You're a man after my own heart," Papa France said. "And I couldn't love you more if you were my own grandson."

Melodye stood a little back from the others, surveying the room. It was so different from the frantic anxiety of last night when Randy had been brought into this room with her hovering over him. The little boy was now on the bed, playing and squabbling with his twin. And Jim had been the cause of it all.

Chapter 19

"Brace yourself to be shocked," Jim said. "I asked you to come down because Lucia wants to talk with you and Manny wants you there when he tells us his story."

Melodye was at the Crystal Lake police headquarters at nine that morning. She stood in the hallway, talking with Jim who'd made that cryptic request. Now that Randy's illness no longer frightened her, she found herself deeply drawn to Jim again in the old, flaming way she'd always been. Standing close to him, she felt heat the way she felt it when she was near him. Her heart beat too fast, but she knew she had to focus on the fact that they were friends now, nothing more.

"What's going down?" she asked him.

"We've arrested Lucia as an accessory to Rafael and Turk's ring of conspiracy, money laundering, racketeering... Hell, you name it. He's locked up for the time being, tight enough that even his high-powered lawyer's unable to spring him."

Melodye's mouth opened with surprise. "And Manny?"

"*He* killed Rafael and shot me. And please don't sit in judgment until you hear him out."

Melodye felt her knees weaken. He placed a hand on each of her shoulders, steadying her.

"I want you to talk with Lucia first and get it over with, then you can focus on Manny."

Sitting in the big, austere room, Melodye had time to reflect on what had recently happened in her life. Jim had returned to New York and had quickly come back to Crystal Lake, bringing Lucia. Randy was on a roll; the doctor was discharging him early. Had it only been two weeks since he'd taken sick?

She found it hard focusing on either Lucia or Manny. The shock was too new. Jim came in with Lucia, who looked disheveled and angry.

Seated, Lucia glared at her. "I'm sure this makes you happy," she sputtered.

Melodye didn't answer, haunted by a lifetime of bitter memories.

"You were always envious of me, but I had my own envy—of you."

"What could you have envied me for?"

"Grandpa France and Grandma Gina's love," Lucia spat. "They never loved me the way they loved you. You had a man in your life and I never did. It left me pretty hungry, but I've made up for it."

Lucia seemed to wither then like the bad witches in fairy tales, but she kept up her facade. "I would've taken Jim from you if things had been different."

"No, you wouldn't have," Jim said easily. "I was Melodye's friend from the start."

Lucia cried then and he let her. She finally reached for the box of tissues on the table and blew her nose, dabbed at her eyes. "Anyway, Mom always loved me best."

"Very true," Melodye acknowledged. "It doesn't matter anymore."

"My everloving husband's deserting me, a rat leaving a sinking ship. But I'm saving myself. I'm turning state's evidence. I didn't know what I was doing. Rafael suckered me into this and staked me to start my own agency. He told me I was the love of his life and I'm sure I was. I always had it on you. I'm beautiful, smart, talented…" She broke down and put her head in her hands.

"You can stop now," Jim said gently, "and the guard'll take you back to your cell."

Lucia rose like a woman many years older and she glared at Melodye as a guard led her out. "I'll be free and I'll be on top again," she told Melodye vehemently. "I was meant to win and you were meant to lose."

Melodye shook her head as Jim caught her eye and smiled at her. Friends again. It wasn't going to be easy, but it *did* feel good.

Funny how she felt nothing where Lucia was concerned. Once she thought about it, she wasn't even surprised. Lucia was an errant ancient queen who believed only in herself and thought the world was hers for plundering. Bettina was the one who was going to be undone by this. Lucia was her life.

When they brought Manny in, Jim turned on the recorders and Manny looked at Melodye hopefully, his eyes grim.

"I'm so sorry," he told her, "but I wanted you to be here

because I want to tell you all about it. You've been so good to me."

Melodye felt her eyes moisten. He looked so haggard. Twenty-two and was his life over? It was certainly blighted.

Manny asked for water and Jim poured him a glass from the thermal pitcher on the table. A policewoman monitored the recording, and when Jim gave the high sign, Manny began.

"At first, Rafael and I were tight. I was a punk kid looking for a job I wasn't finding and that was because I wanted more money than I was worth and wanted it fast. Rafael saw the greed in me because *he* was greedy. Anyway, I was hired to do anything he told me to do and I was willing. I sure wasn't proud of what I was doing, but my old man was a hustler, a card shark, a confidence man. I wasn't particular about what I did as long as the money was right. I didn't know any better."

Manny stopped, breathing hard, and his eyes looked haunted. "I did what they wanted until one day Rafael and Turk called me in and told me they had a truly special job for me to do. Now, Rafael treated me like a son, but I never liked Turk. We just didn't get along. He always seemed evil to me, too much like my old man. At first I didn't think Rafael was like that." He clenched his jaws for a moment before he continued. "I just didn't know."

Manny put his hands in his lap and moistened his lips. "I said Rafael and Turk called me in. The special job was they wanted me to kill Detective Lieutenant Jim Ryman. They spelled it out and laughed about it. They told me we'd all be in prison if Jim stayed alive and they couldn't have that, could they? They pointed out to me that I was part of the team and I'd go to prison, too, if Jim had his way. They said they'd pay me two hundred thousand dollars, and I won't lie, I wanted that money—bad.

"Well, I was a crook, not a killer and I said I didn't think I could do it. But I saw the money in my dreams. I could run with it. Make a fresh start. Turk looked at the ceiling, then he looked at me. 'You'll do it, all right. You don't have a choice. You kill him or we'll kill you.' My blood turned to ice. I knew they weren't bluffing. They told me I was in with them now and they had me tailed twenty-four hours a day. I was in their crosshairs."

He closed his eyes before he continued. "They took me to target practice daily and I spent hours out in Maryland, learning to shoot straight. It was a joke to them. I think they enjoyed the whole thing. Then I was ready and I shot you, Jim. Only I just winged you. I never meant to kill you, but I had to do something to make it look good. I went back to them, told them I'd been frightened by a cop on the beat and had gotten nervous about getting caught. Rafael just looked at me. 'You get a second chance,' he'd said, 'and this time you'd better make good on it, or we'll make good on you.'"

Manny was remembering the whole thing and he had trouble breathing. "I couldn't sleep at night and I wasn't satisfying them at work. I prayed for the first time in my life. My father was a devil, but my mom tried to do right—until they both got drunk. Then it was hell for me and my six brothers and sisters." He shuddered a bit. "I'd gotten to be like my dad, but I was changing, getting what I prayed for."

Manny licked bone-dry lips and his breathing was labored. "Rafael told me one day to come in that night, he was going to give me a foolproof plan to kill Jim. He told me to come in through the back way after everybody had left. It was a Monday and the club was closed. I thought something was fishy and I was scared. I took my gun. I let myself in and went up to his office. He offered me a drink. At first I refused until he ordered me to take it and I did.

"I was scared out of my skull, but I stood up to him, told him I couldn't do it. He told me then he could kill me so I died fast or he could kill me so I died slow with hurt in my gut so bad every minute would seem like an hour. I remember saying, 'Man, be reasonable. Cops hunt you down like dogs when you kill cops. You can't get away with it.'

"And he told me I was twenty, abused, and even if they caught me, I had a damned good chance to get off with a light sentence. He told me they had first-rate lawyers. He said just pretend it was a robbery. He said they'd even pay me the two hundred thousand, but I wasn't greedy anymore. I just wanted out. Then he told me, if I did get caught, I'd better not involve them. 'You think the law's got a long arm,' he told me. 'The New York mob makes the cops look sick.'"

Manny asked for more water then and again Jim got it for him. He looked at the ceiling for a minute or so. "Like I said, I was scared, but I still told him I wouldn't do it. He pulled a gun and pointed it at me. 'After I kill you, I'll weigh you down with steel blocks and they'll never find your body. You'll be thousands of miles from here.'"

The smell of Manny's relived fear was in the room at that minute. "I'd brought my gun and I vowed we'd both die right there. The guy collected guns. This was an old Beretta and it jammed. I drew my gun while he cursed a blue streak and I shot him straight through the heart. I had to do it. He was going to kill me…"

When he'd finished, Manny leaned back. "I'm sorry, Melodye. I had to kill him."

"It's all right," Melodye told him. "Like you said, it was something you had to do."

"But he was your husband. He was playing around with your sister and I knew that. He never hid it from me."

"I know that now."

"Did you love him? If you did, I'm sorry."

"I didn't love him any longer. It's all right."

Manny looked at Jim. "That's about it. I hated like hell shooting you. I'm really glad I drew the line at killing you. You're a good guy."

Jim smiled at him. "So are you."

But Manny wasn't finished. "I was scared and I waited for you guys to come for me. I begged Melodye for a job and she hired me. Then you began to come around and I knew I'd been right to refuse to kill you. I knew I wanted to be a detective because I admired you so much.

"I've been running scared since I killed Rafael. You don't know how often I started to tell you, but I couldn't because I felt you'd hate me. You hadn't died when I shot you and with Turk, I had to save myself.

"I told myself I'd live a clean, useful life for the rest of my life and I'd make you proud…."

He paused and rubbed his hand over his eyes. "I'm glad it's over and, both of you, please forgive me. Thank you for understanding."

A short while later, Manny had been taken away. Jim and Melodye stood near the door in the same room.

"What happens to Manny?"

"I won't press charges and a top lawyer tells me he'll plead self-defense. If it hadn't been for him, I'd be dead."

She shuddered then. She didn't want to imagine a world without him.

"It seems to me we're always near some door." She couldn't help smiling, but her insides were jelly again.

"You thinking what I'm thinking?"

"About that door where you tried to kiss me out of existence."

"I apologized and you accepted."

In a flash of humor and deep feeling, she told him, "If I live to be a hundred, I won't forget it."

"Good, because I sure as hell won't. I'm glad we're friends again. I don't want to upset you, but anytime you want to go back, I'll do it."

"I'll just bet. No, this is more comfortable for me. Are you still taking the job in New York?"

"I'm still undecided but I think so."

"Weren't you at least a little caught up with Lucia?" She was teasing and she wasn't teasing.

He shook his head. "I like my women big and beautiful. Wide-hipped and deep breasted. Yeah, and sweet, like chocolate candy."

His eyes held her and her body smoldered. He knew what he did to her, she thought, and he reveled in it. And she knew what she did to him. Too bad it had to be over, except for friendship.

She glanced at him from under those long black lashes and his heart jumped. They were friends now, he told his heart. Just friends, so knock it off. But hearts can be notoriously uncooperative. His kept jumping. Well, in time—he thought.

She was having trouble, too, letting him go. Her body leaned toward him and her mind had nothing to do with it. It had been a wild and wonderfully wicked ride, the best she ever hoped to know.

And it was truly over, with no regrets, except that they couldn't be different people who could love each other and live together and be happy.

He reached out and put his hand on the side of her face. The electric charge jumped between them. "I'll be leaving day after tomorrow. We'll run into each other when I'm here and you take care of yourself. I'll be coming back for the twins Sunday, one week from this coming one. I have that Monday off."

On impulse she leaned forward and kissed his cheek and he took her in his arms and kissed her thoroughly, setting off the old flames. A goodbye kiss. It had been a glorious mistake, but it made a grand finale. She opened the door and he held it for her. Walking up the hall, she looked back and found him still looking at her. She blew him a kiss that he returned and she walked on.

Chapter 20

Near midnight Jim stood at the guardrail, looking at the Chesapeake Bay out from Crystal Lake. He had one more day before he headed back to New York, one more day to decide on taking the job there. He thought about seeing Melodye at headquarters and got somber. She looked damned good and he was happy about that. Even happier that she still wanted to be friends. That would be easier with him in New York. The twins were delirious with plans to visit him.

In the moonlight and streetlight reflection, he took a small rock from his pocket, threw it into the water and watched the ripples spread. The words of others came back to him. He had read somewhere that the saddest words in the English language were: *It might have been.* When he talked with Whit about Melodye and him, Whit had advised, "Man, the body has a wisdom of its own. Don't play it cheap that you two thrill each other."

No, he didn't play it cheap, but that didn't alter the fact that he was never going to let himself hurt Melodye. Look how torn up she'd been about that simple kiss with Lucia. He felt he couldn't take it if she turned on him for good the way she had for a little while. He wouldn't have believed her friendship could become so necessary to him.

He thought he might as well go in, go to bed and dream the wild dreams again of her lush body pressed against his, making love and making dreams that weren't going to come true.

"Hey, Mommy, when do we go to New York?"

It was only about the hundredth time Randy had asked it. Melodye pulled him onto her lap and shook her head. "Mr. Impatient. Your time will come."

He laughed and asked "When? When?" in singsong fashion.

Papa France let himself in, loaded down with big, bright red tomatoes and a peck of snapped green beans. He gave Melodye and Randy a kiss on the cheek and Randy hung on to him.

"Where's Rachel?" Papa France asked.

"Housekeeping. Playing with her dolls and her toys," Melodye said.

He went to the kitchen, put the vegetables down, came back and stood for a few minutes, looking down at Melodye.

"You're looking mighty happy," she told him. "What're you up to?"

He didn't hesitate. "Miss Belle and I are getting married."

Putting Randy out of her lap, she got up and hugged him. "Oh, that's wonderful! Congratulations! Have you set a date?"

He grinned. "I'm thinking day before yesterday."

They chatted and she offered him coffee. He shook his head as his sharp old eyes got dreamy.

"I'm having coffee with the little woman," he told her. "She said she'd make me some cheese biscuits and you know how I love cheese biscuits. So I can't stay."

"No, of course not," she teased him. "I'll get the chunk of fire you came for and you can hurry off."

He grinned again. "Granddaughter, you're looking at a happy man."

"I'm happy for you."

He stood looking at her, then put a hand around each shoulder. "It's what I've always wanted for you and Jim."

Her eyes felt grainy; she blinked them fast. "I'll be fine and he'll be fine," she said firmly. "Read up on how the world runs today. You might be surprised."

He nodded. "Oh, I'm up to date, but the way the world runs isn't what I want for you two."

She wasn't going to talk about it. "Umm, you're a sweetie, but Miss Belle is waiting."

He didn't need to be told twice. He went to the nursery to kiss the twins goodbye and he was gone.

The big clock on the mantelpiece struck eleven as Melodye sat thinking she had a lot planned today, a Saturday. Odessa would take over the boutique this morning, she would take the twins with her and handle things this afternoon so Odessa and Ashton could go sailing. Her friend planned a December wedding. She felt no envy, just a wish that things could have been different for Jim and her.

She looked down at her vanilla-colored lounging gown. She'd never go back to the somber colors slavery that Bettina and Lucia had kept her in. She'd long ago put away the rings Rafael had placed on her finger. She couldn't help thinking about Jim, and she was sick that he couldn't see that he wasn't a monster who hurt and disappointed those he loved. *She trusted him,* a welcome miracle.

She got up and went to the nursery where the twins happily played with their toys. The door chimes sounded and she wondered because she wasn't expecting anyone.

Looking through the door viewer she saw Jim standing there and her heart got crazy. Why was he here? She spread a hand over her breast as she opened the door.

He stood looking at her for a long while; she couldn't speak at first. Then she got her voice. "Come in," she said softly.

He came in, closed the door and leaned against it. *"I had to come,"* he told her.

"I'm glad you did."

"Melodye, we've got to talk."

"Okay. Let me tell the twins not to disturb us."

He went with her and the twins shrieked with delight to see him. After hugs and kisses, he took two paddles with balls attached to long rubber strings out of a bag and handed them over. She hadn't noticed he carried a bag.

"Play with these a little while so Mommy and I can talk," he told them. "Then I'll come back and play with you."

"You'll come back?" That was Randy.

"Yeah, for absolutely, positively certain."

After Jim showed them how to do it, Randy laughed and they set about playing with their paddles.

Back in the living room, Melodye and Jim sat on the sofa. He wasted no time. "If you tell me what I need to know, I won't be taking the job in New York."

"You want to stay here? But I thought you…"

He turned her to face him and took both her hands in his.

"Melodye, I love you. I realized that last night when I stood on the waterfront thinking about my life. The helpful things you've said to me have haunted me. The night at my house when I cried for the first time about wanting my father's love and never getting it. About feeling I'd failed Elyssa and I'd fail anyone who wanted me."

"I remember." She still thrilled with that memory and what had followed.

He leaned closer. "I'd never cried over anything before, not even at my father's and Elyssa's funerals. I simply felt like an all-time loser. Remember what you said?"

"I said so much. You were in such pain and I saw you as everything I wanted in a man, if I could trust again."

"You told me, *'You did the best you could. That has to be enough.'*"

She nodded. "I remember."

His eyes on her were steady, full of the love he'd felt for so long without knowing it. "I blocked your words at first, but I couldn't forget them. I told myself we had passion and we didn't need love. But all that time, I loved you and couldn't admit it. Now I believe what you said and I'm willing to take a chance. Would you take a chance and try to trust me?"

She looked at him. "I *do* trust you. I've been thinking about that. And it's why I said at the hospital I wanted to be friends again. I realized that if I didn't trust you, I wouldn't want to be friends."

He grinned. "Friends and lovers, a hell of a combination. Now, if we're going to be married…"

She opened her mouth, but no words came, then she stammered, "You—you want to marry me?" Tears stood in her eyes and her heart danced.

"Want me to get on my knees?" he asked huskily.

"No. I love you and you make me so happy."

"Papa France and Miss Belle are gonna be even happier than we are."

Melodye grinned then. "That's not possible. Talk about flying…" Her body felt weightless, warm and wonderful.

"Yeah, you're right. Listen, I want to bundle you three up and take you to my place. We've got a lot of unfinished business to take care of. The twins're perfect houseguests. They sleep hard and they sleep long, so we've got a lot of time."

Melodye sat still and the thrills just kept coursing the length of her body.

He kissed her fingers, feeling thrills of his own. "We have one stop to make on the way."

Her fingers traced his jawline. "What's that?"

"Stop and get a jeroboam of champagne to relive one of many precious nights. I don't care if you drown me in the stuff."

Melodye laughed, throwing back her head. "You're hopeless."

"Hopeless and happy," he told her, "We've got it all, baby *and I'm lovin' it!*"

Two GROOMS and a Wedding

Award-winning author
Adrianne Byrd

For one forbidden night, ambitious attorney
Isabella Kane indulged her deepest passions.
Now she can't get Derrick Knight out of her mind…
and Derrick is equally obsessed. The problem is,
Isabella's engaged to his old college rival.
But Derrick's determined to make Isabella his.

"A humorous, passionate love story."
—*Romantic Times BOOKreviews*
on *Comfort of a Man* (4 stars)

Coming the first week of March, wherever books are sold.

KIMANI™
ROMANCE

*He was the best thing
that had ever happened to her…*

The
FOREIGNER'S
CARESS

Favorite author

Kim Shaw

Determined to change her wild ways, Madison Daniels finds
the man of her dreams in handsome Jamaican billionaire
Stevenson Elliott. But when her past indiscretions earn the
disapproval of Stevenson's family, she must convince him that
a lifetime with her is worth more than his family's billions.

Coming the first week of March, wherever books are sold.

KIMANI™
ROMANCE

www.kimanipress.com   KPKS0580308

A RISKY AFFAIR

Award-winning author

Maureen Smith

Private investigator Dane Roarke leaves Solange Washington
breathless with desire. Hired to do a routine background
check on her, Dane unearths secrets regarding her parentage
that force him to walk a thin line between his growing
suspicions and his consuming hunger for this vibrant woman.

"With Every Breath [by Maureen Smith] is engaging reading
that is sure to provide hours of pleasure."
—*Romantic Times BOOKreviews*

Coming the first week of March, wherever books are sold.

KIMANI
ROMANCE

www.kimanipress.com

KPMS0590308

A compelling short story collection...

New York Times Bestselling Author

CONNIE BRISCOE

&

ESSENCE Bestselling Authors

LOLITA FILES
ANITA BUNKLEY

YOU ONLY GET *Better*

Three successful women find themselves on
the road to redemption and self-discovery as
they realize that happiness comes from within…
and that life doesn't end at forty.

"This wonderful anthology presents very human
characters, sometimes flawed but always
heartwarmingly developed and sympathetic.
Each heroine makes changes for the better that
demonstrate the power of love. Don't miss this book."
—*Romantic Times BOOKreviews* Top Pick on
You Only Get Better

*Coming the first week of February
wherever books are sold.*

KIMANI PRESS™

www.kimanipress.com   KPYOGBI540208

Featuring the voices of eighteen of your
favorite authors…

ON THE LINE

Essence Bestselling Author

donna hill

A sexy, irresistible story starring Joy Newhouse,
who, as a radio relationship expert, is considered
the diva of the airwaves. But when she's fired,
Joy quickly discovers that if she can dish it out,
she'd better be able to take it!

Featuring contributions by such favorite authors
as Gwynne Forster, Monica Jackson, Earl Sewell,
Phillip Thomas Duck and more!

Coming the first week of January,
wherever books are sold.

sepia™

www.kimanipress.com   KPDH0211207

From acclaimed author

DWIGHT FRYER

The evocative prequel to *The Legend of Quito Road*...

The Knees of Gullah Island

A beautifully rendered novel that explores the complex racial dynamics that shaped the South through one family's extraordinary journey to freedom. Born to free parents, Gillam Hale realizes he can never be truly free until he finds his lost loved ones and faces the legacy of his own rash decisions.

"Dwight Fryer's debut novel is a scintillating mixture of love, betrayal, hope and redemption disguised in the incredible human condition of a sleepy little 1930s Tennessee town."
—*Rawsistaz Reviewers* on *The Legend of Quito Road*

Coming the first week of March wherever books are sold.

sepia™

www.kimanipress.com   KPDF1190308

These wo...
has a pri...

NATIONAL BESTSELLING AUTHOR

ROCHELLE ALERS

DISCARD

After Hours

A deliciously scandalous novel that brings together
three very different women, united by the secret lives
they lead. Adina, Sybil and Karla all lead seemingly
charmed, luxurious lives, yet each also harbors a
surprising secret that is about to spin out of control.

"Alers paints such vivid descriptions that when Jolene
becomes the target of a murderer, you almost feel
as though someone you know is in great danger."
—*Library Journal* on *No Compromise*

**Coming the first week of March
wherever books are sold.**

sepia

www.kimanipress.com
KPRA1220308

PAPERBACK